"With brutal elegance and chilling subtlety, Thomas pulls his readers into his dark visions immediately from every opening line."
– Paul Di Filippo, in *ASIMOV'S*

"Jeffrey Thomas' imagination is as twisted as it is relentless."
– F. Paul Wilson

"In time he will, in this reviewer's opinion, be listed alongside King, Barker, Koontz, and McCammon."
– Brian Keene

The Endless Fall
and other weird fictions

by

JEFFREY THOMAS

Copyright Jeffrey Thomas 2017

Front Cover by Nick Gucker

Graphic Design by Steve Santiago and Kenneth W. Cain

Published by Lovecraft eZine Press

Formatting by Kenneth W. Cain

Jar of Mist first appeared in *The Lovecraft eZine* #28, 2013.

The Dogs first appeared in the anthology *The Dark Rites of Cthulhu*, April Moon Books, 2014.

Ghosts in Amber first appeared as a limited edition chapbook of 100 copies from Dim Shores, 2015.

The Prosthesis first appeared in the anthology *The Grimscribe's Puppets*, Miskatonic River Press, 2013.

The Dark Cell first appeared in the anthology *Edge of Sundown*, Chaosium, 2015.

Snake Wine first appeared in the anthology *The Children of Old Leech*, Word Horde, 2014.

The Spectators first appeared as an individual story from Darkside Digital, 2010.

Bad Reception first appeared in the anthology *Atomic-Age Cthulhu*, Chaosium, 2015.

Sunset in Megalopolis first appeared in the publication *Strange Aeons* #13, 2014.

Portents of Past Futures first appeared in the anthology *In Heaven, Everything is Fine*, Eraserhead Press, 2013.

Those Above first appeared in the anthology *Steampunk Cthulhu*, Chaosium, 2014.

The Individual in Question first appeared in the chapbook *The Doom That Came to Providence*, LASC Press, 2015.

The Red Machine first appeared in the chapbook *Black Walls, Red Glass*, Marietta Publishing, 1997.

The Endless Fall is original to this collection.

TABLE OF CONTENTS

INTRODUCTION

In 2003, before the age of Facebook, the happening place for all things Cthulhu Mythos was in the newsgroup alt.horror.cthulhu (it still exists if you ever want to deep dive into its archives). I distinctly recall learning about Punktown from the local maven, James Ambuehl. I tracked down the very first collection, Punktown, from Ministry of Whimsy Press (used copies of this gem are still floating around on the internet). This was my introduction to the wildly creative imagination of Jeffrey Thomas. At first the reader is swept up in the myriad alien races that populate the city of Paxton on the planet Oasis, the clash of culture, foods, languages, all spiced with desperation and violence. The more you settle in for a long stay, the more you browse the anthologies and novels, you realize that what makes the city memorable are the characters that live there. These are real people, mostly on the fringes, barely clinging to existence. They struggle, strive, suffer, live and die. Often the atmosphere is charged with melancholy, as we recognize kindred spirits not quite making it. You can start with Punktown, but as you begin a deeper exploration of Jeffrey's oeuvre, you discover that this is his most consistent theme, real people caught in desperate, bizarre or terrifying circumstances. *The Endless Fall* could represent the descent to oblivion for the protagonists. It could also indicate the turning of the year, as a summer of promise darkens to the coldness and shadows. I was very much struck that even if these characters had been left alone and did not encounter the fantastic, their lives would probably just have become more isolated with the turning of the years.

The Endless Fall collects most of Jeffrey's recent fiction, not any Punktown stories and barely anything that could be construed as Cthulhu Mythos. I sat down one morning to read one or two, and it was evening when I looked up, the book finished and I was wondering why there wasn't more. I was completely absorbed and I hope you will have the same experience. I only want to make a few specific comments and then you can lose yourself in his prose.

"Jar of Mist" is the best Sesqua Valley story I've ever read that was not penned by Wilum Pugmire himself. The imagery is haunting, and, of all the contents, the story is the most gentle.

"Ghosts in Amber" is a brilliant novella that shows the full scope of Mr. Thomas' talents. At first it is all so mundane and reasonable but soon everything spins out of control.

Jeffrey has family links to Viet Nam and has traveled there quite frequently. This comes out in some of his fiction, most notably here in "Snake Wine," where the attention to detail fleshes out the vividness of a wonderfully bizarre tale.

While "Sunset in Megalopolis" is a cautionary tale for a superhero, it also added the right amount of levity to balance out the proceedings.

I struggled to choose a favorite here, arguing with myself about "Bad Reception," where I found the main character so sympathetic, and "Portents of Past Futures," which worked so well on so many levels, and then I read "The Endless Fall," which gives the collection its name. Jeffrey Thomas cut his teeth on science fiction. Here the Thomas everyman is trapped on a distant world, trying to make sense of what's happening. The prose represents the best of Mr. Thomas, showing us how far he has come as a writer since 2000 when the world first met Punktown.

It should be obvious I admire Jeffrey Thomas' writing. I love getting lost in the world he creates, and can empathize with the difficulties his characters face, because they are just so real. I envy those of you making your first acquaintance with this author. Those of you who already know Jeffrey skipped this introduction and are two stories into *The Endless Fall* already!

Matthew Carpenter
November, 2016

JAR OF MIST

He was the one who had to identify his daughter's body in the morgue. He was all she had. She had been all he had. His wife, her mother, had hung herself eleven years ago when Aliza had been ten. Oskar had had to identify her body, too.

The sheet covered her to the waist, so he couldn't see the wounds she had opened high in each inner thigh to sever the femoral arteries. Oskar didn't ask to see them, didn't know if they would be stitched up now or still yawning wide open from the elastic pull of her skin, anomalous deep canyons of raw red tissue in a landscape of smooth whiteness. He doubted seeing those new wounds would shock him any more than the old wounds he could plainly see on both her bared forearms. He drew in his breath sharply when he saw them, and that was when the tears poised at his eyes fell, and when he knew he had neglected his daughter for too long.

Both of Aliza's slim forearms were a mass of uncountable, overlapping raised lines, scar tissue so thick it was like a weave of armor...not to prevent blood from getting out, of course, but perhaps to prevent other things from getting in.

"It's her," Oskar wept then, cupping her cold cheek in his palm. He said it as though that hadn't already been established. He said it as though he had recognized her not by her unmarred youthful face, but by these scars he'd never seen until now. What made him weep so openly was that he *did* recognize the scars, had known they were there all along, though not in the physical sense.

The morgue attendant nodded, and drew the sheet up over her face again, like the edge of an advancing tide that would suck his daughter away to unknown and infinite depths.

Aliza had been living in the town of North Bend, which in itself had mystified Oskar. Previously she had seemed so in love with Seattle, its music scene, its artistic vibe. It was Oskar's understanding that she had relocated there to live with a young man she'd met at an art show in Seattle. Oskar couldn't even remember the boy's name now, though Aliza had mentioned him to her father in their infrequent, brief, and uncomfortable phone conversations.

Oskar had never visited her in North Bend, though she'd lived there eighteen months. Too absorbed in his work, and in his own relationship: a sordid affair with a much younger married coworker that had recently ended messily. Today was his first visit to Aliza's apartment. The landlord had let him in.

It was a small white stucco building on a street corner; just a few rooms above an antiques and curios shop. The floor creaked under his feet in the dusty silence. Oskar drew curtains aside to let light in, and looked out at the forested mountains, the wafting clouds crawling down their bristling flanks. The Snoqualmie Valley. The name meant "Moon, the Transformer," in reference to Native American folklore and the imagined origin of the Snoqualmie people. Oskar didn't know the full story and didn't care to. It was bound to be as inane and deluded as any other human myth of gods, creation and afterlife.

He steeled himself, then turned to a closer examination of the place where his daughter had spent the end point of her life. This murky box held the diminishing tail of a comet, itself gone from view, not to come around again in his lifetime or any other.

He didn't venture into the bathroom, though he had been assured the tub had been scoured by a cleanup crew.

Moving like a detective from kitchen, to living room, to bedroom, Oskar took in countless mundane bits of evidence of his daughter's existence here, but he came across nothing to suggest the presence of her artist boyfriend. No one's clothes or belongings beyond her own. So he had left her, then? At what point? Might that account for her desperate act? It made sense to Oskar, and as guilty as the feeling was, it came as a kind of relief that it was another man abandoning Aliza – not him, her father – who had inspired her self destruction.

He was familiar with this brand of guilty rationalization. It was akin to when he had told himself that chronic depression had been to blame for his wife's suicide. He might even, if he gave in to the impulse now, blame his daughter's suicide on genetics.

It was Aliza, ten, who had discovered her mother's dangling body. Oskar had stayed late at work, but he saw his wife later in the morgue. In red nail polish, on her naked chest she had painted ALL IS NOTHING...though she had presumably been looking in the mirror when she marked herself, because the words were written backwards.

Is existential despair, Oskar wondered, genetic?

He couldn't realistically take all Aliza's possessions back with him to his room at the McGrath Hotel...her clothes, her books and CDs, her makeup, her pots and pans. What was he to do with these things: bring them home to Seattle, to fill the empty place in his life she herself should have occupied? No, he had to distill her entire existence down to a mere few items that he hoped defined her best – if not to herself, at least to him.

He uncovered several scrapbooks and a shoebox stuffed with loose photos, though he clapped the cover back on it as soon as he determined its contents. He wasn't ready to look through them yet; tears threatened to come again just at the thought of viewing them. He set aside her sketch pads and a few paintings, finished and not. Also, a worn stuffed animal his wife had given Aliza: a Doberman Pinscher that resembled their dog Luna, herself long dead.

In the bedroom, however, atop her bureau he encountered a number of items that perplexed him. The way they were placed – with candles and incense holders between them – or perhaps it was something in their esoteric appearance, made the bureau top seem like an altar. One item was a set of pan pipes made from ivory, or was it lengths of animal bone? Another was a pinecone, curiously blood red, all the more curious for not appearing to have been painted. And then there was the stone statuette, a foot in height and stained green as if it had been stolen from a garden, or from deep woods, that portrayed a troll or gnome or other such creature, squatting on its bestial haunches with a wide impish grin on its toad-like face.

Oskar didn't add any of these odd decorations to his pile of memento mori. He couldn't associate them with his daughter, and wondered if they had been left behind by her departed lover. If so, that might explain why Aliza had showcased them in the manner of a shrine.

Having remained here as long as he could bear, at least for today, he gathered up his tokens in her own gym bag, which he'd come across in a closet. Then he left the apartment, leaving the door unlocked, as the landlord had said she would be by later to lock up herself.

Not knowing if he would be returning here tomorrow or if this were a kind of goodbye, Oskar descended the building's stairs to a little front vestibule. Here he encountered the door to the antiques and curios shop that occupied the ground floor.

He hesitated outside the door, with its frosted glass panel. He saw a shadowy form pass across its pebbly surface. On a whim, but without enthusiasm – more like a sleepwalker – he reached for the door and pushed it open. Bells jangled as he stepped inside.

The figure he had seen passing as a watery silhouette turned toward the sound and met his eyes, and Oskar felt his lungs seize up like fists clutching his last intake of air.

It was a man, though so transformed as to almost represent some other kind of being. It was quickly apparent, though, that this man of indeterminate age had suffered terrible burning, with little reconstructive surgery – though Oskar couldn't say what he had looked like before whatever procedures he might have undergone. The man looked to be wearing a stocking mask with lidless holes cut out for his watery, red-rimmed eyes, and another hole for his bulbous immobile lips. He had mere slits for a nose.

When the man spoke it was with a bit of difficulty, owing to the tightness of his thick scar tissue, but Oskar thought there was a smile in his voice, if not on his face. "Welcome," the man said. "Can I help you?"

"I was...just..." Oskar cleared his voice. "My daughter lived upstairs, here." He nodded toward the ceiling.

"Oh...yes, yes...Aliza." The shop's proprietor took a

step forward, and now his muddied voice conveyed sympathy. "Poor girl. I'm so horribly sorry for your loss, sir."

"Thank you. I was just, ah, wondering how well you knew her. And the boy who lived with her."

"Oh...*him*." Now Oskar couldn't tell at all what the proprietor's tone meant to convey. "Julian."

"Yes, that's his name. I'd forgotten. She told me, but I never met him. I was wondering if you knew whether he'd left her very recently."

"Mm, it was recently, I'd say so." The burned man turned to look off into space as if trying to pierce the past. "I can't recall precisely the last time I saw him, but I do know he returned to Sesqua Valley."

Oskar was confused. Had he heard the man correctly? "You mean Snoqualmie Valley?"

The proprietor met Oskar's gaze again. "No, that's here. Sesqua Valley is...another place." Since they still stood near to the open door, the burned man swept his arm toward the interior of his shop. "Please, let me get you a cup of coffee. I was just about to pour one for myself. I'll tell you anything that you might find helpful."

"Thank you," Oskar said sincerely, and followed the man toward the back of the shop, which was a dusty labyrinth of dubious treasures. Furniture piled with knickknacks, framed paintings and photographs filling every inch of wall space. Porcelain dolls and mounted deer antlers, Bakelite radios and books with frayed bindings. At last they reached a glass counter sheltering smaller, more easily stolen items such as old watches, coins, straight razors, hairbrushes, and so on in a museum-like exhibition. Atop this counter beside a modern cash register was a coffee maker, with a half-full pot. When asked, Oskar told the man he took his black.

The burned man made his own with heaps of sugar and far too much cream, and sucked it through a straw. Even so, his awkward lips became slick with his sweet concoction.

"What can you tell me about Julian?" Oskar asked.

"Not much, except I knew he was from Sesqua. He didn't even have to tell me. Not with those eyes of his." The man sounded positively wistful. "Beautiful silver eyes."

Silver? Oskar was beginning to feel a bit uncomfortable with his host, beyond his shocking appearance. "Do you know why they broke up, if not when?"

"Well, he did leave her, but it probably wasn't a breakup in the sense you're thinking. You see, as Julian told me, Sesquans do something similar to the Amish...when young Amish go out to experience the wider world for a time, before returning to their community. The Amish call it Rumspringa. They get all that yearning and youthful restlessness out of their systems before settling back in and accepting their own nature. I'm sure it was simply Julian's time to return."

Oskar found this explanation a bit hard to process. So had Julian belonged to some cult? Was that what this man was suggesting? "Are you sure you didn't hear them arguing up there? They didn't have a big blow-up, or anything?"

"Oh no, they were no bother. The only sound I ever heard from up there was Julian playing his pan flute, and I didn't mind that at all. Such a lovely, melancholy sound it was."

"I saw his pan flute upstairs. I think he left some other things, too."

"He may have given Aliza the flute to remember him by, but if you saw other pieces from Sesqua Valley upstairs, I think you must be talking about the pieces Aliza bought from me herself, after Julian was already gone. Things she felt would keep her connected to him, I suspect."

"A red pinecone? A funny statue of a little...satyr or something?"

"Yes, yes, I sold those to Aliza. I'm very fortunate to have amassed a number of items from Sesqua Valley over the years, and Julian gave some of them to me himself when he needed money. Though sometimes he'd just trade them for some old books he wanted. Here...I'll show you my Sesqua collection."

Oskar meant to decline, as this was becoming a digression, but the scarred man was already moving toward another nearby glass showcase, and a moment later Oskar drifted after him. When Oskar had joined him, the man gestured proudly at the display.

"It's like evidence of Atlantis. Proof of Leng, and Kadath. Look at it!"

Oskar barely glanced at the items within. "So where is this Sequa Valley?"

"Huh," said the scarred man, with a snort meant

perhaps to be a laugh. "Where indeed. You remind me of your daughter."

"How's that?"

"She too was curious about Sesqua, even beyond her love for Julian. She badly wanted to go there...all the more so, of course, after he disappeared...but I'm not sure she ever set foot there. I'd love to visit there one day, myself, but..."

"But?" Oskar was starting to grow irritated with the man's eccentric nature. Had the fire that destroyed his face boiled his brain as well?

"As fascinated as I am by such obscure places, and the *things* that live in them, I confess to being rather apprehensive about venturing beyond a certain point." He motioned toward his mask-like visage. "No doubt you're wondering how this occurred."

Oskar could only shrug.

"As a boy, lying in bed one winter night, I saw strange violet light fluttering through my window curtains. So, I got out of bed and went to the window to look outside. Our house was at the edge of the forest, and the light came from within the trees. As I watched, the light emerged in the form of a hovering globe, large enough to contain a person's body...and I thought I even *saw* a body, curled inside it like a fetus in the womb, but it was indistinct because of the globe's brilliant ultraviolet light. Or maybe the figure was indistinct because it was an unfinished soul, yet to be born into the material world...or else, a departed soul not yet ready for the spirit world. In any case, I was too amazed to feel fear, as this floating sphere moved across the back yard, closer and closer to my window. And then..." The proprietor blew both his hands open.

"What happened?" Oskar asked, to humor this person whom he now knew to be a madman.

"The sphere exploded in a blinding flash. There was no sound, and the glass of the window was unbroken, but this was the result." With both hands, he touched his disfigured face.

"How do you account for that?" If there were anything at all to it, Oskar thought, he could only imagine ball lightning.

"I'm sure it was some manifestation that had strayed from Sesqua Valley. It isn't so far from here."

Oskar had to restrain himself from shouting when he

asked, "So what is it about this Sesqua Valley?" If his daughter had become obsessed with the place, real or imagined, he now suspected it had as much to do with this man's influence as Julian's.

"People talk of places where the veil is thin, or the veil is ragged with holes, but I see it as a tapestry. Woven into the tapestry is a very realistic, mundane landscape that tricks the eye. But the tapestry is a curtain, and if you reach out and nudge it aside, you'll find a doorway behind it."

"A doorway to *where?*"

The proprietor gave a try at a grin, which made Oskar flinch in his guts. "Places like Sesqua Valley."

"I'd better go," Oskar sighed, and he started to turn away. "Thanks for the coffee."

As if he hadn't noticed his guest withdrawing, the scarred man said, "She couldn't afford buying it, but I let Aliza have a whiff of the air of Sesqua. A free sample, if you will. It's all I've ever allowed myself, after all, and God...the things I saw, just from that one taste."

At the renewed talk of his daughter, Oskar wheeled toward the proprietor again, and snapped, "What are you going on about now?"

The man pointed at an object resting inside the glass display case.

The object was in itself not so remarkable, and this was no doubt why Oskar's eyes had merely skimmed over it before. A glass mason jaw for canning, with a screwed on metal lid. Yet on closer inspection, he realized the glass was not tinted with color, as he had at first thought. It was colorless, but trapped within the jar was a faintly stirring smoke or gas, mauve in hue. How was it possible to trap something like that? How long could it be retained? The mauve mist swirled subtly but restlessly, as though it wished to find a means of seeping out of its prison.

"Julian brought that to me. It's a kind of fog that appears when new souls are born into the Valley, or vanish from it forever. Much concentrated, it's the atmosphere...the very *essence*...of Sesqua Valley itself."

"And you let my daughter breathe in some of this...this stuff?"

"Yes," the burned man beamed.

"Yeah? Well, I think you've been snorting too much of it yourself. Or something else."

"I told you, I've only ever had a whiff. I don't blame you for not believing me, sir, but if you were only to experience it for yourself." And having said that, an idea obviously occurred to the man, for he then said, "I'll let you have a taste of it! A gift to the father of my sweet friend Aliza."

Oskar was tempted to erupt again, but as he studied the old mason jar once more, he found himself mesmerized by the way this condensed fog churned, turned in on itself, as if billowing in reverse, like an amorphous flower blooming and decaying and blooming again in a never-ending cycle.

"Let me try it, then," he murmured.

"Yes, please do! Here, sit down." The proprietor dragged over an old wooden chair with an Art Deco design. Oskar did as instructed, while his host went around behind the counter to slide open a panel and extract the glass jar. He came around in front of the counter, set the jar down for a moment, and unscrewed the lid almost all the way. He had to strain at first, so tightly was the lid, with its rubber-rimmed seal, screwed on. Turning toward Oskar, extending the jar, the man asked, "Are you ready, then?"

"Yes."

"Are you certain?"

"*Open it!*"

The burnt man gave the lid one last twist, uncovered the mouth of the jar, and thrust it directly under Oskar's nose. He jerked his head back a little, but before he could protest, or ask how he should do this – if he should draw in a big lungful – the proprietor was already snatching the jar back again, clapping on the cover and tightly screwing it in place.

"That's..." Oskar began asking, but he never got to "it."

When he opened his eyes, it was to find his forward view entirely occluded by roiling mauve-colored fog. So thick, he couldn't tell immediately if it were close to his face, or if he were observing a wall of clouds miles away.

Having gained consciousness to discover himself

squatting on his haunches, he leaned forward from this crouch and in looking down found that the fog lay below him, too. Vertigo swept over him, as if he teetered at the edge of a skyscraper's roof, and he jolted back. His spine came into contact with an unyielding solid surface, and he twisted around to examine it.

Oskar found an immense black column at his back. It appeared to be covered in many layers of blistering and peeling black paint. As he watched, new tears appeared in the black skin, shredded strips falling away into the writhing mist below. But then he realized that at the same time, old tears were healing up and smoothing out. This continuous, seething phenomenon was like an endless process of growth and decay, creation and destruction, occurring simultaneously in an unknowable balance.

Looking up, he saw shadowy dark limbs branching off from this immense central pillar. Chancing a look down again, as brief rifts appeared in the fog he spotted similar branching limbs below him. It was then he understood that the vast column was in fact a colossal tree trunk, and he was balanced on one of its mighty boughs.

Though, he considered, maybe this wasn't so much a tree itself as one great root of a tree, burrowing through a nourishing soil of ether, and feeding something much more vast up there beyond these clouds.

The restless black bark of the tree or root made no rustling sound, as he might expect, but he did begin to detect a sound from somewhere apparently high above him. It was faint, muffled by distance or the fog or both, but it seemed to be piping music, as from a flute or group of flutes.

The music inspired Oskar, as if its very intention was to call to him. He was reminded of Julian's pan flute in Aliza's apartment. In fact, might that even be Julian playing up there? If so, Oskar needed to see him...talk to him...

So Oskar looked around him for smaller branches he might use like the rungs of a ladder, in order to climb higher into the fog. He didn't find any, and the nearest bough was quite a ways above him. At last, though the thought of touching it with his bare skin initially repulsed him, he reached out and found handholds in the sloughing/reforming bark. Hoisting himself up, he dug the toes of his shoes into the bark as well. He pulled himself upward, one hand over the other. At one point, a wound in the bark began closing on his hand, tightening around his fingers like a mouth, so that he had to jerk his hand away violently lest it become trapped. He crawled up, up, until at last he reached that higher bough, and he threw a leg over it, swung himself up and straddled it, huffing from his efforts.

When he lifted his head to survey his immediate surroundings, he saw that he was not alone on this titanic tree branch.

A naked woman crouched on her haunches further away from the trunk than he. All around where she was hunkered, smaller limbs branched off from the bough like capillaries from a major artery, but none of them bore leaves. She held onto one of these thin branches with one fist to help support herself in her perch. The woman's head was lowered so that her long inky hair fell in curtains to obscure her face. The skin of her body was not just pale, but white as paper. Yet little black veins appeared and disappeared across her bare skin, looking like fleeting swarms of centipedes. Oskar realized it was a phenomenon like the tree bark: tiny cracks opening and just as quickly healing in the whiteness of her skin.

"You are lost," the woman spoke from behind her obscuring hair.

"I'm following the music," Oskar stammered, trying not to sound afraid.

"You must go that way," the woman replied, pointing downward...back the way he had come.

"But what's up that way?" Oskar asked her, motioning at the mists above them.

She lifted her head, and the hair slid away from her face to reveal a beautifully formed nose and mouth, the latter with blue lips, but there was only blank skin where eyes should have been. Yet even as Oskar took this in, eyes did open in her face – not as if eyelids were parting, but more as if entirely black orbs had surfaced in a bowl of milk. There were three of them, the third obsidian eye being in the center of her forehead.

"That is one way to Sesqua Valley."

"One way?"

The sphinx answered him only with cryptic silence.

"Who are you to tell me which way to go?" Oskar

asked her, trying to sound challenging to bolster his courage. "Which way are you going?"

"Neither way," she replied, staring unblinking with her three black eyes. "I am an In–Betweener."

"Why shouldn't I keep climbing?"

"It isn't for you."

"Maybe my daughter has gone up there."

"She hasn't. I'd have seen her."

"Did you see Julian go that way?"

She tilted back her head to gaze upward. The shifting mists cleared somewhat between Oskar and the woman, and he realized that behind her white body two great wings were folded against her back, layered in feathers the same glossy black as her hair.

"I know that boy...but he went back to the Valley another way." She fixed him with her eyes again. "You must return now."

"Why?" he demanded.

The woman's three eyes sank back into the bowl of milk. She lowered her chin to her chest, and the hair fell in front of her face. She answered, "Because the air returns to your lungs. The blood returns to your brain. Your eyes open to *your* world."

Oskar's eyes opened to see the terrible and tragic visage of the burned shop owner, hovering directly above his own face. Staring intently into Oskar's eyes, the man asked, "Are you all right?"

"My God," Oskar croaked.

"Mm," the scarred man said, nodding in satisfaction. "You saw. You know it wasn't just some drugged vision...you know it in your gut. Now you believe me."

He moved back to allow Oskar to sit up. Oskar found himself on a narrow twin bed, in a room in back of the antiques and curios shop. It had the looks of being the shop owner's own apartment.

Oskar lowered his head into his hands – his palms pressed into both eye sockets, his elbows propped on his knees

– and sat that way for long minutes while the burned man silently watched him.

At last, Oskar said, "I never believed there was anything beyond here."

"Make no mistake...there is no heaven, there is no hell. Not the way we were taught. It's nothing like that."

"But beyond here..." Oskar said again.

"Oh yes. Beyond here there's so very much."

"It's where she wanted to go, to be with him. But she didn't know the way. Or...or she knew the way, but that one taste you gave her...like the taste you gave me...it wasn't enough to get there."

"I'm sorry," the shopkeeper moaned, spreading his hands. "If I'd have known what she was going to do to herself, I would have given her the entire jar – free of charge. I swear it!"

At last Oskar sat up straight, removing his hands from his eyes. "How much do you want for it?"

"Well, I..." It appeared as though the man now regretted having said he would have given away the mason jar for free.

"Just tell me," Oskar said firmly.

"Uh...so rare a treasure..."

"I said *tell* me."

"Three thousand?" the burned man whimpered, cringing back a little as if he expected Oskar to explode in wrath.

Instead, Oskar only nodded thoughtfully and murmured to himself, "She never even thought she could ask me for the money."

His sister and his niece did most of the work decorating the funeral parlor for the wake, mounting many of the photos Oskar had found on boards supported by tripods. Aliza as a baby in her dead mother's arms. Aliza on a tricycle. A bicycle. Proudly leaning on her first car. Oskar ached to see how few of these photos included himself.

They had also mounted some of Aliza's sketches and oil

paintings. One of these showed a vast black tree swathed in gauzy mauve mist, with a group of diminutive satyr-like beings clambering up its flaying/mending bark. Another painting was a portrait of a young man who was both handsome and odd-looking at once, in an indefinable way. When Oskar had first seen this in her apartment, he had thought it was unfinished because of the boy's seemingly empty eyes. Now he realized the eyes were not unfinished: they were meant to appear as brightly silver.

Oskar had with his own hands added only three items to the mementos present in the room. On a small table near the head of the casket he had placed a flute made of slender lengths of bone, a red pinecone, and an odd greenish-stained statuette.

Oskar and his sister wept in each other's embrace. His sister, a Catholic, whispered in his ear, "She's in a better place now."

Years ago when his wife had taken her own life, his sister had tried to console him with these same words. At that time he had muttered back to her, "All is nothing."

This time, he replied gently, "Not yet."

When the viewing hours came to a close, Oskar told the funeral director that he needed a few minutes absolutely alone with his daughter, so he could say his personal goodbye. Of course, his wish was respected.

Alone in the room, Oskar stood over the open coffin, gazing down into his daughter's face as if with some expectation he couldn't fully define. As if she might yet open her eyes. She didn't look as unnatural as some corpses he had seen at wakes. Those had been mostly old people who had succumbed to wasting diseases, their faces unnaturally packed and painted. Aliza didn't appear joyful – which was what her name meant – but she did seem to be smiling in a very subtle and enigmatic way.

Oskar produced the glass mason jar from a pocket of his overcoat, and began unscrewing its rubber-sealed lid. As he did so, he said to her softly, "I don't know where you are right now, my baby. But I know where you wanted to be."

He held the jar close to her face, just under her nose, and then gave its cover a last turn.

The mauve gas billowed out eagerly, like a genie released from its bottle at long last. The mist obscured Aliza's face entirely for several moments, like the caul sometimes found covering a baby's head at birth, before it began to disperse. Oskar held the jar at arm's length, and he held his breath until the mist finally thinned out and mostly vanished from sight. When he could no longer hold his breath, however, he gulped in a deep swallow of air.

Opening his eyes, Oskar found he was already situated on that higher branch upon which the In-Betweener squatted, as if he had earned a more advanced starting position as a return explorer.

"You again," the woman said, her three eyes materializing out of blankness. "Lost again."

"Not as lost this time," he replied.

The entity nodded, as if she could see this. "A few moments ago I saw the woman you asked after last time." She pointed into the swirling mists above their heads. "She was climbing in that direction."

Oskar smiled. "Thank you," he told her. "That's all I needed to know."

This time he knew better than to try climbing up in pursuit of that constant, distant piping. Instead, he sat on the bough to keep the In-Betweener company for a short time, until his lungs were clear, and the blood flowed back into his brain.

Curious about the long silence, the funeral director returned to the room fifteen minutes later to find Oskar slumped unconscious on one of the room's leather-padded chairs.

"Sir?" the director asked, patting Oskar's arm. "Sir? Are you all right?" He sounded increasingly frantic. "Should I call you an ambulance?"

Finally opening his eyes, from which tears had flowed down the sides of his face, Oskar looked up at the man and his lips spread in a tremulous smile.

"It's okay now," Aliza's father told the man. "She's found her better place."

– For W. H. Pugmire

THE DOGS

There were two conditions March needed fulfilled when he entered into his search for a new apartment. One, was that pets be permitted. Some places, he had found, allowed dogs under a certain weight, or only of certain types, excluding such breeds as pit bulls, Akitas, and so on. This apartment building, a former factory in the heart of the city, followed the latter policy, but fortunately March's dog was a three-year-old retired greyhound, Snow, white mottled with faint brown. His wife had stayed on in their house. She had let him take the dog.

To determine the second condition, March took a sheet of paper out of his pocket, unfolded it, and held it against the brick walls of the apartment he was shown in the old factory, which like his dog had outlived its original purpose. He placed the sheet against one spot, spread flat under his palm, then another. Progressing from room to room, though the third-floor loft was mostly all one large room. The worn boards creaked under his feet as he shifted about.

"Is that a witchcraft symbol or something?" his prospective landlord asked as he watched March, chuckling nervously as he tried to make his apprehension sound like a joke.

"I'm an artist," March lied, though he had spent quite a lot of time getting the complex geometric figure on his sheet of paper just right. "This is one of my designs. I was just trying to get a feel for how my work would look hanging in here. I love the look of artwork hanging on brick walls." He turned to smile at the older man, to allay his fears. "It's great that you haven't over-gentrified this place. I love these old exposed pipes, the original wood ceiling and support beams." He gestured around him.

"They give the loft character, yes," the landlord said.

"You wouldn't be the only artist who lives in this building."

March resumed pressing his sheet of paper to various places on the rough walls. The bricks had been painted over thickly, white, looking like scales in the flank of some immense reptile. Then, when he held the intricate design he had drawn against a windowless stretch of wall in the sprawling main room, he sucked in his breath sharply. He hoped the man standing behind him hadn't heard his little gasp, wouldn't ask if something were wrong. March could feel a current vibrating up his arm…spreading down into his chest and up his neck, as though some heavy piece of factory machinery – left behind, forgotten – still thrummed with power on the other side of this wall.

He snatched the paper away from the spot quickly, before the vibration could spread up into his head. He wasn't ready for that. Not yet.

March looked around to smile at the landlord again. "I'll take it."

It had been three years since that day.

One wall of March's main room faced onto the gray street, admitting gray light through the large windows that ran its length. The other walls were covered in taped-up sheets of drawing paper, all of them crowded with arcane symbols and geometric patterns either copied from the esoteric books that filled his shelves and stood in precarious piles on the floor, or of his own design. Seen all together, the sheets of varying size partly overlapping each other, they looked like a strange web of ink surrounding him, enclosing this space in which he lived.

This space and the little it contained – himself, his six-year-old dog, his books – was all that he had left, all that might define his forty-two years on this globe. Two months ago he had been laid off from his job of the last nine years. He was experiencing frustration in finding another that would pay adequately. Of course, he knew he wasn't the only one experiencing life's difficulties. Somewhere beyond the walls of his little cave, with their inked caveman's graffiti, right now someone was setting off a bomb strapped to their body in a crowded outdoor market. Some teenager was walking into his school's cafeteria at noontime with his father's shotgun in his hands. Someone was being burned as a witch and stoned with cinderblocks while other townspeople stood around taking videos of it on their cell phones. All the while, men in expensive suits sat around tables as large and glossy as ponds, laughing and laughing, like gods looking down at the entertaining cruelties of their playthings.

Thinking these things as he paced his creaking floor, with a mug of coffee in hand, March stopped to look down at Snow, curled on the floor near the foot of his bed. "If only we could aspire to be like your kind," he said to the animal. She lifted her head in her gently timid way, her protuberant brown eyes fixed on his. "But humans will never be as loving as you are. As devoted. As loyal. As noble." Snow perked her ears up. Was he babbling something about going for a walk, perhaps? He smiled at her fondly. "Isn't that right, my noble little girl?"

He still couldn't understand why his former wife, whom he had once thought was so in tune with his mind, his spirit – now the wife of a man she had met online twelve years into her marriage with March – hadn't understood his desire to know if there were other, better worlds or realities than this. Was it really "crazy" to hope for and seek such possibilities? Was it really "nuts" to be dissatisfied with the limitations of this floating ball of miseries? In the end she had flat-out called him "insane." As if it wasn't this world that was insane.

Just last night, in fact, according to a local news web site he had been perusing on his computer, a young woman had been found murdered in the city's largest graveyard, Hope Cemetery, savagely mutilated. Yes, right here in this very city. Hope indeed, he thought.

He hoped for something better. Or if he couldn't have that, he hoped for this all to end.

Still holding his coffee mug, he turned away from Snow, leaving her to lower her long snout onto her paw again, her hopes for a long walk for the moment crushed. March faced the wall where he had on that day three years ago held the page of a sketchbook, and known that a window could be opened on this blank space where no window existed.

It had taken him over a year to accomplish it. He had taped up innumerable drawings, which had since been moved to other walls or destroyed in frustration entirely. Now, only one large sheet of paper was mounted there, by thin nails driven into the mortar between the bricks. He had learned that instead of erasing certain lines and drawing new ones – in order to modify the view this window offered him – he could alter the configuration with lengths of black thread instead. So he had driven other nails into the wall (fortunately his landlord had never needed to set foot in his apartment again), and he would unwind one end of a thread from a nail, shift the line of thread to another location, creating a new angle, and loop its end around a different nail.

The design as a whole was enclosed within one large circle extending to the edges of the paper, but other circles overlapped/intersected it, and complex angles created stars that subdivided into triangles. At various critical points and vertices in all these angles and curves he had handwritten words learned from his obscure personal library. Without these words to imbue the formula with power, it would all have only been black ballpoint on white Strathmore.

At the very center of the design there was a decagon formed from strands of black thread. This was, in effect, the window pane itself. It put him in mind of a porthole, which he now approached as if to stare out at a storm-tossed sea from the relative safety of his ship's cabin. But first, he picked up a pair of sunglasses from a little side table and put them on, resting his coffee aside.

March put his face close to the window, but he never touched it. He didn't even know what the sensation would be like. He didn't believe his hand would pass through – after all, he felt no breeze from the scene beyond, no whiff of air or scent from another land, and he never even heard sounds from the other side – but some intuition told him it was better to limit his curiosity to observation.

Ah, he thought, peering through, soon he probably wouldn't need the dark glasses anymore. Day by day the nuclear blaze of white light continued to diminish, where it showed between the vast black shapes that hung like continent-sized boulders in the sky. When he had first succeeded in opening this scrying lens, nearly two years ago now, nothing at all had been visible past the light streaming into his apartment like a concentrated ray beamed from the molten heart of a star, from which he had shielded his face with a cry. He had been blinded for over an hour, had feared he would never see again. The skin of his face had been burnt red and tender.

Gradually, over the weeks and months thereafter, as the brightness of the light grew less intense, he had been able to make out a city on the other side. And those looming black forms that hovered above it.

He couldn't tell how many there were; the one in the foreground blotted out most of his view of the sky, but other, similar shapes were suspended behind it. Slight adjustments he had made by shifting the angles of his threads had afforded him other views from the city's streets, but the position of the dark shapes crowding the sky hadn't noticeably changed, so tremendous in size were they.

It was not only a city out there...it was *this* city. His own gray city, grayer still, at some unknown future time. He had recognized the buildings, or the shells of them at least, since many had been burned charcoal black from within or without, while most had simply been abandoned to disrepair, their windows broken into silently howling fanged mouths.

When he had finally been able to make out the details of his city, he had realized that lying strewn throughout its streets were the bodies of its former inhabitants.

At first, disregarding the titanic hulks levitating in the sky because he couldn't yet process them, he had thought a nuclear war had transpired and these people had perished in the initial blast. But then he had grasped, scrutinizing the corpses from various different views of the city's streets as he tweaked his window's perspective, that all of them – whether man, woman, or child – bore the same strange injuries. Quite simply, their heads appeared to be smashed into unrecognizable pulp, bone and all, as if they had actually exploded... as if a grenade had been implanted into every skull.

Yet when the glare of light dimmed further over time and he was able to make our finer detail, he noticed that thin black cords, not so unlike the black threads he utilized in his formula, streamed out of each exploded head like sticky strands of web. These strands extended straight up into the sky. Though the silhouetted hovering mountains were too far up for him to see it, he felt intuitively that the far ends of the strands were connected to the amorphous titans themselves. It was, of course, not that these black strings had reached up into the sky from those myriad shattered skulls, but that the cords had been extruded from the shapeless shapes that almost occluded the sky above this dead city.

But the city, the Earth, wasn't entirely dead.

Whatever cataclysm had befallen humanity, it had apparently not annihilated other forms of animal life. Pigeons would waddle about this nightmare world as nonchalantly as if awaiting bread crumbs in the park. Gulls still wheeled in the sky, white motes against the unmoving black giants. March occasionally saw cats. But mostly it was the dogs that captured his attention. They skulked through the streets singly or in packs, their ribs showing ever more vividly through filthy coats. They looked lost, disoriented, and March imagined they were searching for their masters. He had always felt it was cruel that beautiful animals like his Snow were used for racing, so that humans might wager money on these sensitive unquestioning creatures, but seeing the stray dogs wander the stilled future city made him feel it was just as cruel that human beings had made dogs dependent upon them for food, for shelter, for the love they craved…too often, in vain.

Night never fell in this world beyond the brick wall; the steady radiance in the sky prevented that, or had the Earth been jolted to a stop so that it no longer even turned? The dogs stole about constantly, flitting from alley to alley. Sniffing through the streets, searching. Hunting, March thought, for cats and squirrels. He once saw a collie pounce upon a pigeon, successfully snatching it in its jaws then shaking its head wildly to kill it. Iridescent feathers floated to the ground.

Finally had come the day when the dogs had lost their inhibition, their sense of the previous order of things. March suspected, though, it had more to do with their desperation than any kind of breach in their loyalty. He saw a mongrel creep up on one of the corpses lying on a sidewalk – the body of a young woman in a short skirt turned to rags – sniff at a withered and discolored leg warily, as if the woman might sit up suddenly and scold it as a bad boy, then lean in at last and bite into the half-mummified flesh.

After that day, he had seen the dogs eating human bodies on a regular basis. They fought over them, savagely. They dragged them off whole, like a leopard with a broken-necked antelope, or in dismembered pieces. The tethers that bound the near-headless humans to the overhead colossi snapped free and trailed across the ground.

Watching the starving dogs go mad with desperation, knowing how unnatural it was that they had been driven to feed off their very masters, made March's heart ache. As for all those dead humans themselves…well, their extinction was a fate they had earned, through their actions and their inaction and their unworthiness. And if his own future self lay in one of those streets out there, his own head turned to mush, cables of black web running up from it to connect him to one of those Outsiders in the sky, that had manifested to reclaim this world – for he had later come to admit to himself that that was what those leviathans were: the beings that the rarest of the books in his collection had foretold – well, then that was okay, too. He didn't count himself all that much better than the rest of his breed. To his way of thinking, his own dog Snow was superior to him. And if Snow were out there hungry and afraid, then he'd *want* her to feed from his corpse rather than starve to death.

Today, March turned away from the scrying window and removed his sunglasses. Not much had changed out there over the past two years but for the slow dimming of the light that had heralded the appearance of the Outsiders. He felt a familiar itch, a deep grumbling hunger like that which had started him on this quest for knowledge back when he had still been married.

The need to know…to *see*…even more.

He had been too long content with his success in opening this window, doing nothing more radical than changing his street view from time to time. But now, finally, he had determined that he had to make more dramatic adjustments to his formula if he hoped to understand the destiny of his race more clearly…and exactly when it was that the Outsiders would tear their way into this reality. Once again, he had to truly experiment.

Then one day, more through that sense of intuition he

possessed than through his exhausting reexamination of his book collection, he struck upon the answer. It was so simple he hadn't even considered it until now. What had really inspired him, ultimately, was a dream he had had the night before, in which he had been standing on the deck of a ghost ship at sea, the *Mary Celeste* perhaps, the only human aboard but with Snow faithfully by his side. He had taken up an incongruously modern pair of binoculars so as to scan the gray, stormy horizon for land. His view through the lenses had been blurry, so he had had to turn the diopter adjustment ring to sharpen his focus.

Yes! An adjustment ring!

First, with white correction fluid he painted over the ten words of power that accompanied each of the ten points on the formula's central decagon. The moment he painted over the first word, for the first time in two years the window was gone, leaving only an area of blank paper. He didn't panic, however, or bemoan his decision. As soon as the white fluid had dried he wrote the same ten words of power...but this time he advanced their position by one degree, clockwise, as if adjusting the focus of a lens.

The window opened again, and this time he had his dark glasses on from the start just in case he got kicked back to the beginning again, and that blasting column of light.

But no...his instincts had been correct. The lens gave him the same view of the city as last time, but from a point further, deeper, into the future.

He no longer needed the sunglasses, and removed them. The sky revealed in the spaces between the blob-like masses of the Outsiders was now a subdued, almost twilight violet. Faint rags of mist wisped between the buildings, and grass had grown up lush, if gray, through cracks in the pavement. Sizable trees had even sprouted, their roots displacing cement slabs, leaves dull and waxy. Walls were choked thick with grayish vines. Many buildings had crumbled in on themselves, turning into ivy-choked rubble. The city looked like a vast graveyard, overgrown, its long-dead occupants without surviving mourners.

He expected to see bones scattered in the streets. Surely no intact skeletons, but at least stray rib cages or femurs, for instance. No skulls, of course, though the occasional lower jaw was conceivable. Still, there was nothing. Had it all turned to dust?

He unwound one end of a string, shifted it to another nail an eighth of an inch over. It was like changing the channel on a television, with only a brief interruption of fluttering light/darkness between. As a result, he was given the view of a different street in the same demolished city.

Not only did he discover bones, this time, but he was introduced to the descendants of the city's orphaned canines, as well.

At first it was just the bones. They lay in the very middle of the street, heaped up in a neat cairn. He might have believed that dogs would leave them that way after having gnawed the last shreds from them and cracked them for their marrow – just as a dog will bury a bone for future use – maybe even as some new territorial behavior, but what then about the flowers?

The pile of bones was surrounded by a ring of plucked flowers of a type March couldn't name, with white petals. This was without question no accidental drift of uprooted flowers blown here by a windstorm. The circle was nearly as perfect as those he himself had inked on paper to design this magic lens.

So, there had been survivors of the apocalypse, after all! He was almost disappointed, but still anxious to see them…what they looked like, how they lived.

In the next moment, he did. And he gazed through his window with his jaw hanging slack.

A large dog, so thin it was emaciated – rather like an albino greyhound, but rougher in outline, more feral-looking, with striking pink eyes like a rabbit's – came loping out from between two tall mounds that had once been buildings. In its jaws it carried a human pelvis. Its intention was clear: it was going to add this prize to the cairn in the center of the street.

But as the dog neared the cairn, it rose up onto its hind legs. It walked upright the last few steps. With its front legs, which March now realized had something more like human fingers than the toes of a dog's paw, the animal removed the pelvis from its jaws and added it to the very top of the pile.

"Dear God," March said aloud.

Behind him, he heard the tinkle of Snow's dog tags as she lifted her head at the sound of his voice.

He placed a kitchen chair close in front of the window. Outside the actual windows of his apartment, night had fallen, galaxies of windows alight as if each building in the city had begun to burn up from the inside.

He saw other dogs come and go, as fleet and furtive as white ghosts in the unending violet twilight. Some galloped along on all fours. Some tiptoed past on two legs. No more bones were added to the monument to their dead, beloved masters while March watched, but one dog – and they were all of the same, strange new breed – did come forward to push the ring of flowers into a neater arrangement after the breeze had made its rim untidy. She bunted the blossoms with her nose and also patted them with her white-furred hands.

Was this, March wondered, a mutation caused by some emanation, conscious or accidental, generated by the Outsiders? Or could it even be that, having lived among human beings for so many generations, in their absence the dogs had begun to adopt human characteristics and behaviors as a matter of natural evolution? Even, in imitating humans, to *replace* them in some kind of tribute?

After a while March saw no more dogs in the street. He became conscious that his rump was sore from the hard wooden chair, and he realized he had neglected Snow for too long. He took her outside on her leash. She released a small pond of urine only a few steps from the old factory's front stoop. As he stood over her, March caught himself glancing up and down the dark street nervously…as if he expected that at any moment, some crouched figure as gaunt as a bundle of birch branches would come tiptoeing out from around a corner, its vivid pink eyes fixed on him hungrily.

When he was back inside he shuddered, bolted the door, unhitched Snow from her leash, and set about microwaving himself a poor excuse for a Thai dinner. While he waited for it to cook, he walked over to his computer idly and glanced at the local news.

He spotted the headline immediately: "Second Ghoulish Murder."

The body of a sixty-four-year-old homeless man had

been found at the back of Hope Cemetery. He had been horribly savaged. A police spokesman was not confirming that these two murders were the work of a single perpetrator. They did not want to use the term serial killer at this time.

It wasn't the first time there had been murders in this city, March reflected. It was a big enough city, and the more people you lumped together, the more harm they did each other. It was just the law of nature. Shadowy predators had always accompanied what passed for civilization, and always would. But somehow these two killings resonated with him on a deep level, unsettling him in a way he couldn't articulate to himself.

Naturally, the next thing to do was to white-out the words of power again, then draw them in anew, rotated one more degree to the right. He did this the following morning, after first making sure Snow had had her walk and her food and water bowls filled. He expected to be seated in front of the two-dimensional crystal ball he had created a long while.

He didn't know what increment of time had passed – any more than he could judge the time that had transpired between now and the first view, and the first view and the second – but it was obvious that it was a great many more years (if one were still to portion time into a man-made notion such as years).

Buildings had lost more of their orderly shape, become more like natural formations of the earth; he might not even have recognized them as having been buildings if he hadn't gazed on this scene from his apartment building's perspective previously. More trees had risen, almost forming a grove. Their leaves, and the grass and underbrush and rampant creeping ivy, still had that grayish poisoned look, but somehow the vegetation flourished. It wasn't so much that Nature was reclaiming the city, but that a new Nature had come about.

Yet all of this was secondary to his interest, because there was a new development that made him lean forward on his chair and murmur, "What the hell is this?"

In the center of the street where the evolving dogs had

erected a monument to their masters – and he had decided it must only be one monument of many dispersed across the city, if not dispersed across the globe – the cairn of bones was gone, replaced by something which he couldn't identify. It appeared to be a two-dimensional black disk maybe six feet across, floating a foot or so off the split pavement, angled slightly away from March so he could see it wasn't a sphere. Its surface was flat black, featureless, but the edge of the circle appeared to be rimmed in a fringe of wavering cilia like that of a paramecium. In addition, maybe a dozen strands varying in thickness – from thread-thin to cables as thick as a wrist, perhaps – streamed upwards from various points in the disk's outer rim. Just like the strands that had once connected the decimated heads of human corpses to the Outsiders overhead, these various cords ran up into the sky to disappear in the distance, but March had no doubt they connected with the immense bodies still hovering above the Earth.

The sky showing in the gaps between the Outsiders was still that violet hue of early evening, and against its subtle glow he could see that after centuries or millennia of immobility the silhouetted outlines of the Outsiders appeared to be pulsing, throbbing amorphously. He noticed that long whip-like flagella had been extruded by the Outsiders here and there, lazily wavering as if the entities swam in place in the Earth's atmosphere.

He returned his focus to the hovering disk the Outsiders had apparently manifested. Just as in the case of the cairn of bones, March strongly suspected this wasn't the only such tethered disk that had appeared in this city, or upon the face of the Earth. Were those god-like entities at last, moving with the unhurried pace of the immortal, endeavoring to transform this reality into an environment that better suited their needs or desires?

A low rumbling behind March caused him to spin around on his chair's wooden seat to look back at his living space, jolted like a man abruptly awakened from a dream. For a disoriented half-second he didn't recognize his own surroundings, as if someone had bricked him alive in this box while his spirit had been elsewhere. Then he saw Snow. The white greyhound stood just behind him, her gaze fixed hypnotically on the lens as his had been. Her upper lip was quivering. At first he had had the odd notion that she was growling at him, but she had obviously sensed something in the scrying window. Up until this moment, over the past two years that it had remained open, she had never even appeared to acknowledge the window's existence.

March faced his lens again to try to ascertain what it was that had caused his pet to take note of it after all this time. The appearance of the levitating black disk? The undulating bodies of the Outsiders?

New movement, and March flinched as a figure entered the scene from the right, like an actor stepping out from behind a curtain onto a stage. It was one of the dogs, but that much further evolved from the last time he had watched them. It bore no vestige of a tail, and walked more erect than the tiptoeing creatures he had seen before, its upright posture no longer seeming tentative or unnatural. Though still lean, its musculature appeared more like that of a human than a dog. It was still covered in short bristly white hair, its snout still elongated and canine, its eyes still an almost luminous pink, but the creature's overall aspect conveyed a palpable intelligence.

The creature was carrying an armful of tinder, perhaps to start a fire. March had no doubt at all that these beings were now capable of creating fire. He realized, however, that it wasn't bare branches in its arms but a bundle of human leg and arm bones.

The strange being was moving straight toward the hovering disk. It didn't bend its path around it. Snow growled again, showing her teeth now, as the creature drew closer to the inky circle. March reached around behind him, without taking his eyes off the viewing screen he had called into existence, and stroked Snow's neck to calm her. Was the creature going to offer its burden of bones to the disk as a tribute, to appease its new masters?

Having created this scrying pane from a once empty sheet of paper, March was not surprised when he comprehended the black disk was a portal – though whether it was an intentional creation of the Outsiders, or merely a hole stretched open in the fabric of space and time as a byproduct of the Outsiders' new activity, how could he judge? However the portal had come to be, March's first impression when the dog-creature arrived at the disk was that it was going to throw the bones into it. Instead, the thing stepped over the rim of the disk and slipped its whole body into the blackness. In a fraction of a moment, the dog-being was gone, as if it had plunged into a vertical pool of ink.

No sooner had it disappeared than two more of the canine-things emerged from the same direction, their arms also full of human bones. Snow growled again, as the pair of creatures approached the disk as the first one had. They too, one after the other, hopped up into the black circle and were swallowed.

Like him, the dogs had figured out that the disk was the mouth of a tunnel.

"They're...migrating," March whispered to Snow, in awe. "And taking their masters' bones with them."

But, he wondered, migrating *where?*

Over the next several hours he saw one more dog-being disappear into the disk with a load of bones in its grasp. After that, March was too impatient to watch for more of them. Too impatient to wait until tomorrow to forward the words of power another notch. He decided to do that now.

First, though, he sat on the edge of his bed and stroked Snow and talked to her soothingly. He told her he was going to tear up some hotdogs for her and add them to her bowl of dry food as a treat, to keep her distracted while he inscribed the last of the ten words of power that would reactivate his decagonal lens. He said, "You're a good girl, Snow. You're the only living thing on this planet that I can count on. That I can trust. The only constant in my life. The only living thing in this world that truly loves me. The only thing that *I* truly love." His eyes were filling up in self pity, but also with the enormity of his affection. He understood he not only loved this animal, but admired her...and all her kind. To his mind, dogs were already the pinnacle of evolution.

He went on, "You don't live as long as we do. What will I do, someday, when I don't even have you anymore? I'll be alone. But I guess...I guess we're all of us alone. Most people just don't think they are." He smiled, and ran his hand along her neck again. "We'll just keep being alone together, I guess, huh? And see what the future brings."

She turned her head to lick his hand.

With Snow digging into her bowl of food at the other end of the long, single room that doubled as March's bedroom and living room, he penned in the last of the ten potent words.

March's initial impression was that he had been unsuccessful; that he had written one of the words incorrectly. The window only showed unbroken blackness. He was reminded, uncomfortably, of the disk he had seen floating above the street in the last view. He imagined a dog-creature's head suddenly thrusting out of the portal into his reality, pink eyes blazing, to snap at his face. But then he considered that perhaps night had finally descended over that future landscape.

Eventually, though, he realized he was seeing a churning sort of blackness within the blackness, a restless pulsing almost sensed more so than actually seen. Seen with his mind rather than his eyes. Thus, trusting more to his intuition than his paltry organs of sight, March came to understand that the Outsiders had descended from the sky at long last. Descended, and consumed. They had swallowed up all, until they *were* all.

He advanced the ten words another notch, to the fifth configuration he had attempted, so impatient that the correction fluid hadn't dried fully and the inscriptions were smeary. They still did the trick, but the resulting view was the same as before: only churning, sentient blackness. Nevertheless, he continued this way – sixth configuration, seventh, eighth, ninth, tenth, as though he were the master of time himself, forcing the arm of a clock – until the only position that remained was the original one, setting number one, which had showed him the Earth still blazing with the white light of the Outsiders' eruption onto this plane of existence.

For now, he left the dial set at view number ten. For now, his mind couldn't assimilate any more than that seething black emptiness. It was almost soothing, that living oblivion. A kind of relief, like an afterlife of blissful nothingness.

That night, after he had walked Snow and then made himself a sandwich, he sat down in front of his computer to look in on the news. He almost expected to see that there had been a third killing in his city in or around Hope Cemetery, but there hadn't. He extended his search to other cities, then other countries, but of course gruesome murders committed in or around graveyards were so prevalent that they could have been the work of a never-ending supply of madmen. Still, wasn't it possible that some of these crimes he skimmed had been committed by another kind of predator? A predator that had lived in humankind's shadow for generations, maybe since the earliest days of human civilization? Going back as far, perhaps, as the time when primitive humans and wild canines had first begun living in conjunction?

The cosmic clock come full circle?

With the world all peacefully black outside the windows of his third-floor loft, March swiveled his computer chair to watch Snow as she slept, her snout propped on one paw as always.

"They don't eat us because they hate us," March whispered to the dog, while he wondered about the dreams that made her twitch one hind leg from time to time. Was she dreaming the primal dream of hunting prey? Was she dreaming of stalking on her hind legs alone?

He said, "They eat us to commune with us. Because they still love us."

GHOSTS IN AMBER

His boyhood terror of spiders, as electrically vivid as any feeling pleasant or unpleasant experienced by a child, had in middle age dulled to a quiet aversion. Even fear becomes mundane with time.

There was a small, dark and otherwise undistinguished type of spider in the rustic areas on the periphery of Gosston, and in the woods beyond that sprawling town, which in cooperation wove great filmy tents high in trees. From time to time as their community swelled some instinct triggered them and a great number of the spiders would slough off from their tribe and extend the tent upwards into a bloated protuberance, until this tumor-like shape would break off when sufficient wind was aroused, a perfect orb rising aloft and borne on the current, maybe the size of a baseball but perhaps large as a beach ball, eventually coming to rest on the crown of some other tree. If that tree was untenanted a new shroud-home would be knitted. If it was already overpopulated a fresh web globe would be fashioned to further their migration.

This type of spider abounded in the area where he now lived, and he was always scanning the trees that hemmed the apartment house's parking lot whenever he set out in the morning for his car or upon his arrival home from work. He remembered being teased by his older sister as a boy that he'd better be careful outside lest an extra-large specimen of those ghostly bubbles descend onto his head and enfold him, trapping him within and bearing him into the sky when the wind gusted again. She said they might never find his body, mummified in the top of some tree with spiders swarming in and out of the tenement of his husk. For years his parents had had all they could do to get him to go play outdoors instead of hiding inside with a book in his hands and a low, solid ceiling over his head.

As an adult he knew the venom of these spiders was not dangerous to humans and that their woven balloons would never support a field mouse let alone a small boy. But he had never shaken off that image of looking up to see one of the misty spheres lowering onto him, too late to avoid, its collapsing parachute like a white cloth draped over the head of a blind-eyed stone bust in some house where people no longer lived.

There were nineteen banks in the town of Gosston, and he'd forgotten now which one they'd originally taken their home loan through, but whichever one it was they had now lost their house to it. It hadn't been a large house, but they'd had a little fenced yard in the back. After the first couple of years they never went out there, and the grass and weeds swallowed up their picnic table till just the top showed like a raft adrift, but the yard had been *his* little piece of the universe and he'd liked its summer green glow through the little window over the kitchen sink. There had been a scrap of front porch warped as the deck of a listing ship with a busted railing where he'd sit out on golden evenings to read a book until the gold turned blue and he couldn't make out the words any longer, and he'd have a coffee or beer at his elbow. He'd driven by his little old house a few times since they'd left and these days the front lawn was mowed to a stubble like a nappy carpet with a for sale sign stabbed in it and he could see around the side of the house that the back yard was the same. The new owner would probably fix the busted rail on the porch and never once sit outside to read some old book.

Now he and his wife lived in another part of Gosston in a big house up on a woodsy slope overlooking the narrow road, but they only rented one of four sections of this house, an apartment that was sizable enough with nice wooden floors, but the young woman who lived downstairs from them was either a drunk or had a mental disorder or both. They had had to stop using one of their two bedrooms except for storage because the woman had left a note in their mail box complaining she could hear their bed at night, and their alarm clock in the morning woke her up, too, though she left for work about the same time they did. He didn't understand what she heard from their bed, since he and his wife hadn't had intercourse since moving into the apartment and for a long time before that. Just getting in and out of it and shifting position while they dreamed? The woman below pounded on her ceiling if they walked around too much in the kitchen after about eight-thirty, though one night she'd pounded as early as six-thirty. So he and his wife tried to stay out of the kitchen after dinner, just as they'd moved their bed into the smaller of the two bedrooms.

His wife left for her job a half hour earlier than he did so she never seemed to encounter their downstairs neighbor in person. He himself tried to avoid running into her when he left for work in the morning and often peeked down from the window over the kitchen sink to see if she was outside getting into her black beetle-like car before he left his apartment. Sometimes he watched her walk to her car and start it and leave before he did the same. Though apparently unattached she was not an unattractive woman, young and with long, curly dark hair, and evidently a nurse because she wore a white uniform under her coat and white pantyhose. Under other circumstances he would have found that beguiling but she was too unsettling for him to desire her overtly.

Despite his efforts to avoid contact sometimes they set out to start their cars at precisely the same time and on one of these occasions he'd asked her just exactly what she was hearing that upset her so much. Did the floorboards in their kitchen squeak too loudly? All she said with an intense and meaningful expression was, *I hear you moving around up there.*

One weekend night around eleven when he closed a sliding drawer in the bathroom after removing nail clippers a wrecking ball crashed against one of the walls downstairs. Another boom followed and another with a rhythm as if this wrecking ball were swinging as a pendulum. A ululating shriek rose up to accompany it. This giant's booming heartbeat and banshee screaming went on for minutes. His wife looked into the bathroom at him from the living room where she had been watching TV and both of them were paralyzed unblinking while they listened. At first he wanted to call the police because he thought the woman downstairs was being raped or murdered by an intruder. Then he realized she must be lying on her bed or maybe on the floor pounding the wall with both feet and screeching out all the air inside her because she hadn't liked the sound of the bathroom drawer on its slides.

He missed when his wife would work nights because he'd liked coming home and having their little house all to himself, but just before the move she'd switched to a day shift like him. She scolded him if he came home too late. *You know we have to eat and clean the dishes before she starts complaining.* But he still customarily didn't come home until an hour or more after he'd got off work. He'd find an excuse to pick up a few things at the market or he'd go to the library to soothe himself with the smell of old books and maybe take one home guiltily like a pet he'd found. Or he might walk in the rambling cemetery where his mother would take him for picnics as a boy. Cemeteries had never frightened him because of that. He just thought of them as beautiful parks full of sculpted blocks and tablets. (And that particular cemetery had never been infested with tree spiders, though others in town were.) He sometimes drove to look at his old childhood home, that is until it was razed and a bank was built in its place. One would think the citizens of Gosston were rich for all the banks but he knew that wasn't the case for most, just as it wasn't in any other town besides Gosston. The banks didn't so much safeguard the money of Gosston as horde it.

One early evening when he'd finally come home from driving aimlessly around town after work, as he was getting the mail out of their box in a row of four boxes at the bottom of the steep hill the house perched atop, he glanced across the street at an old mill or factory nestled against a pond that from here looked man-made. Maybe the water had powered a turbine in the distant past. Gosston boasted even more ill-fated, shut-down factories than it did banks, as if the latter had sucked the life out of the factories for their own and left the carcasses. Some of these factories had been repurposed for apartments or offices while others had not. He'd never gone across the road he now lived on and over the guardrail to have a closer look at this apparently disused building, but gazing at it now he felt the compulsion to do so stirring. It was as though he was running out of other places in town to go before he had to come home.

He determined then, before he got back in his car and drove it up the precipitous driveway to the parking lot of the house he rented a quarter of, that tomorrow after work he would park his car on the other side of the road and hope his wife, having come home earlier than him as always, wouldn't look out a window and spot it there. He planned to step over that rumpled guardrail barrier and go down the incline with its shabby trees and brush-snared rubbish into the great deep hollow where the pond lay, and the factory looming from its edge.

He turned from the factory and reached his hand to the door of his car, and flinched when he saw a great white snowball come bouncing down the curve of his driveway. It was a silk globe as big as a boulder and he feared it would impact with the nose of his idling car, explode and shower his vehicle and himself with swarms of small dark spiders. Before he could open his door and duck inside, however, a surge of breeze swept the rolling balloon up into the air and it sailed over his head. He swiveled to watch it float higher and saw it was followed by a chain of a half dozen smaller bubbles in a retinue of gauzy full moons, all of them drifting off into the sky in the direction of the factory and then beyond until they either flew off into purpling dusk or alighted in the silhouetted tree line that was like the fanged mandible of night.

Without turning from the kitchen sink where she stood washing and breaking apart something green and slippery, as if she were trying to drown and dismember some giant insect with veiny wings, his wife simply said, *Late.* He wanted to say he couldn't be too late since she was still preparing their meal, but he refrained and only stood staring at her from behind for a moment as if he hadn't looked at her straight on, rather than merely peripherally, for a very long time. She was short and had a block-like shape, with hair dyed blond and tight blue jeans on a sexless body in an attempt to look much younger than she was, and thus so resembling so many of the women he worked with that every day he could conceivably mistake a dozen of them for his wife from the back. He understood the same could be said of himself, in regard to all the bespectacled round-bellied men with graying and thinning hair at his company who looked like they had been mass produced at the very plant where they worked.

He and his wife had never had children and he wondered sometimes how their life might have been different if they had. Would they have been happier or would the additional financial stresses and commitment of time and energy have caused them to divorce by now? As it was they had never fought badly enough for either of them to have even uttered the word divorce. They didn't seem to possess the passion to become that angry or discontented. Sometimes she criticized him for remaining in the same relatively low-paying job for these many years, for lacking ambition to the point of apathy, but he supposed it was this quality of acceptance that had kept them united. He wondered which was the worse condition of the two for a person to possess: apathy or dissatisfaction.

He wondered if he was dissatisfied with his apathy, or apathetic about his dissatisfaction.

As he eased himself down the incline, occasionally holding onto the bone-white trunks of birches to help maintain his balance, he speculated as to whether the extensive hollow in which the factory resided could be a crater where a meteor or asteroid had collided with the world tens of thousands of years ago, with the pond having formed at its nadir. If a heavenly body had created this depression, might it have carried radioactive elements that today polluted the pond's water, or even primitive alien life that had evolved into secretive creatures that throve in the pool's murky depths? Already a boyish sense of adventure had taken hold of his mind, his curiosity becoming more intense the deeper he descended into the pit.

At one point while catching his breath he twisted to look back up the incline to check if he could see the house he rented an apartment in, balanced high on its hill across the street. He feared his wife might be watching him in confusion and disapproval from one of its windows even now. He found he could not see it, however, as he had ventured far enough into the bowl that its upper edge blocked his view of his home, not to mention all the intervening trees. He faced forward again and continued downward until the ground leveled out and he stood before the pond, with the factory on the other side of a stream that disgorged into the body of water. He realized this stream must be the Gosston Canal. It separated him from the factory like a castle's moat.

The left flank of the long brick structure abutted a desolate-looking road that vanished into dense trees. Running the length of the right side of the factory was a narrow strip of parking lot, entirely empty and with long weeds growing through cracks veining its pavement. The parking lot bordered the edge of the pond with its black surface as undisturbed as a table top. A clock tower rose above the rest of the factory's flat roof and was twinned in the obsidian pond as if painted on glass, but where its face should have been there was only an empty black skull socket now as though the clock itself had dropped out and been lost under the water. His imagination still stimulated, he pictured the clock lying on black muck at the bottom of the pond with its arms even now turning unseen as the years passed.

A metal bridge with blistered paint spanned the drowsily flowing canal from this side to the other side and as he started across it he chided himself for not owning a camera to capture these intriguing images, but he hadn't felt sufficiently motivated to preserve his memories in photographs for quite a few years.

He reached the far side with the factory now rising more imposingly above him, especially its blind tower. From here it looked as though the front entrance lay directly below the tower, within an archway, but he spotted another door nearer to him on the left side of the building and it was toward this that he started walking. Even as he did so, though, he asked himself, *You don't mean to try to go inside, do you?*

He assured himself he would only test to see if that metal side door was locked. Purely out of curiosity.

He found the door was unlocked. He also found that his curiosity was not quenched.

He pushed the metal door open with his clothed forearm not so much because he needed to put the weight of his chest against it but because he was reluctant to touch its rust encrusted surface and possibly abrade his skin. It screamed on its hinges like a dying animal aroused to one more complaint of misery before subsiding into unconsciousness again. He pushed it open only far enough to pass through the gap without his body touching.

The smell packaged up inside the building was profound. It spoke of machinery and oil, of moldering cardboard and garbage and something like the damp leaf litter of a forest floor, combining into a kind of dumpster smell, but with other elements lingering like leather and tanning chemicals. He knew those smells because in the early years of his long and varied work history he had been employed as a leather cutter for a boot manufacturer and then later a pocketbook company, both here in Gosston and both long since closed down. Whatever the individual source of these olfactory strata, they combined into one stench so complicated and pervasive that it oppressed him almost to the point of queasiness. But he was not to be dissuaded and tried to breathe shallowly only through his mouth.

He had entered the building into a shipping area with a pair of shuttered garage-type doors further along a wall of bricks painted white with a second coat of grime upon that. A third and more irregular covering for the walls was graffiti done in the cartoonish manner of tagging, as if the rural outskirts of Gosston might actually be home to dangerous gangs marking their territory instead of simply bored white teenagers romanticizing a harder way of life. Coherent words were hard to distinguish in this garish overlapping jumble that was like a visual representation of the miasma permeating the room. One word for instance, ballooned purple and blue to deformity like a bloated corpse, apparently said GOMEZ but it might have been GONEZ or even GONE?.

Across one of the shuttered shipping dock doors someone had painted in red letters, easier to read than any of the others: DON'T GO OUT THERE! He contemplated this with a little smile of perplexity and muttered, *Too late for that now.*

Other than the preponderance of graffiti the room was stripped down to only heaps of debris and trash that seemed to have mostly crawled into the corners to huddle, perhaps adhering there to the sticky tar of shadows. High windows were covered in torn membranes of plastic once perhaps meant to retain heat but now only cataracts that dulled the already overcast sunlight to a foggy glow.

Crunching pebbles of beer glass under his shoes he crossed to a doorway in the opposite wall from which he had entered and found himself in a corridor with a high ceiling of bare joists and exposed pipes and lights with their fluorescents smashed out, but more narrow windows let in that weak milky light. He moved down this corridor, poking his head into various rooms along the way where doors stood open or had been taken off their hinges probably to facilitate the removal of machinery. Most of the rooms were bare but for more debris more shadows more incomprehensible graffiti.

He jerked his head of one room quickly, though. In here one of those web orbs hung down from where it was affixed to the ceiling like a gigantic mold-white heart, at least the size of the one that had come rolling down his driveway the day before and he might even believe it was the same one, having somehow made its way inside this building and squeezed down this corridor, squeezed through this doorway. The room was dimly lit but the sphere seemed to pulse subtly with the movement of its many denizens, like a living breathing planet. He reached in timidly and hauled this room's door shut before continuing on.

The corridor ran the length of the whole ground floor and toward the front of the building he took the rooms he peeked into to be former offices. In fact he next encountered one large area subdivided into cubicles though any computers and filing cabinets that might have been in them were gone as were the chairs except for a couple of specimens cast into gloomy corners. He walked among the cubicles and in one he came across a photograph from an instant camera thumbtacked to a mounted corkboard. Its colors all faded to shades of yellow, it showed a baby smiling up from its crib but its eyes had been scratched out in the photo with a pin or maybe the point of a razor knife as if to obfuscate its identity.

At the back of this large office area just beyond the last row of cubicles he discovered a bare mattress on the floor, so discolored with mold and variously stained he felt he might become diseased just from looking at it too long. More than disgust he experienced a kind of resentment that teenage boys were apparently making love to attractive young girls, unappreciatively, in this place just across the street from where he lived in abstinence. When he was a teenager it had seemed that sexual matters were the secret province of adults, from which the very young were excluded. These days it was as though the situation had reversed.

He felt he could almost discern the sweat and juices of young bodies now in that complex mix of scents that formed the atmosphere of this place.

He spotted something poking out from under one corner of the blackening fungoid mattress and bent down to delicately pinch it and pull it out. As reluctant as he was to touch anything in here with his bare hands he suspected this might be a pornographic magazine or, judging from its thickness, book and that possibility engaged his keen interest.

What he lifted into his hands as he straightened, though, was a photo album. With the hope it might still contain pictures of a titillating nature, given the setting in which he had come upon it, he opened its cover.

It was immediately apparent that what he had uncovered was a wedding album, its pages filled with photographs preserved under clear plastic sheets. The colors of the photographs were faded though not to the extent of the baby photo he had discovered in the cubicle. Why this object would have been abandoned here he didn't try to fathom but he paged through the album slowly with gaze flicking from image to image. Finally half-consciously he dragged one of the office chairs out of a corner and righted it so as to sit down as he continued poring over the album.

He was charmed by these photos and especially by the bride, a youthful beauty whose white dress and veil set off all the more her long dark hair and dark eyes. Her fresh face and petite figure had struck him from the first image. The groom was similarly young and attractive and he was jealous of this man though he couldn't be bitterly resentful, because the groom's smiling face conveyed how happy he was and how lucky he knew himself to be.

He stared hard at how the corset bodice of the wedding gown clung to the young woman's slender waist and how the skin of her arms showed through their sheer lacy sleeves. Her hair spilled in permed coils over her shoulders and the proud mounds of her breasts. Toward the back of the album were a series of pictures that showed the groom kneeling in front of the bride so as to remove the ruffled garter from her leg before tossing it over his shoulder to the unmarried males, perhaps infused with her scent. Her shapely leg with its firm thigh and calf muscles was thrust out in front of her sheathed in a white stocking. He found himself growing aroused as he focused on her extended leg in this group of shots.

Whereas the wedding photos looked to have all been taken by a professional, the last page of the album featured several pictures yellowed like the baby photo, on the thick film of an instant camera. These appeared to have been taken at a hotel or motel at a later time, though not much later because the bride's hairstyle and makeup were the same as in the wedding series. They had to be honeymoon shots taken by her fortunate husband that same night.

In one photo the brand new wife was posed on a bed with both arms propped behind her, leaning back on them with her legs together and cocked to one side. No white stockings this time just bare flesh and toes pointing toward the camera like her shy but mischievous smile. She wore a short nightie of silk and lace, valentine red. In another photo she was on hands and knees facing toward the camera and he looked into the darkness between her hanging breasts. In the last shot she was under the covers with one arm thrown back behind her head to expose her smooth underarm. She was waiting for her husband to put the camera down and join her.

He wanted to slip into that photograph with her. Slip under those covers with her and press his nose and lips into her underarm. To take her small round toes into his mouth and suck them one by one. She was watching him, watching him through time, waiting for *him*.

He looked up from the album spread upon his lap and listened. Back when he had spent many peaceful hours alone in his little house while his wife was working he would hear tiny furtive sounds of wood creaking, the shower faucet dripping, a branch stirring against a window like a ghost child's nails, but in this solidly built old building there was not the slightest sound but for those he made himself. Aside from the graffiti and the musky human traces he thought he detected he felt certain that presently he was alone in the old mill or factory. So he opened his fly and freed himself and began working himself to release as he returned his attention to those three last photos in the album.

Having reentered the main corridor he came to a reception area and the front door to the building situated under the clock tower, the unseen but towering presence of which he could almost feel as an increased gravity pressing upon his body. Continuing past the reception area he arrived at the corridor's end and a shadowy flight of stairs ascending to another level. He stood there gazing up into the murk of the stairwell and considered climbing but a glance back at the dimming light bleeding from the high windows along the corridor told him that the day was too far in decline. He had best get home, which was only across the street but seemed very far both in space and time, and continue his exploration of this structure on some other day.

He tried leaving through the front door but it was locked so he retraced his path down the central corridor and into the shipping area and out through that side door. Under one arm he carried the wedding album.

For several more days and through the weekend he refrained from revisiting the factory. He would merely glance over that way before mounting his driveway as if he hoped no one, maybe himself included, would notice he was looking, the way he stole glimpses of young women at work. Part of him was eager to resume his exploration of that place of solitude but after his first visit he had experienced a strange sensation upon returning home, like a mental version of a diver's decompression sickness, as he readjusted to his usual environment.

One night as he sat absorbed in an old book he felt a hand materialize upon his left shoulder and slide down his chest, and seemingly disembodied lips brushed against his ear. He flinched in aversion. His wife's voice too near spoke to him. *Look what I just found in your bottom bureau drawer, under your dress shirts.*

Her right hand appeared in front of him and she rested the wedding album from the factory atop the open book he had been reading. He stared at it in a kind of implosion of numb panic. He began to scrabble blindly for an explanation. His wife went on: *I was wondering where this had disappeared to. I should have asked you.*

I'm sorry, he mumbled.

She came around in front of him to sit on the arm of his chair and shifted the album onto her thighs to open its first page. *Oh, weren't we cute? Wasn't that just the best day of your life?*

He stared a long time at the first page, which was filled with a single enlargement of these strangers when they had been young, before the groom had grown a rounded belly and the bride had chopped and dyed her hair.

Yes, he mumbled.

His wife went through page after page, photograph by photograph pointing out faces and giving them names that came back to him now, and sighing again and again as she remembered this dead parent or grandparent or aunt as if the two of them moved from grave to grave in a cemetery.

He dreaded her arriving at the last page with its three final instant photos but she did and she leaned down against his shoulder and cooed, *Do you remember that nightie?*

Of course, he told her.

She closed the album and placed it on a small table and took the book from his lap and lay that on top of the album and lifted him from his chair by the hand. She smiled at him all the while that she pulled him toward their bed.

He eventually became hard and struggled valiantly atop her as if pushing a boulder up his steep driveway. He thrust with more and more force determinedly, wheezing and encapsulated in a membrane of sweat. Apparently repulsed by the sweat his wife didn't put her hands on his back but she moaned when her orgasm came. He drove himself more forcibly yet and the bed squeaked and jounced and a terrible booming arose from within the wall like an awakened monstrous heartbeat.

He wanted to press his palms against his ears. He wanted to clamp his eyes shut as if to be alone in a small room taking comfort in its darkness and silence. He stopped thrusting and subsided heavily upon his wife and whispered, *That bitch down there. I swear someday I'm going down there with a hammer to shut her up.*

Silly! his wife said to him. *That wasn't her; it was our headboard hitting the wall. She hasn't been home for a few days...haven't you noticed her car hasn't been here?*

He hadn't been conscious of it but now that he thought about it he realized his wife was right. Still, despite this reassurance he melted away inside her and thus was not able to achieve a climax. He rolled off her and lay panting and unfulfilled.

I'm sorry, he said again.

It's okay, she reassured him. *It's late and we're both tired.*

During the night he got out of bed to empty his bladder, still tiptoeing despite his wife having reassured him their neighbor was away perhaps on some vacation. When finished in the bathroom he crept across the living room, poked his fingers through the blinds and looked out in the direction of the factory. There were no lights to indicate its presence, of course, and he saw nothing but a little bit of streetlamp glow reflected on the surface of the pond as though a viscous black void were slowly flooding in his direction.

It was a brighter day than it had been the last time, the sky still clear and crisply blue even after his interminable work day. Having parked his car opposite the apartment house crowning its little hill he descended the slope as before and once again came to the pond into which the Gosston Canal spent itself.

He stopped halfway across the scabrous metal bridge that spanned the canal to peer down into the water, being able to see into it more easily today. He thought he might be able to see fish. Perhaps, remembering his theory about a meteor creating this hollow, mutant or unknown breeds of fish. Past the epidermis of reflected sky he could just make out a multitude of shadowy tendrils all reaching toward the pond like a migration of eels but he figured them for aquatic plants squirming in the dreamy current. He turned to look off the opposite side of the bridge and what he discovered there surprised him. A large form crouched below the water's surface: the body of a black automobile, the canal just deep enough to have submerged it entirely, its roof humped like the back of a small whale basking in the penetrating sunlight. Had the car been driven or pushed down the wooded slope in the past by some of those teens who rutted inside the abandoned factory?

He continued across the bridge and toward the elongated red brick building with its faceless clock tower and went again to that unlocked side door that let him into the shipping area. He stole in quietly, listening for any indications of others. Though he had seen no cars in the parking lot teenagers from the area would likely come here on foot. Yet only that previous silence as solidly rooted as the brick walls greeted him. It was as though even sound had been stripped from this place of unknown industry along with its machinery and all the rest.

Leaving the former shipping area he tested a closed metal door at the start of the central corridor and confirmed his suspicion that it opened onto a stairwell identical to the one at the other end of the building. He was grateful that in order to explore the second level he would not have to pass the door he had closed last time to shut up that massive ball of spider silk suspended from the ceiling, in case it had burst in the interim and its cargo was crawling free, slipping out around the door's edges.

The door screeched as he opened it further, the noise amplified by the stairwell. If anyone else were here they would now certainly know he was here too. Not that he expected anyone who came here would physically harm him though one could never fully rule out such a threat, but he wanted the place all to himself.

He entered the stairwell and eased the door shut again behind him on its pneumatic cylinder to minimize a repeat of the metallic shriek as best he could.

The stairwell was lit feebly by one narrow window up near the landing, which he soon reached. He stepped through a threshold from which the door had been removed and entered one end of a corridor that ran the length of the building as did the one on the ground level. The floor of this corridor was wood with bolted down metal plates presumably for hand trucks or carts to move more smoothly across and to prevent further wear of the warped old boards beneath.

The floor just ahead appeared to be strewn with dozens of severed human feet gone brown and petrified with age, with more of the same heaped up innumerably in bins to either side of the walkway. He smiled with recognition. They were wooden lasts for shoes or boots to be formed around. He'd been correct when he thought he'd smelled leather and tanning chemicals the first time he entered the place. He didn't know why the lasts would have been left behind unless it was because they were an obsolete make, scuffed and gouged old wood, whereas nowadays he assumed it was more likely they were fashioned from plastic. He knelt to pick one up. Yes – the last, hinged through the instep, was much like those he had seen every day in the old boot factory he'd begun working in at the age of nineteen, his first fulltime job, except those lasts hadn't had a grooved suggestion of toes like these scattered and piled specimens did. He figured the kids who came in here were responsible for the ones knocked all over the floor. He placed the wooden foot he had been examining into one of the bins, after first conscientiously making sure the number stenciled on the bin corresponded to the last's size.

He supposed by now every shoe or boot that had been manufactured in this place had gone the way of the cows that had died to make them, and maybe every one of the people who had worn them besides.

As he proceeded further along the corridor, passing through slants of late afternoon sunlight entering through windows that were larger than those downstairs but still fogged white with dust, he took note of something odd about the ceiling. The ceiling here on the second floor was much lower than the one below and its bare wooden timbers were bedewed with a profusion of yellow droplets. He stopped again to tilt his face toward them. Were these dirty drops of rainwater that had soaked down through the building's flat roof? It hadn't rained for a number of days but it seemed the best explanation. He speculated that the tar covering the roof must be in very bad shape for so much water to have leaked through, since the whole of the ceiling as far forward as he could see was jeweled with these hanging drops. He noticed, however, that nowhere did the floor seemed puddled or even wetted by the water having dripped down. The drops simply hung suspended like millions of beads of glistening honey.

Past the bins of lasts piled in cairns he came to an open area with empty bolt holes in the floorboards. His guess was that there had been rows of benches here supporting sewing machines, where canvas linings had been joined to leather vamps and all the leather panels had been assembled into shoes or boots.

Beyond this, he knew from its wide work bench and slotted racks like roomier letter holders was the leather room, where tanned and finished skins would have been grouped by their dyed pigments and rolled up into tubes to be inserted into the rack for the leather cutters to pick their next job from.

And there, toward the end of the corridor, a row of leather cutter's clicker machines lined either wall making for a total of a dozen. He recognized the clickers because for several years at two companies he himself had stood up all day at such a machine, swinging it into position on its arm, depressing the two buttons that caused it to press heavily down upon bladed metal dies, the outlines of which represented the various panels that would compose a boot, driving these dies through spread cow skins like cookie cutters pushed into sheets of dough. He was surprised to see the clickers remained whereas the sewing machines and other machinery downstairs had been removed but he supposed the clickers might have been harder to transport or too dated for future use.

Yet there was another thing toward the end of the corridor that commanded his attention more so than the clicker machines and he stood poised like a deer that had emerged from the forest to confront its first human being at the opposite end of a clearing.

Was this other figure contemplating him as he contemplated it? For a human form stood on the raised little platform that supported the last of the clicker machines along the left row. This figure was, at once, both darkly silhouetted against the window behind it and yet luminous from within.

He watched this human outline for long seconds in a silence thorough as deafness, as if he expected the figure to swing the arm of the clicker machine, simultaneously push the buttons set into its two handles, and stamp a die through a cow's flayed skin. The figure did not move, though, nor produce the slightest sound.

He stole forward again in the manner of a person afraid to awaken one who is sleeping.

Though he mostly kept his eyes on the human form standing at that machine in the corner he was peripherally aware that the drops on the ceiling dangled progressively lower here, some of the strands a foot or more in length, making them appear more solid than liquid, like strings of rubber cement. Was there an attic space in which glue for shoe soles might have been stored, ruptured over time or overturned by vandals? Or were these seemingly gummy extrusions related to the roof's deterioration, some sealant gone liquid during the hotter months only to solidify again when the weather grew cold?

He walked between the rows of clickers and approached the last machine on his left. Still the figure mounted there on its little pedestal did not shift or emit a sound. As he began to study it more clearly he no longer expected it to move. Nevertheless he spotted a small weighted cobbler's hatchet stuck in one of the clicker machines' heavily scarred plastic tables and he pulled it free if only to give himself some physical sense of security. A familiar weight in his hand. These hatchets were used to chop away the web of leather remaining after the dies had punched out their panels and the cow hide was advanced across the cutting block. He had once accidentally chopped his thumb with a similar hatchet while hacking away such scrap and still bore the depressed white scar today.

Here at the terminus of the corridor, the back wall bearing pegs that once would have supported the variously sized and shaped dies, some of the strands depending from the ceiling had dripped so low they were like thin icicles glowing yellow with sunlight, and at last there were even a few thickly mounded pools on the floor where the gunk had collected in overlapping folds. A couple of the ceiling's delicate stalactites were connected to the top of the largest of these heaps. He tapped this pile with the toe of his shoe expecting from its translucent golden appearance that it would be gelatinous and resilient but in fact the mound clicked solidly like hardened resin.

At last he turned his full attention to the human-shaped thing standing on its wooden platform with its hands wrapped around the clicker's double handles, though if there had been a cow hide spread across the cutting block it was now absent, leaving only the table's badly chewed up plastic surface.

It was the form of a man as rendered in the same golden-brown translucent material that was seeping down everywhere through the old wooden ceiling. This statue was anything but crude in execution. Rather than merely being roughly anthropomorphic it was beautifully sculpted, or molded perhaps when the resin had been softer and pliable, detailed to such an extent that the strands of its hair and the folds of its clothing were convincingly suggested. The figure was that of a slender young man though of course the matter's uniformly honey-like color prevented one from telling the model's hair or eye color, the effigy's eyes just blank golden orbs in a glassy golden head that seemed to glow inside with the mellow light that angled in through the window behind.

All alone now, huh? he said aloud to the statue. He waited a beat as if an answer might come. *Working overtime? Good luck with that. I worked a lot of overtime, too. Still lost my house, though.* He cocked his head a little. *Who left you here?*

It was far too artful a creation to have been fashioned by the teens who had sprayed graffiti on the walls of the ground floor. It was in fact too masterful an artwork to imagine anyone having abandoned it here. Which made him wonder then if this posed mannequin of glassy resin was a piece of artwork at all.

Was it possible that some freak mishap or grave calamity had occurred here, and that was the cause of this factory having been abandoned and stripped down? Could some dangerous chemical have poured down from an attic upon a poor unsuspecting worker at his station, encasing him alive? Then, the tissues and bones of his body having burned away or rotted over time leaving only this fossil-like shape of him in his place? A physical echo, a solid shadow?

Or might it be that this golden matter – this perhaps

celestial matter – was or had been organic, even sentient, a protoplasmic mass of communal cells that had found the loneliness of the dead factory so troubling that it had shaped itself into the form of one of the beings that had once populated it, raising up this monument in tribute, like the skeleton of an extinct creature erected in a museum? Or, had it been an ill-conceived shortcut in evolution…a noble but failed attempt to aspire to something greater than was within this primitive life form's capacity to attain?

If so, apparently those living cells themselves had died off and become a fossilized residue of their former existence.

He reached out and lightly ran his fingers along the petrified figure's forearm, bared by the rolled up sleeve of its mock shirt. The young man's body was as smooth and glossy and dead as the face of a granite gravestone.

A thin cry started up like a teakettle's whistle as its water begins to steam. It was distant but growing louder and seemingly closer like an approaching train. He drew his hand back from the arm of the resin mannequin and gooseflesh pebbled up all over his own arms and still the wail grew louder and closer and he was certain it was coming from that placid lucent face with its unmoving lips held in a possible half smile.

An explosive boom caused the boards under his feet to tremble or was that only the startled spasm of his heart? Another heavy boom followed and another with the terrible mounting howl stringing these detonations together.

He realized this sustained shriek was not coming from the frozen figure but, along with those evenly spaced out reverberating thuds, from downstairs instead.

He turned from the solid yet empty effigy, which was like a tainted window with no particular view, and crept toward a doorway in the opposite wall beyond the last of the clicker machines there, for above it was a sign reading EXIT except someone had spray-painted a question mark after the T.

The door was off its hinges and he went down the further of the building's two stairwells with his hatchet held at the ready. The pounding went on unabated but sometimes the wailing dipped and almost stopped only to ascend to full power again as the screamer drew new air into their lungs.

Having reached the ground floor he stuck his head out a little into the central corridor and determined the screaming/pounding came from a good distance further along. So he slipped into the long gloomy hallway and started creeping in that direction with his heartbeat all but suspended lest the screamer hear it nearing like footsteps.

He was past the front door/reception area and the office section when he guessed or intuited where the booms that sent vibrations skittering along his nerves, like rhythmic blows against a gong, were coming from. He didn't know if he could bring himself to open that door which upon his last visit here he himself had closed.

He made his way slowly, hesitant and uncertain, wondering if he should continue on past the shut door and out of the building and up out of the crater to his waiting car. As he was contemplating this, torn between trepidation and curiosity in equal immensity, the noises abruptly ceased and the contrasting silence caused him to freeze in his tracks and his heart to stagger out of its pattern.

Should he go to the door or past the door and had the scream and thumps been more terrifying or was this sudden absolute quiet even worse?

Ultimately he had to give in to his curiosity, the curiosity that had brought him to this desolate location in the first place, the curiosity that was all that really motivated and sustained him now.

The door's tongue was not engaged so he pushed it open with his forearm wide enough to be able to see inside.

Of the great sphere of silk that had bulged from the ceiling like a distended belly now only burst tatters remained, hanging down in shredded gauzy curtains. Under these remnants like the torn and faded flags of extinct countries lay a figure curled on the bare floor almost in a fetal position. It was the nude body of a woman. Not far from her in a corner lay a crumpled and discarded garment. He shifted closer to this and knelt down to pick it up and it was like a slippery membrane in his hands edged in intricate web work. The red silk and lace of a nightie. Absently, he shoved it into his pocket in a ball and studied the woman again.

She lay facing away from him and she was petrified like a figure that had been molded in plaster after having been buried under volcanic ash ages ago except that she was beautifully crystallized in honey-colored matter marred by not even a bubble within, as far as he could tell. Though her long hair, spread so realistically onto the floor around her head, was also honey-colored he imagined that if she were an actual human being that thick curly hair would be dark and fragrant with life.

He had expected to find his mysteriously tormented neighbor here and at first in a way he thought he had but the figure now reminded him more of a woman he had known and loved many years ago as if in another life. Her identity dodged and blurred in his mind and he knelt down to reach out and touch her as if that might help remind him. He ran his hand along the bare curve of her waist, up the slope of her hip and it came to rest on the smooth globe of a buttock clear as a scryer's crystal ball. He was becoming aroused and wondered whether the orifices and channels of her body had been reproduced as well but he knew that would be like kissing a mirror for want of soft lips.

He edged closer to the figure to look down at her face reposing in profile but as he did this his gaze slid down her body instead and for the first time he noticed her interior was not empty after all. A dark mass was lodged inside her low in her body and hard to make out in this windowless room with only pale light misting in from the corridor without. She was too hardened for him to roll her over but he leaned in closer still and moved to the side a bit so his body wouldn't block the anemic light, and though her belly was only sensually rounded and not gravidly swollen he saw that this dark mass was in the shape of a child curled inside her as if to replicate her own position.

No sooner had he recognized the shadowy outline in her abdomen for what it was than he thought he saw it move, kicking out with both of its feet at once as if to pound them against the constraining wall of her womb. At the sight of this there was an inaudible boom in his mind – a realization. The child was alive within this ossified form, with no chance of being delivered. Surely it would suffocate and die trapped within her.

A sense of desperate urgency came over him. He had to rescue the child, set it free.

He still gripped the heavy little cobbler's hatchet in his fist by its stubby metal handle and he raised it above his head.

Brought it down. It gouged the side of the woman's body between where her ribcage and pelvis would have been had she possessed bones inside her. He hacked at her in the same place again then again, creating new gouges and deepening existent ones. This activity seemed to trigger the child into kicking out again in whatever space it occupied in that body which glistened like hard butterscotch candy.

With more blows, the hatchet almost slipping out of his hand several time as his palm became sweaty, fine cracks began spreading out from the area he was chewing into. Then, a deep cleft appeared and a large fragment of the woman's waist betrayed that it was loose. Seeing this, he worked it from both angles as if chopping a wedge to fell a tree and then he was able to lever the edge of the blade under the chunk and pry it free to clatter on the floor. He was that much closer to the shadow baby's womb.

Seeing his success with the first sizable piece he continued in the same manner, hacking in from opposing angles and prying out more chunks with the blade or sore fingers, widening and deepening the wound but mindful of the vulnerability of the baby within.

Finally he shattered his way into the hollow core wherein the baby lay on its side. A few shards and jagged pebbles fell onto the child and he was just ready to toss his hatchet aside and reach in to sweep the debris from its body and lift it out into his arms and perhaps take it home for he and his wife to raise as their own when he saw the black shape of the child break up into myriad tiny components that came swarming up out of the exposed hollow.

He cried out and fell onto his rump and then he was scuttling backwards with his hands as the thousands of spiders that had tightly amassed themselves inside the effigy's belly swept toward him in a black wave.

He didn't recall leaving the forsaken boot factory or climbing the basin's slope or crossing the road and ascending his steeply inclined driveway or trudging up the wooden steps to his second floor apartment. He came to himself standing at his kitchen sink looking out the window above it at the parking lot below. He realized he must have left his car parked by the side of the road across the street because he didn't see it down there. As his wife had pointed out, the car of the young woman downstairs had been missing for a while now and even his other two neighbors weren't home from work yet apparently. And though his wife was usually home before him making dinner she must have gone out on an errand because he didn't hear her moving around anywhere in the apartment behind him and her car too was absent from the parking lot. The lot was completely desolate.

That was okay though. He liked having this place all to himself.

His feet were numb and if he directed his consciousness toward them, without taking his gaze off the parking lot, he couldn't sense where they contacted the floor beneath them, as if he either floated above the floor or was one with its solidity. His feet might as well have been wooden lasts inside his shoes.

As if a paralyzing venom were at work within him, a subtle wave of feeling or rather a negation of feeling was spreading up his ankles and into his calves, as his nethermost cells one by one seemed to fade out like stars in morning's firmament. As each cell crystallized he became that much more deadened and hence that much more at peace like one who feels the dark cloak of sleep lowering over them.

He watched several large balls of spider silk race and bounce across the parking lot in a breeze like tumbleweeds and his only regret as he became rooted there, and so emptily transparent that the world could be observed through his absence, was that the view below him was not the green overgrown back yard of his sadly lost house which had been, for a flicker of time, *his* little piece of the universe.

THE PROSTHESIS

He should be proud of himself, his supervisor had assured Thomas, because he was performing an important service for people.

He was no physician or therapist, and yet he and every other employee of Gale Therapeutic Appliances no matter their function was part of a healing process. Other departments than his created prosthetic arms and legs for victims of mishap, and upon his initial interview he had toured the entire plant and viewed these processes. He had seen yet other departments where glass eyes were produced, or portions of faces lost to accident or disease. A nose, a whole upper section of face or perhaps a bottom jaw, these facial appliances held in place with magnets.

The products his own department fashioned were similar, and yet different. His was an especially, perhaps even *more* important function, his immediate supervisor had told him with pride upon that first tour through the plant six months earlier. The healing process they were a part of, in their department, was purely psychological rather than physical – and wasn't emotional suffering worse even than somatic pain?

What their particular customers experienced, Thomas's supervisor explained in words that no doubt came from promotional literature, was a "phantom pain of the psyche."

"Did you hear about Lucinda?" Bao asked him during a lull in activity. She was smiling, which meant it couldn't be pleasant, as he knew Bao disliked Lucinda. She disliked all her female coworkers, but seemed to like chatting with him. Bao was short and thickset, with a broad ruddy face and long slitted eyes; she had once told him the name of her home country but he'd forgotten it and hadn't recognized it anyway. Somewhere small and obscure on the border of somewhere big and desolate.

She left a space hanging open for him so he obliged her and asked, "No, what?"

Bao whispered, "She got fired for smuggling out a wee-wee!"

"Oh no," Thomas said. He was going to ask what Lucinda had needed that for, but stopped himself.

"Isn't that stupid? She could buy herself a toy for next to nothing – it's like getting fired for stealing paperclips." Bao supplied the answer to the question he had nearly asked. "But you know, her husband died in that accident and all, so I guess she's lonely." Instead of sounding sympathetic, however, Bao snorted a little laugh.

Having been divorced for a few years now, Thomas experienced an unpleasant, sickly craving for Bao when she was near him. It was an unsolicited kind of desire. She was sufficiently exotic to stir him, with her scissor-cut eyes and long frizzy-black hair – and the fecund pendulous breasts that pushed out the front of her white lab coat – but she smelled of hot plastic when she was close to him. She'd once told him that she had six children, but her husband had recently left her for a younger woman. Her pain, anger and loneliness were as plain as the smell of hot plastic.

At the time Bao had revealed this personal information to him, she had said, "Some people have too many children, and some people don't have any." This comment was in regard to the work they performed in their particular department. "Nothing is balanced, is it?"

Knowing that Bao hadn't liked Lucinda, Thomas didn't want to sound too concerned for her, but nevertheless he mused, "It's like when Paul got fired for stealing those two breasts." Their coworker Paul had been the quality control inspector for the department that created artificial breasts for women who had undergone mastectomies.

"Oh, poor Paul," Bao said, sympathetic because she had liked flirting with Paul, too, "that was different. You didn't hear? He lived with his mom and she had cancer."

"Did she lose her breasts?" Thomas asked, confused.

"No – she died. He lost all of her."

The baby was still warm in Thomas's hands as he used scissors to trim away the irregular fringe along its seams. They called this extra plastic, squeezed out where the two halves of the mold fit together, "flash." The baby was heavy, solid, though it wasn't one of the more expensive models with the articulated steel skeletons inside. Its limbs jiggled a little as he handled the doll. But the employees were sternly instructed never to use the word "doll." It was "prosthetic infants" they produced in their department – for women who had lost their own babies to illness, accident, or Sudden Infant Death Syndrome. They were a therapeutic product and many insurance companies covered their expense. They might only be utilized for a short while, after which the mothers might donate their baby to another needy mother, though Thomas had heard of women who had cared for their prosthesis – even walking it in the park in a stroller – for decades.

As he clipped the seam that ran over the top of the infant's as yet hairless, healthy pink head with its closed eyes and peaceful smile, he heard Bao speaking to the babies at the end of the line where she inspected them. He glanced over at her. She wasn't cooing baby talk to the infants, however, but grumbling such comments as, "You're an especially ugly one, aren't you?" He saw her give the baby she held a good loud smack on its jiggly bottom before she tossed it through the air into a big bin full of babies waiting to be pushed out into the packaging room before they went on to the shipping department or the warehouse.

"Hey, Thomas," a voice behind him said. He recognized it as belonging to his coworker David, a muscular black man, and turned toward him. He saw that David had acquired a big pink pregnant belly. The black man was grinning.

Thomas smiled, but in a low voice advised, "Be careful Bao doesn't see you fooling around with that stuff or she might say something to Derek."

"Do you think Bao was bigger than this when she had her six kids?" David said, setting the plastic belly aside. Women who had suffered miscarriages and had never even had the chance to see their baby come into the world were said to benefit from wearing such a prosthesis – sometimes for a few months. Sometimes for years. David went on, "I think the bitch carried all six babies in one litter."

"Shh, David," Thomas warned.

David picked up the next tiny golem Thomas needed to trim and turned it over in his big hands. In a more serious tone he observed, "It must be a horrible thing to go through, losing a baby – I don't want to even think about what it would be like if I lost my son. He's my whole life."

"I know what you mean," Thomas said. He looked up at David with a worried eye as his friend began trimming the baby he held. David was trying to help him stay caught up but Thomas felt his coworker was a bit careless when he trimmed, leaving too much flash here but snipping into the flesh a little bit there. While observing him, Thomas added almost unconsciously, "I've always mourned somebody I never even knew."

"How's that?"

"I was supposed to be a twin, but my brother was stillborn."

David reacted with a pained expression. "Really? Oh wow, man."

"We were going to be Thomas and Mason. I guess I'm the one who got to be Thomas. But it could just as easily have been him."

Thomas walked home every evening from Gale Therapeutic Appliances, the tenement building that housed his flat being only fifteen minutes away on foot.

He carried a thick plastic shopping bag, black with the name of a clothing store in gold lettering. He had done his best not to look over his shoulder nervously while he was still close to his place of employment, but it was out of sight now and he relaxed somewhat. He had made sure to remain in the restroom for a good fifteen minutes after clock-out time, so that when he finally emerged the parking lot was all but empty. Earlier, as always, he had declined offers of a ride home from both David and Bao.

Normally he enjoyed the walk, but as autumn deepened the days were growing more chilly — and on top of that, this evening it was beginning to drizzle. From past experience Thomas was prepared for this eventuality, however, and carried a small plastic flashlight in his coat pocket. He left the sidewalk and approached a deceased brick factory with its arched windows boarded up and covered in menacing black graffiti like hordes of giant insects. Since he had been a boy most of the industries in his hometown of Gosston had closed down — largely for economic reasons, but there had also been chemical spills, gas explosions, fires. Gosston seemed to have more than its share of accidents, and a disproportionate number of citizens with artificial limbs, and that might well have had something to do with the fact that Gale Therapeutic Appliances, at least, continued to thrive.

Thomas had moved out of Gosston over twenty years ago, swearing never to return, but he had moved back to care for his mother after his father had passed away. Last year he'd lost his mother, too, and yet he had stayed on. As much as he had come to despise the town, it was all he had now. The town and the "phantom pain" it held for him.

Thomas waded through overgrown weeds, wary of debris concealed in the tangles like booby-traps, until he arrived at one side of the derelict factory building — a spot just past its loading docks.

As a boy he had become familiar with the tunnel system that connected a number of the town's old industrial sites, and one of the openings to this system lay before him now. Thomas ducked through a bulkhead door that had once been boarded up, flicking on his flashlight as he did so.

After descending a short flight of steps thick with fallen leaves he entered a straight tunnel with an arched ceiling and walls scaled in grimy tiles, rusty train rails laid into its damp cement floor. More graffiti abounded, rubbish and smashed glass scattered everywhere. A bare mattress had turned to a mildewed sponge from water that had trickled down the wall. Thomas walked quietly for fear of alerting any teenagers or homeless people who might currently be partying or sheltering down here, but he heard nothing. Even on the few occasions he had seen people down here they had only watched him as he passed without accosting him. Maybe they had feared he was a ghost, even as he had half-wondered the same about them.

Only once had he had a frightening experience down here, as a youth many years earlier when some of the plants the tunnels connected had still been operational. He had been alone and exploring out of simple curiosity when a shadowy figure had lunged out of a narrow stairwell that led up to one of the factories. The figure had chased after Thomas, never calling out to him and its intentions unclear. A security guard chasing him from a place he didn't belong, or a madman with terrible desires? From the figure's short stature, maybe just a bully of his own age. Whatever the case, a panicky Thomas had glanced back once or twice but the figure remained a silhouette, its features indiscernible. The most he could make out was that it held its arms out in front of it, as if to embrace him.

For years afterward – until he'd moved out of Gosston, in fact – in dreams the figure had continued to pursue him, as if some part of him had never escaped from the tunnels.

The tenement building he lived in had formerly been a factory building itself, just as other defunct factories in town had been portioned into office space. The tunnel delivered him only a three minutes' walk from his home. The rain was moderate and he arrived in the tenement building's vestibule only a little worse for wear. On the brick walls of the vestibule were an old punch clock and empty racks for punch cards. The landlord must have felt they were charming souvenirs of bygone days.

Up squealing wooden steps that sounded like each one trapped a dying animal inside, which Thomas pressed beneath his heels. Up to his apartment on the third and topmost floor. He quickly moved from room to room (which was all there was – two large rooms) pulling shades and drawing curtains, as if to hide from eyes that would emerge with the night. Then, at a more relaxed pace, he put on a kettle of water for instant coffee and changed into comfortable pajamas and his faded flannel bathrobe. When his coffee was in hand, he turned to stare across the combination living room/kitchen at the plastic bag resting on the table. The morning paper, *The Gosston Mirror*, was still spread there as if ready to soak up blood.

Thomas sipped his coffee a few more times, slowly, with long stretches between, before he finally padded barefoot – as if with a need for stealth – over to the table and opened the mouth of the plastic bag to draw out what he had folded double and hidden inside.

It was an adult-sized human arm, minus a hand at its wrist, heavy and solid. The expensive kind, with an articulated steel skeleton inside.

"Did you hear about that customer the company turned away?" Bao asked Thomas at lunch. She sat across the table from him, making him self-conscious as he slurped up his instant noodles. She left one of her open pauses for him to step into.

"What happened?" he asked after sucking up one particularly errant strand of noodle.

"He contacted GTA directly with a request. He said he'd lost his daughter and he was having a hard time dealing with it. So he showed our order department a photo of a girl of maybe sixteen – and she didn't look anything like him." She laughed. "And he never once mentioned that he had a wife, either."

"Huh," Thomas said, and then to give her a better reaction, "Wow."

"He probably thought if we okayed it, he might even get his insurance company to pay for it."

"Huh," Thomas said. Poking around in his noodles, he hesitated but then said, "It might not be what you think, though. Maybe she was someone he loved when he was the same age and could never forget. Maybe even someone who died a long time ago."

"Oh Thomas," Bao chuckled, wagging her head. "You're so sweet and naïve."

He had just finished his meal when the time came for them to return to work. He excused himself to go to the men's room, and Bao went on ahead without him. All the rest had already returned to their respective work areas and he knew his supervisor Derek would chastise him when he was late to his post, but he could deal with that.

He had come into the men's room earlier with the object hidden inside a roll of used bubble wrap Derek had given him permission to bring home. He had seen someone's shoes under the door to one of the stalls, however, so he had been afraid to go through with his plan all the way. He had quickly dug the object out of the bubble wrap, then pushed it down deep into the trash container – knowing the people who came to empty the trash and clean the floors wouldn't do so until closer to the end of the shift.

There was no one in here now – only his own furtive-eyed face staring back at him from the big mirror over the row of sinks.

He knew there were cameras focused on the front doors, making him apprehensive about smuggling out anything that way. Furthermore, there was that stooped gnome of a security guard, Bill, sitting up front at his reception desk, lost in his baggy uniform like a child dressed for Halloween – holstered pistol and all – even if he did frequently doze off in front of his monitors. Likewise, Thomas suspected there were cameras in the coed locker room because no one actually changed their clothes there, only stored their coats, pocketbooks or phones in the lockers. But surely there were no security cameras in the restrooms.

With one more glance over his shoulder to be assured he was alone, he thrust his hand down into the trash and felt around until he retrieved his prize.

There was one small hinged window at the back wall, and it was already cracked a little bit open. He went to it, pushed it open more, and reached out the hand that held the object. He let it go, and heard a soft thud and a crackle of leaves below.

As he had last evening, he waited until all his coworkers had eagerly left for home before he emerged from the building and walked around to its rear. Here, where the company property bordered a strip of gray woods, drifts of fallen leaves drained of their bright colors had washed up against the back wall of the building. Thomas knelt before one such heap, directly below a small hinged window, and sifted through until he once again uncovered his prize. From the pocket of his coat he produced the same balled up black plastic bag with gold lettering, and he dropped the adult-sized human hand inside it.

"What happened to your hand?" David asked Thomas in the cafeteria, pointing at a nasty red burn across the back of his wrist. It looked like his hand had been severed and reattached there.

"Oh...I did that today with a sealer wand. One of the hip joints on a baby popped out of its socket – it mustn't have been connected securely – so I had to cut the leg off, reconnect the joint then seal the leg back on. And when I did, the wand slipped and..." He made a hissing sound like sizzling flesh. The electric-powered wands melted the pliable plastic to an almost liquid state so that pieces could be joined together, and if skillfully smoothed out the place of joining was virtually undetectable.

It was true that he had had to repair one of the infant prostheses in this way, today, but the heated wand hadn't slipped. The accident had actually occurred last night in his apartment, with a sealer wand he had smuggled home from work.

A shrill cry behind Thomas caused him to spin around with jolted heart. Bao had opened one of the refrigerators to retrieve her lunch, to be greeted with the sight of a human head resting on one of the shelves.

She whirled to glare at all the workers seated at their various tables. Some were trying to repress their smiles but others were laughing outright. "You think that's funny? If I find out who did that I'll be reporting you to Mr. Gale himself! I'll ask security to play back the tape!"

"I don't think there are any security cameras in the caf," Thomas said, subtly glancing around at the ceiling tiles.

"I sure hope not," David muttered.

Thomas gave his coworker a look.

But only a minute later, the old security guard Bill shuffled into the room, his fissured face one big grimace. "I saw that," he grumbled. "Where's the head now?"

"Damn," David whispered, "so there are cameras in here. Why did the old geezer have to be awake for once?"

Bao handed Bill the adult-sized head. It was a male with realistic looking hair punched into its scalp. Its eyes were closed as if in sleep. Not many were produced at GTA, but occasionally an accident victim who had suffered decapitation was able to be kept alive indefinitely with life support. A lifelike prosthetic head, fashioned in the likeness of the victim, made the family's visits more bearable. Other times, though, such heads were merely created so a family could view and bury an intact representation of a truncated loved one.

Bill cradled the head in both hands and held its face against his chest protectively. Rather than retreat with it to his desk in the foyer, though, he addressed the assembled workers. "You people need to take your work more seriously! You don't know by now what these things mean to the people who buy them? You still think they're only so much plastic? They have a magic to them, a magic to heal. They have soul in them...the soul of the lost loved one and the soul of the person who grieves for them."

"Listen to him," Thomas heard a worker murmur behind him, "the senile old fart is going to cry."

Another worker replied in a lowered voice, "Watch out or he'll start shooting us."

Thomas could hear it now...either later today or tomorrow, once the camera's tape had been reviewed, Bao saying to him triumphantly, "Did you hear what happened to David?"

David's termination was inevitable, and Thomas felt sorry for him, but in a way he was grateful. If any of his own thefts had been noticed, there was now a person to take the blame.

Of course, now it might prove more difficult to steal one of the prosthetic heads for himself, and his work was not yet finished.

It happened sometimes in autumn – an early snow – but it was only a light snow and Thomas was one who enjoyed walking even in driving blizzards. It was almost just an excuse for him to take the underground path home from work. Surely it wouldn't be much warmer down there.

But of course, he had to be honest with himself that he was nervous his theft might already have been detected, and people were just waiting to catch him walking home with his heavier than usual shopping bag.

He dug out his flashlight and slipped through the bulkhead opening as always. As he descended the snow-dusted stairs his breath steamed, looking like ectoplasm churning before his face in the beam of his flashlight. He moved forward along the rails of the old trains that had once unloaded cargo down here, barely glancing about at the familiar refuse: a stack of rotting cardboard boxes filled with ceiling tiles for a repair job that never came, several metal trash cans filled to the brim with little pieces of coal intended for some long disused furnace, a chaotic pile of rusting dismantled machine parts. No teenagers partying, no homeless sheltering – just the one figure that stepped into view at the far end of this stretch of tunnel.

Startled, Thomas stopped in his tracks. His beam had begun waning recently, the flashlight overdue for fresh batteries, and so he only made out the barest outline of the figure in the murk. But it was standing directly in the path he was taking – neither advancing nor retreating, and not stepping to one side – in a stance that appeared challenging.

Thomas didn't want to appear nervous to this person or to himself. He thought to ask, "Can I help you?" or something of that nature, but instead he found himself blurting, "Who are you?"

His voice echoed back to him: *"Who are you?"*

As if these words prompted the shadowy figure into action, it suddenly lunged forward and came running straight at him down the center of the rails, arms extended as if to seize him in an embrace. It loped along with an uneven, awkward gait.

"Hey! Hey!" Thomas said, trying to sound authoritative. But the figure kept rushing toward him, and every dream he had dreamed about his boyhood encounter in these tunnels crashed upon him like bricks in a collapsing wall.

Thomas lunged forward himself, but bolted in a new direction – at an angle toward the left-hand wall, where he recalled there was another set of stairs leading up to an old textile mill. He prayed he could reach those cement steps and pound up them into the open air before the running figure intercepted him.

His flashlight beam danced ahead of him wildly as he ran, so he couldn't see the stranger advancing – just heard its frenzied limping approach – but only a few more feet remained before he reached the stairwell. He knew he would make it just a bit ahead of the stranger.

And he did, shining his light up at the bulkhead doors.

He had never used this bulkhead entrance in his adulthood, and maybe the situation had been different when he was a boy, but now he saw that this particular bulkhead still had its original metal doors – and that they were padlocked shut.

Terror passed through him like a cloud of liquid nitrogen. Thomas spun around as if he might still escape the dead end of the stairwell, but of course it was too late. His pursuer stood at the bottom step, blocking his escape. Crowding his back up against the locked metal doors, Thomas pointed his light directly at the stranger – now close enough to sufficiently illuminate.

Now Thomas understood the cause for the figure's extreme limp: its left leg ended in a stump rather than a foot. But more than that, his confronter was lacking a head.

It wasn't that Thomas' fear faded away then, but other emotions pressed in alongside it. Tears rose to his eyes. A smile quivered on his lips. And this time he didn't think of escape, as the headless stranger held out its arms to him.

He lifted his head with a start from the kitchen table, across which was spread a copy of the *Gosston Mirror*, and looked around his kitchen area with frantic eyes. Slowly he calmed himself, but found that he was gripping the table edge. Was it that odd smell in the air that had roused him from his doze, a smell like something burning? Maybe an electrical fire?

He vaguely recalled pulling his comfortable flannel bathrobe around his cold, shivering body. Seemed to recall scrabbling noises outside his apartment door, its knob rattling.

He believed he had staggered to the door and called warily, "Who is it?" without a response, finally opening the door only to find the morning paper bound with elastic and hanging from his doorknob in a plastic bag.

He might have dismissed these blurred memories and lapses of unconsciousness – dismissed that before donning his robe he had awakened naked on the floor of his apartment – had he had too much to drink the night before. But he wasn't a drinking man.

What time was it? Should he be at work now? The thought that he might be late to work sobered and sharpened his mind. He realized he didn't even know what day it was, and located the front page of the disordered paper before him.

It seemed that his place of employment, Gale Therapeutic Appliances, had in fact made the front page of the *Gosston Mirror*.

The company's security guard, sixty-four year old William Crampton, had caught an employee attempting to steal one of the plastic prosthetic appliances the company produced – in this case an adult model left foot. This employee had at first vehemently denied that he had possession of this article, at which time Mr. Crampton seized hold of the bag in which the appliance was concealed. A struggle ensued and the younger, larger employee was able to wrest his bag free and dart for the exit.

It was at this point that Mr. Crampton pulled his licensed handgun and fired twice, striking the employee in the back. The employee, forty-three year old Thomas Capgras, was pronounced dead at the scene.

"Killed a man for stealing a plastic foot," he mumbled aloud, wagging his head. That crazy old fool; they had him in custody for it, too. And the other, the victim; he again said out loud, "Got himself killed over a plastic foot."

His brow furrowed, then, and he scanned through the article again. He might have expected the thief to be David, joking around again, not this other man...this Thomas...

Mason involuntarily crushed the paper, wadded its inked words in his hands as if to unmake them. For a few moments he stared across his combination living room/kitchen, but focusing on nothing in particular. Vaguely he noted that smell in the air again – a smell like melted plastic.

Then, reluctantly, hesitantly, he pushed his chair back from the table a bit. Just enough that he could look beneath it.

And Mason saw that his left leg ended in a stump instead of a foot.

THE DARK CELL

"You're mighty young," Rose said to the newcomer. She didn't really want to start up a conversation, but one of them had to. She was being polite to mask her resentment. She hadn't been hoping for company, and this pretty but surly-looking Mexican girl didn't appear enthusiastic about the prospect of making new friends, either.

The girl looked out through the cell's door, as if she hoped the guard who had locked it only a minute earlier might have a change of heart and come back to release her. "I'm sixteen," she mumbled.

At least the girl understood English. Rose said, "Sixteen, huh? Lord almighty. Twenty-eight, here. I'm Rose."

"Yeah?" the girl said. But after several moments, without looking around, she said, "Maria."

Maria. Well, Rose felt that was enough of an effort on her part. She didn't want to ask what a sixteen-year-old girl had done to be sentenced here – lest Maria ask her, in turn, what her own crime had been.

At the time of her arrival at the Yuma Territorial Prison, on October 22nd, 1899, Rose had been given the designation 1551. This number was worn on the front of her respectable blouse with its puffed sleeves and cinched waist, which also bore a tight pattern of thin horizontal lines – a demure and apologetic indication of her status – unlike the men's uniforms, striped with broader bands of black and white. There were more than three thousand male inmates at the Yuma Territorial Prison, but at this time only eleven females were incarcerated. Their small group, as of today, increased by one.

The men were stacked six to a cell with one chamber pot between them, but Rose had been fortunate to have a cell to herself these past nine months. *(Nine months...nine months...she could have carried a child in that time, and yet it was only the start of a thirty year sentence.)* "Fortunate" was a relative consideration, however. The prison was located in the Sonoran Desert, atop a bluff overlooking the Colorado River, and on summer days like this the temperature could reach 120 degrees. Rose had no window in her cell. And she hadn't truly been alone these past nine months, when one considered the company of lice, bedbugs, and cockroaches. But she had had the luxury of suffering her indignities alone. She had been able to deal with that suffering by sending her mind away, sending it afar, into memories of good times from her childhood and dreams of good times that had never happened. Now, she felt her privacy had been compromised. Now, after having found a way to adapt to her situation, acclimate to it – to accept this existence as her life – she was experiencing an acute sense of punishment all over again. It was as though she, Rose, were the new prisoner, not Maria.

"I killed my brother Emilio," Maria muttered with her back to Rose, as if talking to someone out in the hallway. "He called me a whore." At last she turned around so that Rose, seated on the edge of her bunk, could see that pretty but surly face again. "What about you?"

Rose hesitated only a second. This had been inevitable, hadn't it? Best to get it over with. "I killed my husband...William."

Maria grinned then. The toothy grin didn't make her look more pretty; in fact, Rose preferred her looking unhappy.

Rose decided she hated her.

Conditions at the prison were unavoidably harsh, owing to the heat and overcrowding, but efforts had been made to enrich the lives of the inmates and one of those efforts was the library. The staff kept the male and female prisoners separate, and so presently the only inmates using the library were women. Rose sat at one of the tables that ran through the center of the room in a long row, while framed portraits of Thomas Jefferson, George Washington and Abraham Lincoln watched over her like benign guardians. She had been hunched over the book spread before her – its subject being the marvels of natural history, her favorite book in the library – losing herself in strange untamed lands, open vistas without cages, without men holding guns, when someone sat down on her right so close that their arms touched. She looked up into Maria's face with its sneering smile...a smile that curled her lip up and exposed her gums, like an animal baring its fangs.

"So how did you do it, *hermosa Rosa*? How did you kill your husband?"

Rose returned her gaze to the book, but could no longer walk within its pages, trod upon distant soil. The book was once more a closed window. "That's none of your business. I told you all I'm going to say on that."

"You didn't tell me nothing more than his name. *William.*" Maria drew out the name with mock wistfulness. "Come on now, Rosa," she purred, "don't you want me to tell you how I killed my brother Emilio?"

"No." Rose didn't look up. "I don't want to hear that."

"We're stuck in a cell together, the two of us. Don't you think you ought to be polite to me?"

"If you want polite, be polite to me, and don't ask me about my husband again."

Peripherally Rose saw Maria sit back a little in her chair, felt the girl's glare burn on her skin like the hellish sun that baked them in this oven of adobe and stone. "Maybe I'll just ask the other girls what they know about it, then."

"You do that. I can't stop you. But you won't be hearing anything about it from me."

Rose continued flipping through the book, feigning nonchalance, waiting for her cellmate to move to another chair to strike up a conversation with someone else. But she didn't. Maria was now staring down at the book, also, and Rose thought she could sense the anger circulating through the girl's veins without release. A turned page: picture of a leopard. Another page: cougar.

"Ah!" Maria said when Rose turned the next page. She reached in front of Rose to tap the black and white illustration with a fingernail. "*Tigre.*"

"Jaguar," Rose said.

"We say *tigre.*"

The densely detailed engraving portrayed a wild-eyed, startled jaguar apparently in the act of clambering up a tree. Rose knew that – though their numbers were diminishing, owing to the guns of man – jaguars could still be found in Mexico and as far north as Arizona. Rose's husband had had a friend who claimed to have shot one, once, and sold its gorgeous pelt with its camouflage of intricate rosettes. "But you get a black one sometimes," William had told Rose. He had been drinking when he related this story about his friend, and had reached out suddenly to take Rose's chin and jerk her head around to face him. "Just like I got me a black one right here. All beautiful on the outside…but a black soul inside."

Rose broke free of the memory with a little start. This was not the way she had hoped to be transported when she cracked this book open today.

"Tepeyollotl," Maria whispered, as if speaking only to herself, still staring at the jaguar. "He is the god who looks like *el tigre*. He is the heart of the mountain…the god of dark caves and echoes."

Rose didn't meet her eyes but asked, "Why echoes?"

"I don't know. Maybe a long time ago, people didn't understand who it was talked back to you when you were talking alone."

"This is the stuff you Mexicans believe?"

"The Aztec people. You ever read about them in your books, Rosa?"

"No…I haven't."

"That's where we come from. A magic people. But the only magic you believe is *Jesús Cristo*. That magic…and the magic of *love*. You loved your William so much, huh? That's why we kill people, right, Rosa? Because we love them too much, or we hate them too much. You…I think it was love."

"You don't know a goddamned thing about me, little girl. What I'd love is for you to go bother somebody else right now."

As if she hadn't heard her, Maria went on, "I hated Emilio. Always hated him, because he thought I was nothing. He couldn't see inside of me. I'm not just this raggedy little girl people think they see." She thumped her breastbone, thrusting out her jaw defiantly. "I don't like it when people see me as nothing, Rosa. I hope you don't make that mistake, too."

Rose finally cranked her head up slowly to regard the girl. "Why can't you leave me alone?"

Maria leaned her face in close. "Because you ain't alone, pretty Rosa. I'm like your echo."

"Get away from me," Rose said in a barely audible voice.

"Can't."

Rose broke their gaze, looked down to close the book – like a barred door clanging shut, locking her out – and maybe Maria felt Rose was dismissing her, saw her as nothing, because that was when the Mexican girl picked up another heavy book from the table and swung it in both hands against the side of Rose's head.

The guard who walked alongside Rose had hold of her arm, but not roughly; it was more that he was helping to hold her up. She seemed to hurt all over at once, as if every nerve were a glowing hot wire. Fistfuls of hair had been pulled out of her scalp, her cheeks were plowed with long claw marks, and her muscles felt deeply compressed where Maria had bitten her in the side of the neck. In the prison infirmary they had wound gauze around her throat.

"That wasn't smart, Rose," the guard said. His name was John and he was tall, husky like her William had been, but his voice was soft and more regretful than accusing. "It ain't often we got to put you ladies in the Dark Cell."

"It's her you ought to be throwing in the hole, John, not me," she mumbled through her purple, swollen lips.

"She's already there, Rose."

Rose turned toward him as they walked. "You can't put the both of us in there!"

"The both of you were fighting...the both of you have got to pay. People get put in the Dark Cell for less. I'm sorry, but it ain't up to me."

"I was only protecting myself! Look what she did to me!"

"You gave her some, too, Rose. You closed up both her eyes pretty good. Busted her lip, bloodied her nose. Her face was red from eyes to chin. Course, it wasn't all her blood. That girl's an animal, I'll give you that."

"Do you know how she killed her brother?"

"Don't know much about that story. Just heard that she made a god-awful mess of him."

They were coming close to the chamber they called the Dark Cell. Because it was near to the women's cells and the library, Rose knew its location well enough, though she herself had never been inside it before. She had heard troublemakers might spend anywhere from one day to a few weeks in the Dark Cell, but she'd also heard of one inmate who had spent over a hundred straight days in there.

To change the topic of conversation, or maybe to somehow make Rose thankful that she was secure on the inside rather than outside these walls, John said, "Hey, you should see the dust storm moving in out there, Rose. Looks like a solid wall rolling across the world, tall as a mountain. A mountain made of cotton." He struggled to convey it. "Can't see past it. Must be quite a thunderstorm stirring up all that dust, pushing in behind it."

"Seen them before," Rose said bitterly.

"Well, I'm sure you have."

"John... I'll take the blame for the fight. It was all my fault, all right? I'll do my time in the hole myself, all alone. But you can't put me in that little cage with that girl."

The big guard stopped walking, and thus so did she. Looking down at her with sincere concern etched on his face, he said, "Rose, like I told you, it ain't up to me. Look, I don't think that little senorita will go at you again no matter how loco she is...nobody wants to do any more time in the Dark Cell than they have to."

Rose sighed, and then asked, "You have a wife, John?"

"Yes, I have. Married twelve years."

"You love her good?"

"Good as I can."

"I reckon she's a lucky lady." She gave him a tremulous smile.

"You'd have to ask her that." He took her arm again gently. "Come on, Rose...let's get this over with." And they resumed their march.

Only a little further along they came to their

destination, its entrance gated by a door of riveted metal bands. Like the women's cells and the library, the Dark Cell had been carved directly into the rock face of Caliche Hill. Another guard, Martin, stood waiting for them outside the metal door, carrying a Winchester loosely in both hands. John nodded at the rifle and asked, "What's that for, Marty?"

"Heard stories about that little Mexican girl," and he tipped his chin meaningfully toward Rose's marred face, "but she didn't give me no trouble. Bob helped me lock her in, but he's gone back to his post." Martin returned his attention to Rose as he stepped aside to unlock the door. "We emptied eight men out of the cage before their time to make room for you, Miss Rose. Don't that make you feel better? Maybe they'll say a prayer for you tonight."

Beside Martin's boot was a kerosene lantern. John squatted by this to light it, and when he straightened he carried it before him.

The gate screeched as John pushed it open, and he ventured first into the narrow passage with it rough, leprous walls. Rose followed, with Martin behind cradling his rifle. At the end of the little tunnel, a room opened up like a hollow pocket in the granite, about fifteen feet by fifteen feet. And in the center of this room was a cage fashioned from metal bands, like the gate. Aside from the shifting glow cast by the lantern, only a miserly portion of light leaked into the cell through a small air vent in the stone ceiling.

The restless lantern light caused a crosshatched pattern of shadows to move across the cage's sole occupant, who was crouched down in one corner because the cage was only five feet in height. Through the shadowy stripes on her face, Maria glared out at the trio. No, Rose knew, glared at *her*. Even in this insufficient light, though, Rose could see that the young girl's eyes were swollen almost shut from the blows she had landed in self defense. Maria's contused eyes put Rose in mind of a drowned man she had once seen fished out of the river, dead in the water for days, his face bloated and monstrous...transformed into something inhuman.

Having set his lantern on the floor, John bent forward to unlock the cage's door. As he did so, he said, "You got three days in here, ladies. I suggest you don't add to that. It would be a good idea for you to use this time to talk out whatever it was got you so fired up in the first place."

"Bread and water every day," Martin added. "That's it. No blankets, no pillows, and you see that grate?" The grate formed the floor of the cage. "That there is where you'll be taking care of your business." But he hadn't needed to explain that part; the hot, boxed-in air reeked of urine and excrement.

Rose thought of the man who had spent over a hundred days in this room, in this cage, and shuddered. The door of the cage squealed open, and then Martin was giving her a nudge forward with the length of his gun. For one hallucinatory moment – a disorienting fragment of memory, like a suddenly remembered nightmare – Rose thought it was her William behind her, pushing her with that shotgun of his. And then she was bending down to step into the cage. Too cruelly small, she thought, even for an animal.

The wind howled past the air vent in the ceiling of the Dark Cell, like ghostly lips blowing into the mouthpiece of some hellish instrument. A ululating wail, rising and falling as the gusts rolled past like the titanic phantoms of dead gods in an otherworldly procession. Though evening had not yet fallen, the dust storm had blotted out whatever meager light the vent offered. The man-made cave might have been the bottom of a well filled with inky water.

Rose could even feel the desert sand sifting into the cell, a gritty pollen against her face in a nearly imperceptible caress. It got into her nose, her mouth. She became conscious of how thirsty she already was. When would they bring them water, as Martin had said they would?

Pitch black. Had Rose ever known such a blackness? A person could not close their eyes to approximate this profundity of darkness...unless perhaps they did so in a room at night with all lights extinguished, curtains drawn, but Rose thought even that might not approach this total lack of light. Perhaps if one's eyes were burned out with a heated poker. Perhaps then. Perhaps if a person floated in the heavens after the last star had burned out.

But she was not alone in the void. Though she could

not see her, not the slightest reflected glistening of an eye, she knew Maria was still there squatting on her haunches in the far corner of the cage. In lulls between the wind's banshee cries, she could just barely hear the girl's raspy breathing. Sometimes, the faintest tinkle of metal links as she shifted her position slightly. The two of them had had shackles affixed to the ankles of both legs, their shackles chained to opposite walls of the cage.

Yet the cage was small, and Rose knew that Maria could reach her if she wanted to.

Rose sat with her arms wrapped around her knees, her skirts doing little to cushion her behind against the hard grate of the floor. She wanted to change positions, to try lying on her side with her arm as a pillow, but feared the sound of her own chains moving might startle Maria into action. And she was afraid that if she reclined, she might fall asleep.

Three days. Could she go without sleeping for three days? Of course not. Well, if she did sleep, how would Maria know the difference? But then, though she had never heard it herself, Rose remembered William complaining about how she snored at night. In the early days – before the drinking had got bad, before the pain of the toothaches that he said were demons excavating their own little hell inside his head – he had teased her about her snoring in a good-natured way. Later, however, he would elbow her awake irritably. Tell her the sound she made was so loud and ugly it gave him nightmares. "My Daddy used to snore," he said, "and it always scared me at night. I didn't know what the hell that was. I thought it was some animal outside the house...or in the house, prowling around." And he said, "I swear some night I'm going to wake up and grab my shotgun to shut you up for good."

Then, without really planning to, Rose said aloud into the darkness, "I don't want any more trouble." She heard her voice echo. It sounded like a ghost imitating her, mocking her. "I'll tell you about William...about me and William...if that's what you need to hear."

She waited for some kind of response or acknowledgement, even a grunt, but there was nothing. Could the girl have fallen asleep? No...no...even through the blackness between them, Rose could still feel that unabated glare boring into her.

She resumed then, and told the silent spot where she figured Maria to be how handsome William had been when she had first met him at a church dance. How sweet he had been, or seemed to be. But after their marriage the drinking had escalated, in response to the pain in his jaws that he could at least put a name to, and the pain in his mind or soul he could never articulate to her, and perhaps not even to himself. "He hit me time to time," Rose related. "Afterwards, when he was sober, he'd say, 'I'm sorry, Rose.' Course, he'd just do it again. And then it was, 'I'm sorry, Rose' again. Well, I took it. But I had some pets. I had me a cat named Tom and a dog named Rascal, and a horse. I always loved animals, ever since I was a child. I brought home birds with broken wings, pollywogs in a bowl of water. One time our family cat even knocked a snake cold, batting it with her paws, so I took that snake and put it in a bureau drawer until it came to and could move around again, and then I took it outside and let it go, and my Momma was never the wiser. I felt closer to animals than I did to people. I felt connected to them. See, animals ain't evil like people are. The harm they do each other...well, it ain't like the sins we do. They only kill to feed themselves. Or to protect themselves."

Only the echo answered. Only the banshee song. But still she went on.

"Sometimes William would give Rascal a kick. Most times I bit my tongue about it, and other times I spoke up, but of course then he'd turn that anger on me. Which was probably what he wanted to happen, anyway. But one day he saw Tom sitting on the kitchen table and he picked him up and threw him right against the wall. Then he stomped on over to Tom and gave him a kick. Such a kick." Rose paused for a moment to contain the emotion that threatened to seep out and stain her words. "Well, he killed him with that kick. And so I went at him. I pushed him away and slapped him in the face. Slapped him good and hard right across his jaw full of pain down deep in the bone, and I didn't care.

"But then he went in the other room and got his Spencer twelve gauge."

A slight jingle of metal chains. Rose paused in her story, waiting tensely, but the sound was not repeated. Still wary, at last she continued.

"Rascal was outside, so William stomped out into the

yard and called him, and when the dog came around the corner of the house William shot him. Then he walked right on past what was left of my Rascal, walked straight to the barn, with me chasing after and crying and screaming. And before I could get my hands on him to try to pull him away, he shot my horse.

"When I tried to hit him again, he turned around and struck me right in the chest with the butt of his gun. Knocked me onto the ground. And he stood over me and pointed that precious pump-action of his right down at my face..."

A new sound caused Rose to pause again. It was not the shifting of chains, but another sound, at first barely heard until a momentary ebb in the roaring dust storm exposed it for what it was.

Tiny, whispery giggling...coming from some uncertain point in the utter blackness.

The surprised anger that welled up in Rose left her speechless. Fury had knotted in her throat, even as it sent electric currents crackling through every nerve in her body.

She did not finish her story.

In the dream, Rose had taken shelter in a cave in a mountain side to escape the pummeling of a monsoon rain. For several moments she stood at the edge of the cavern's opening, watching the torrents punish the jungle canopy below her, before turning away and following a passageway eroded by time through the mountain's flank.

When she came to a hollow chamber in the rock, she crouched down with the granite wall pressed against her back for a sense of security, wet and shivering and hugging her knees for warmth. She would wait out the storm. Wait for many long years if she had to, before she could emerge free into sunlight again.

But slowly she became aware that she was not alone in the Stygian darkness. She did not hear the beast that sheltered in this cave, did not even smell it, but simply sensed its presence as if the savage blood in its veins radiated heat through its hide. Sensed its feral eyes – which she knew could see her clearly, even though she couldn't see her own hand in front of her face

– summing her up cunningly, as the beast waited for just the right moment to spring.

"Don't do this," she said to the black beast camouflaged in the darkness, her own voice echoing back to her. "Go back to sleep...please..."

She thought the beast replied with a low growl, rumbling deep in its throat, but it was difficult to tell as the sound of the rainstorm drumming against the mountain side swelled in intensity...became deafening...

The crackling sound that had awakened Rose was so loud that for a moment or two it made her think a fire raged all around her, cooking her alive. She was wildly disoriented by both the strange sound and the impenetrable darkness, not aware of when she might have fallen asleep or for how long. She was sure she had let out a gasp or unintelligible exclamation upon coming awake. As far as the darkness was concerned, she might have believed she was a spirit without a body drifting through oblivion were it not for the pain in her bottom and back from the pressure of the metal bands, like a giant waffle iron, against her.

The tangible contact of the cage at least helped ground her thoughts, gave her mind a handhold, and she remembered where she was – but what was that ungodly sound? Now it put her in mind of a vast audience clapping their hands, as if the Dark Cell might be filled impossibly with countless people, all applauding her punishment...but that wasn't the cause of the great clamor, either.

Then something like a pebble thrown in the darkness ticked her thumb, stinging her skin, and she drew her hand back as if bitten by a scorpion. While she had heard scorpions did indeed venture into the Dark Cell, and occasionally snakes too, she realized that what had struck her hand was a piece of ice. Hail stones the size of bird shot were finding their way in through the little vent in the ceiling, but the clicking sound of their impact was drowned out by the thunderous onslaught of frozen pellets against the roof of rock above. The dry hot dust storm, whipped up by the rain storm behind it, had moved on and been replaced incongruously by this.

Had night fallen while she dozed? Again, there was no way to gauge the passage of time. Rose once more recalled that one prisoner had spent over a hundred days in this cell. She wondered who he was, and if the experience had driven him to madness.

But more important right now was a different prisoner: the one who was chained across from her in this cramped box. Did Maria realize that Rose had fallen asleep...been vulnerable? Perhaps she herself had drifted off. Well, the girl certainly couldn't be sleeping now, not with this cacophony raging above their heads.

Rose arched her back, stretching her aching muscles, and repositioned her legs to one side so that she sat on the outside of her left buttock. This series of movements caused her chains, unavoidably, to clatter across the grated floor.

Immediately, she heard a sound that seemed to be a reaction to her movements. It was hard to distinguish over the skeleton dance of the hail – and might she even have imagined it? – but she thought she'd heard a deep throaty rumble.

Rose froze like a startled deer, breath clenched in her lungs' tight fists. The sound, real or imagined, had been less than human...*bestial*...and it made her recall Maria touching the engraving in the natural history book and evoking the name of Tepeyollotl, the jaguar god of a magical people.

It was easy to believe in magic in the absolute absence of light. Easy to believe in magic when it sounded like the sky outside had split asunder, the fabric of reality ripped wide open and all the tumult of the universe pouring in through the rift. The four elements all cascading through the fissure in a chaotic state, raw material to remake this sad little world...to *transform* it...

Again, a deep bass growl, maybe not so much heard as transmitted through the metal bands of the cage, like a vibration through a tuning fork. The warning growl of an animal that feels threatened...or hungry.

"I know you," Rose whispered so softly that she couldn't even hear the words herself. "I know who you are."

Somewhere in the darkness, the rattle of chain links as they dragged across the floor grate, like a delayed echo of her own movements.

"You've killed before," Rose said, louder this time, maybe loud enough to be heard above the hail storm. "But you don't have to do this again. Please don't do this again."

A different kind of sound then, veiled by the hail, veiled by the dark, but it still cut straight to the heart of Rose. It was that giggling laughter again, though closer this time. And on the tail of it, a voice croaked, "Poor Rosa." Once more, mockingly: "Poor Rosa."

Then, she flinched when an unseen hand touched her cheek, as if in a tender caress. "I'm sorry, Rosa," that voice said, near and intimate. But it was a lie...his love was a lie...and the beast roared.

John and another guard, named Bob, arrived at the entrance to the Dark Cell at a run. Bob had drawn his Remington revolver when he came within sight of its gated door – which unsettlingly stood open and unattended – but John stopped his companion from plunging into the passageway until he could light the kerosene lantern he'd brought with him.

The men found their fellow guard Martin standing at the end of the passageway staring into the cell, just short of its threshold, as if he had never quite entered the room – or as if he had retreated from it.

"What did you do, Martin?" John asked, smelling the gunpowder that still hung in the confined air. "What in God's name did you do?"

The fusillade of hail had ceased, leaving an unearthly stillness in its wake. Though the storm had passed on, evening had descended and no light shone through the vent in the Dark Cell's ceiling. Martin had brought his own kerosene lantern, however, and it rested on the floor in front of his feet. Between its wavering light and the illumination cast from John's lamp, the three men could see enough of the two prisoners chained inside the cage at the center of the room to know that they were both dead.

"I thought it was something else," Martin said in a weak, stunned voice. "What I saw...I didn't know how it got in there, but it had a hold of the girl's neck..."

John squeezed past Martin into the chamber, pushing down the barrel of his Winchester rifle as he did so, to get a better look at the bodies. He held his lantern up higher, and hissed, "Dear God."

"It looked like something else," Martin repeated, as if he stood before a doubtful jury. "I *swear* it did. It wasn't a person, John. It was some kind of...animal. But after I shot it...after the smoke cleared..."

The sixteen-year-old named Maria lay on her back, eyes gazing emptily at the vent in the ceiling as if her spirit might have ascended through it. Her tightly striped blouse was saturated with blood from the ragged wound where her throat had been torn out, the larynx exposed and carotid artery chewed through.

Chewed was the word John thought, when he saw how blood was smeared thickly across Rose's nose and lower face. But it was Rose lying there across Maria's body, Rose with three bullets fired into her back, not some animal as Martin claimed to have witnessed.

"Look what she done to that girl," Bob said, wagging his head. "Just like I heard she done to her husband."

"It wasn't Rose," Martin insisted, and he was beginning to quake with sobs now. "I swear it wasn't, boys!"

Gently, Bob took the rifle from the other man's hands. "She was killing that Mexican girl, Marty. You did what you had to do."

"But what I *saw*, Bob!" Marty cried.

"It was dark, Marty," Bob reassured him. "It was dark."

John couldn't take his eyes from Rose. Couldn't stop thinking about their conversation when he had been escorting her to the Dark Cell.

"She was afraid to be put in there with Maria," he said. "I thought it was Maria she was scared of. But now I think maybe she was scared of herself."

He thought of Rose asking him if he loved his wife, and there was a deep contraction in his chest. He reminded himself that her punishment hadn't been up to him...and there was nothing he could have done to change it...and that there was no denying the woman had been both dangerous and mad...

And yet he couldn't help but murmur, "I'm sorry, Rose."

SNAKE WINE

Gorch wasn't sure which source of pain had awakened him: the headache that felt like his skull was ready to give birth to a full term baby, or the throbbing of his left hand, which was black in a glove of caked blood and missing its index finger.

He blurted muddled curses, sat up too quickly on the edge of his bed and nearly blacked out for his trouble. He shut his eyes to will the elevator of his stomach not to rise up and disgorge its contents. With his eyes clamped shut, sizzling phosphorescent blobs swam on the insides of his lids like amoebas on a microscope slide.

When he cracked his eyes again, his innards under a semblance of control, he raised his hand in front of his face. He hadn't imagined it, dreamed it, misinterpreted what he'd glimpsed upon awakening. His left hand's index finger had been removed at the base. A glance at his bed showed no severed finger lying there, but the sheet was soaked thoroughly with drying blood. How long had he been passed out? How long would it take for blood to dry to that extent?

Gorch's apartment was on the third floor above his bar. The second floor was where his bargirls, called *bia om* in Vietnam, took amorous customers for more than the hugs that *om* alluded to. A sliding glass door gave access to a balcony. Through the door's sheer curtain he could see that the sun had risen, an orange ball buoyed on the sea.

He remembered the woman then.

She had come into the bar with another man, a British tourist in his sixties, his formidable belly like a cask and his sweating and wheezing head like a fat clenched fist. He boasted of having been a professional wrestler in younger days, but Gorch didn't volunteer his own past as a fighter. He hadn't fled to this country – as a result of some paid fist work outside of the ring – only to draw attention to his bloody past now.

The big man was already drunk as he raucously ordered a round of Saigon beer for himself, his lady friend, and a number of other white tourists and ex-pats seated at the bar or clustered around the billiard table.

Himself an ex-pat from Melbourne, now four years in Vietnam, Gorch had opened a bar catering primarily to the many Australians who visited the seaside city of Vung Tau. The bar looked across the coastal road toward the South China Sea, where the surf was iridescent from the Russian oil ships punctuating the horizon. Despite this pollution, along the coast where there were strips of beach swimmers could wade far out into the water, or lounge on the sand eating crabs while clouds of dragonflies hovered above them.

The Australian tourists found the *Down Under Pub* a welcome oasis when they tired of the indigenous fare. As if the bar's name left any doubt, live rugby played on the TV and boomerangs hung .on the walls along with photos of boxing kangaroos (Gorch's private joke) and a large painting of Ned Kelly in his bizarre armor and helmet, firing his revolver rifle from the hip.

The British tourist became enamored of one of Gorch's girls, No, and the drunker he got the more he seemed to forget the one he had come in with. Rather than act jealous or insulted, however, his companion appeared to take it in stride and cheerfully switched her own attention to Gorch as he tended the bar. Her English proved more than adequate. She told him her name was Hong.

Gorch thought the old man was a fool for neglecting her. Hong was more beautiful than No and probably a few years younger, he guessed between nineteen and twenty-one, but he supposed it had to do with the old man being jaded and gluttonous. Dolled up for their date, Hong wore a clingy red silk dress with a high Chinese-style collar, cut to the tops of her thighs, her hair falling to the small round posterior her dress so artfully encased.

No took the ex-wrestler upstairs to "nap" for a bit and recover from imbibing too much. Gorch hoped No didn't try to support him if he lost his balance on the stairs, lest she be crushed in the avalanche. Hong didn't bat an eye. Instead she asked Gorch where he was from. He swept his arm around the bar. "Uh, Australia," he said. She asked him what it was like there and he spoke in generalities, told her about Sydney – where he had also lived for a time – instead of Melbourne.

Atop the bar, she took his left hand and held it in both her much smaller hands, turning it over and examining it as if to read his future. "You have strong hands," she observed. "You have worked hard with them."

"At times," he admitted, uncomfortable. Then he asked himself why he was always so wary. Did he think she was a spy hired by vengeful enemies back in the city he had exiled himself from?

She didn't let go of his hand, and that was when he was certain they were going to fuck. Which was fine by him; he had already slept with every one of his *bia om*, repeatedly. Gluttony and all that.

He invited her upstairs to see his apartment. "Do you have photos of your country?" she asked him with shiny-eyed interest, though he suspected what really interested her was the money he'd doubtless have to pay her.

"No," he answered. "But I have a camera. Maybe I could take some photos of you."

"Ahh," she said, smiling. "But I don't like people taking pictures of me...I'm sorry."

"Okay, so we'll skip that part."

Gorch got one of his girls to take over behind the bar, but before he could show Hong to the stairs she said, "My motorbike is outside. In the seat I have a gift I bought today for my father, but I think I'd like to give it to you."

"Really? I wouldn't want to deny your father his gift."

"Oh, I can get him another. Please wait a moment, will you? I will go get it."

In his flat on the third floor of the narrow building he had bought with all his savings, ill-gotten and otherwise, Hong pulled a bottle out of the plastic shopping bag she had fetched from her Honda's seat compartment. "My father likes to drink this sometimes," she told Gorch. Smiling with charming if unconvincing coyness, she further explained, "It's good for a man's baby."

"Baby?"

"You know," she said. She pointed toward his crotch and giggled.

"Ah, I see. Makes baby grow up big and strong, yeah?"

"Yesss."

"Let's have a look." He held out his hand. "I've seen these things a million times here but I've never really wanted to try it before."

"Oh, but you will drink this one, won't you? Because it is from me?" She passed him the bottle.

"For you, and for my baby, I'll do it."

It was a bottle of *ruou*, or rice wine, and he had drunk that on its own. But this type of *ruou*, which he'd seen sold at gifts shops such as those at the Cu Chi Tunnels and the Saigon National Museum, had conspicuous extras stuffed into the bottle. Usually it was a cobra, preserved in the yellowish wine as if pickled in formaldehyde, maybe with a huge black scorpion or a fistful of smaller snakes and some herbs added for good measure. Hong's gift did have some blanched-looking herbs at the bottom, but no scorpion, and the snake coiled inside wasn't a cobra, unless its hood was closed.

Gorch turned the bottle around slowly to see it from all angles, and held it up in front of the fluorescent ceiling light. His brows tightened. Definitely not a cobra. And maybe it was a result of the animal's saturated tissues being distorted, but he almost questioned whether it was even a snake. He was reminded of the animal called a worm lizard, an amphisbaenian, which possessed a long pinkish body that looked segmented like an earthworm, with only a rudimentary pair of forelegs. It almost seemed this creature had such forelimbs, if withered, unless those were just bits of sloughing skin. Its eyes were bleached dull gray. It was looped in on itself within the glass, coiled around and around in a spiral as if chasing itself unto infinity.

"A dragon fetus, perhaps? Ace." He handed her back the bottle to open. He took down a shot glass. "Are you going to drink it with me?"

"It's a drink for men," she told him. "I don't have a baby." Her smile was a mixture of carnality and passable innocence that made his stomach squirm with hunger, as if he had his own dragon fetus coiled inside him.

She filled his shot glass, and he took a tentative sip. He tried not to show his disgust lest he insult her. After all, her father had unknowingly sacrificed this elixir for his benefit. It tasted just as he had expected: crude rice wine mixed with the essence of a reptile terrarium.

"Do you like it?"

Gorch didn't think he'd be stocking this beverage in his pub anytime soon, but he said, "A fine vintage. Cheers." He took another sip.

He and the woman Hong were naked and stood waist deep in the sea. It was high tide, and it was perpetual dusk, the bloody fleeces of clouds strewn upon a sky like magma.

The horizon was punctuated by a number of silhouetted metal ships – or the resonance of ships that had occupied those spots eons ago, or would occupy those spots in some far future epoch – in this realm where Gorch sensed steel was as transient as shadow. Hordes of dragonflies dangled above their heads, their wings a chorus of low humming.

His left arm lay limp at his side, submerged to the elbow in the lapping water. Hong held his right hand in both of hers, to her breast. Gorch felt her brown nipples pressing erect against his forearm. She was smiling up at his face, but he was looking down at the water, if it was water. It was yellowish, a color like piss, with a tang that was sour and rotten. Not so much polluted as venomous.

A whispery touch brushed repeatedly against his submerged left hand, along with the subtlest tugging, which might only be the movement of the yellow fluid itself. Gorch was reminded of the Dai Nam Van Hien amusement park, when he had taken one of his new bargirls there as a prelude to seduction. For a fee, the park's visitors could slip their bare feet into tubs in which fish would gently nibble away dead skin. He had tried it, though his date had been too squeamish. It had felt like this...an almost nonexistent sensation, unnerving all the same.

Hong squeezed his right hand tighter, and he raised his

eyes to her slowly, as if he'd been stunned by a blow in the ring. She said, "That fat man has brought pain and drawn blood, but your hands have taken life. I can feel it."

Fat man? Gorch blearily managed to conjure the image of a British tourist in his sixties, with a belly like a cask and a head like a clenched fist. The man had boasted of having been a wrestler in his younger days.

Hong went on, "You are still young and strong. You can spare a little of your youth and strength, can't you?"

"I'm not so young," he slurred.

"Compared to my father you are." She tilted her face downward suddenly, and looked around them at the yellow sea rocking against their torsos. Gorch saw her gold skin turn pebbled with gooseflesh, like tiny hard scales. "He is here," she said.

Then the tide went out, but not gradually; it was sucked back violently like a bed sheet torn away, with a roar of rushing water. At the same time, the swarms of dragonflies churning above them were all swept back as if a powerful wind had come along, though there was no powerful wind.

His lower body unveiled, Gorch lifted his left arm to find that his index finger was missing, blood sluicing from the base and diluting with the water on his skin. He contemplated his hand almost calmly, detached, turning it over and back to view it from different angles. But his gaze came to focus on something else, beyond his hand, and he looked instead to his feet and the wet sand beneath them.

Turning slowly in a circle, Hong turning with him obligingly, he saw that there was a wide groove or channel imprinted in the sand, surrounding them in a giant C. But whatever had dragged itself through the sand, coiled itself around the spot where they stood, had gone out with the tide.

Because No was the most accomplished of his *bia om* at English, Gorch had her accompany him in the taxi and stay at his side in the nondescript little hospital he chose, to translate. The young doctor who saw to his hand was pleasant and barefoot, having left his sandals outside his examination room.

Various tools like instruments of torture soaked in a pan of what looked simply to be water, on the floor in a corner of the room. A gecko was stuck to the wall near the ceiling. Gorch instructed No to tell the man he'd lost his finger in an accident, though he knew it looked too neatly severed for that. The doctor was too polite and shy to express any doubts. Gorch had to repress his curiosity about how his wounding had been accomplished: knife, shears? The word *bitten* bobbed up in his mind, but that would have been too messy a result, he was sure.

Talking to No past the attentive doctor's shoulder, as he bandaged his hand into a mitt bulky as one of his old boxing gloves, Gorch said, "I should have known something was off when she didn't bring up money. She took what was in my wallet, but it was like an afterthought. What she wanted was to mutilate me. Got to be someone I pissed off back home, reaching out to me. I haven't made any enemies here that I know of."

"Mm," was all No could contribute.

He considered his list of old enemies, and how to interpret this message from any one of them. But the dream, or vision, he'd experienced under the effects of the rice wine came back to him, not so much in a clarity of detail but as an overall impression. For no reason he was conscious of, if he had to sum up what had transpired in the vision in one word, it would be *ritual*. He asked No, "There isn't any rite in Buddhism I'm unaware of, where you might take someone's finger?"

No looked horrified by the suggestion. "No," she said emphatically. "Not Buddhism."

He pocketed the baggies of antibiotics and painkillers the doctor gave him, though he had no intention of taking any of the latter until he found out why this woman had taken a part of his body. He wanted his head clear. Pain he was used to working around.

Back in the reception area – a dotted trail of someone else's dried blood leading them toward the front desk, where their waiting taxi driver flirted with a nurse – Gorch said to No, "All right, then, did that big British guy happen to mention where he was staying, when you had him upstairs?"

"Oh!" No replied. "Yes...yes...he told me!"

Gorch didn't recognize the place's name, but No appeared familiar with it, as she was no doubt intimate with many of Vung Tau's innumerable hotels, from before she had come to work for him. The frugal tourist had decided against one of the bigger establishments like the Sammy or the Imperial, opting instead for one of those narrow, pastel-colored structures of a half dozen floors or more, looking all the more elongated for being crushed cheek-to-jowl in the side streets off the main drag, where for under ten US dollars a night one could get a clean room and HBO with a minimum of ants.

Gorch gestured roughly for the taxi driver's attention, surly from pain, and said to No, "Tell him that's where we're going. If that Brit's still there, maybe he can tell us where to find this woman."

No asked him warily, "Are you sure you don't want to tell the police what she did?"

"Why would I want to do that, if I might have to kill this little sheila when I find her?"

No's eyes widened, but she nodded quickly. "Oh. Okay."

Crowded beside No in the back of the toy-like taxi, Gorch was almost tempted to dull himself with some of those painkillers. The doctor's numbing injections had already worn off, and steady waves of pain were telegraphed up the lines of his nerves. In addition, he realized he was experiencing phantom signals from his absent index finger. At least, that's what he took it to be, this whispery sensation of brushing caresses, and an odd subtle tugging, as if he had inserted his missing finger through a hole in a wall, and on the other side little fish were nibbling at it.

He even dozed, for what was probably only several minutes, but long enough for him to find himself standing on a damp beach, though the ocean itself had drawn back so far that the water might as well have all poured off the curve of the world. Above him he heard a chorus of low humming, and he looked up expecting to see swarms of dragonflies. Instead, dangling overhead – suspended upside-down by their feet, via ropes that vanished into the fiery sky – were countless young girls in virgin white *ao dai* costumes like students, their arms crossed on their chests. Their long hair hung down in black flags, their eyes closed and mouths gaping wide – from which came the humming chorus, a wordless chanting, lips unmoving. Gorch saw what appeared to be a pinkish tentacle emerge from the mouth of a girl in the far distance, whip around searchingly as if probing the air, then withdraw into the girl's throat out of sight. Transfixed with fear, Gorch continued watching as the single limb reappeared from the mouth of another girl in the middle distance, closer now, again thrashing in the air for a moment before it was sucked back inside its host. This time he had noticed that the thing appeared vaguely segmented, like an earthworm. And then, in a flash, the appendage or rubbery body shot from the mouth of a girl hanging directly above him, seeming to lash around for him blindly. Gorch held up a four-fingered hand to shield his face, and cried out.

He opened his eyes to find No shaking his shoulder. Her expression told him she wished she was anywhere right now but beside him, even working the cheap hotels again. "Are you all right, *anh?*" she asked him.

Gorch sat up straighter. "How much longer?"

"We're almost there."

Just as the taxi was about to turn into the mouth of a shadowed corridor of interchangeable hotels, they came to a snarl in traffic. Pedestrians had gathered on the broad sidewalk, craning their necks, chattering and pointing. Diligently nudging his way through, palming his horn to urge onlookers aside, the taxi driver said something over his shoulder to No.

Gorch began to ask what was happening, but when he gazed out his passenger's window he understood. The first thing he saw was a pool of blood on the pavement, standing as thick and tacky as a bucket of spilled nail polish, already congealing under the sun. As they continued to crawl forward, he saw the source of the blood. A motorbike, now lying on its side in the gutter, had been struck by a truck overloaded with red bricks, apparently as the bike rider had been turning out of this side street to join the main road's traffic. Gorch had seen other accidents in his time living in Vietnam; they were inevitable in a country choked with motorbikes. The recent law requiring riders to wear helmets hadn't saved this victim: the truck had run directly across her head, splitting her helmet into hinged halves, and her skull identically inside it. In contrast, her body was mostly untouched, her schoolgirl's white *ao dai* almost pristine. The young girl lay on her back with her head in the wide corona of blood. Someone, maybe one of the city's many Catholics, had crossed the student's arms onto her chest.

A hard shiver went through Gorch. The dream he had snapped awake from only a few minutes earlier came back to him like a punch to the stomach that he hadn't tightened up in time to lessen. He looked away from the poor girl, resisting a deep down yawn of nausea, and the taxi managed to get the knot of chaos behind it and enter the chasm of hotels.

They pulled up in front of a tall, oblong hotel with its ground floor open to the street, at the top of a flight of steps. Gorch and No disembarked, while the taxi driver settled back to wait for them. No must have seen Gorch was feeling queasy, either from his careful step or his grayish complexion, because she put a hand on his arm. "You okay, *anh?*" she asked him again.

He nodded brusquely, gestured for her to climb the stairs. They did so, stepping into a little reception area that from the street had appeared as dark as a grotto. Now that its contents came clear, it presented them with another knot of chaos.

Heavy wooden chairs, ornate and lacquered, were arrayed along the side walls, the reception desk at the far end of the room. A wall-mounted TV played a Chinese costume drama dubbed into Vietnamese, *Journey to the West*, with an actor in makeup as Sun Wukong the Monkey King. A granite staircase swept up in a curve to the second floor. And at the foot of these stairs, a group of people had gathered, speaking noisily all at once in agitation. They stood around a bulky white mass heaped on the floor.

When the people – the couple who owned the hotel, their grown son, and several hotel guests – noticed Gorch and No, they whipped around looking nervous, as if they might be blamed for what had occurred. The hotel owners pointed at the hulk on the floor and babbled to No.

Gorch stepped past them all and stood directly over the

dead man. As if overseeing the scene with celestial amusement, the trickster Monkey King let out a wild cackle.

It was the British tourist in his sixties, the former wrestler. Staring up past Gorch, he lay on his back naked, his immense hard belly a white-haired boulder. Vomit was slick on his jowls and the front of his chest. The vomit smelled like the venomous yellow sea in Gorch's vision.

The index finger of his left hand was missing. Lifting his eyes, Gorch saw drops of blood on the granite stairs, blood smears on the banister. He turned to face No. "Did he fall down the stairs, or was it a heart attack?"

No relayed this question to the hotel owners. The couple spoke simultaneously, both of them dramatically gesticulating. Facing her boss again, No explained, "He fell down the last steps. Maybe it was a heart attack, but maybe he hit his head. He was chasing a girl who ran down the steps before him."

"Yeah. The little witch should've used more of her potion than she gave me, to subdue this big pommy." Then Gorch jerked around to face out the open front of the hotel toward the street. He heard the continuous drone of motorbikes from the long, sinuous coastal road. "I'll be stuffed," he hissed. Then, despite his lingering queasiness, he was bolting across the reception area, down the hotel's front steps, past the tiny waiting taxi, and down the shadowy side street toward the sunny and open main drag.

When he reached the mouth of the narrow street, huffing, the dead girl was on a litter being loaded into the back of a truck. Gorch caught a glimpse of her lolling head, the red gape of her face. She didn't need a face for Gorch to know her. Either Hong had been even younger than he'd guessed, or had dressed as a student to excite the old lecher, or had donned her snowy *ao dai* as a disguise to fade into the masses.

Policemen in green uniforms and military caps had appeared on the scene, talking to witnesses. So far, the Honda still lay neglected against the curb. Gorch skidded to a stop beside it, intending to crouch down and open the seat compartment, but he found that it already lay open.

Several articles that had been stored inside the compartment had spilled into the street. A plastic poncho, for those sudden drilling rainstorms that came out of nowhere, and a student's book bag that had in turn spilled some of its contents. Glass shards sparkled wetly.

Gorch snatched up the bag and dumped its remaining contents onto the street. Having noticed his actions, a policeman called out. Gorch ignored him. In a stream of rice wine, at his feet tumbled more shards, a few blanched herbs, and two bloodless index fingers looking like some kind of wrinkled worm, glistening from having been submerged in *ruou*.

Gorch peered into the bag again, but found nothing more. He hunkered by the bike, leaned in low to peek under it, didn't see anything there. The policeman had come close, speaking to him sharply, but Gorch still acted as though he were deaf.

Finally he spotted something. A thin wet smear like a snail trail. It led from where the book bag had been ejected from the bike, to an opening in the curb for draining rainwater into the sewer.

Straightening up, but finding himself unsteady on his feet – close to blacking out from pain and blood loss and more than that – Gorch experienced a renewal of those phantom signals from his absent index finger. A whispery sensation of brushing caresses, and an odd subtle tugging, as if he had inserted his missing finger through a hole in a wall, and on the other side little fish were nibbling at it.

THE SPECTATORS

I was lucky. The Spectators didn't arrive at the same time, so the first people who encountered them were not forewarned. I can only imagine waking up to find one of them standing at the foot of your bed, or in the shadows of the basement when you went downstairs to do your laundry, or waiting inside your bathroom – maybe standing in the tub – when you groggily went in to brush your teeth that first morning. There was panic, people running out into the street screaming. There were heart attacks. Many people assaulted the Spectators, even shot them.

I was lucky in that I was one of those later people who were ready. But could you really be ready? You could try not to be surprised, but you were still shocked when the day came that you acquired one of the Spectators, too. So waiting for them was really just traumatic in another way. I was nervous in those days of anticipation, sleeping with the lights on, creeping stealthily from room to room like a homeowner searching out an intruder. And wasn't that what they were?

My Spectator was waiting for me in my daughter's bedroom, but since I no longer used it the thing might have been standing there for hours or maybe even several days before I finally discovered it. I had gone in looking for something...I can't recall now what. It might be that what I really wanted to do was just stand in the room and stare at the border of cute animals my wife and I had stuck onto the walls together. It was all that remained of the nursery, but I could still see the crib in my mind's eye, the changing table, the little bureau. All gone now, but in the place where the crib had been, a figure now stood on the bare floorboards, almost in the corner. I experienced an intense jolt. I had seen other people's Spectators – the three spaced throughout my sister's house, for instance (one for her, one for her husband, one for their son) – but this one was mine. I owned it. Or did it own me?

"Fuck," I said to it when I finally could draw breath again. "Fuck you, okay? Fuck you!"

I hadn't been expecting it to appear in here, simply for the reason that I seldom came in my daughter's former room. Why not the living room? The bedroom? Not much going on in those two spaces either, though, truth be told. What would it have done in the living room – watch me surf porn or flirt in chat rooms on the web? In the bedroom, what? Watch me masturbate to some skin mag, or a set of sexy photos I'd taken of my wife long before our child died of SIDS? Long before we split apart, and she moved down to Florida to be close to her parents?

The Spectator did not turn its eyes to me at my curses. Somehow they seemed to see everything without looking at anything in particular. They resembled us in general outline – that is, they appeared like humans. Was this their true form, or one chosen for our benefit? Might their true appearance have been too horrible for us to bear inside our homes? Though to me, I would have preferred them not to be human, because they hadn't got it quite right. And that wrongness was very unsettling.

They all looked the same. Whether you were an old man, a young woman, a toddler…your Spectator would look like a tallish man of good build, standing erect as if at attention. No clothing or sex organs. Mannequins, they looked like, with no hair anywhere on their bodies, and their skin pitch black. Not African black; no human has ever been that black. It was the black of obsidian, and glossy like obsidian as well. It was the black of space. The gulf, or maybe the hell, from which they came.

Their eyes were black, too, except for their silver pupils, as bright as mirrors.

Expressionless, immobile, my Spectator seemed unaware of me, but that would have made no sense. They came to observe us, on that we could all agree. But some said, in order to study us. Others said we were a form of entertainment for them. Each one picked or was assigned one human being to study or be entertained by. Well, I wasn't going to be a particularly fascinating subject for this creature…but then, how many of us were?

"Good," I told my new guest. The only other person – person? – who shared my apartment now. "You stay in here. Enjoy." I shut out the light, closed the door, and chuckled bitterly. I knew once they had elected their position, they would not choose another.

At first, people had picked them up (when they'd satisfied themselves that the beings would not resist or fight back), and carried them out of their houses. Many had been piled up and burned by angry villagers – in India, in Africa, in American suburbs – but a new Spectator (or the same one, reconstituted?) would appear in the same spot from which the first had been taken. If you shot one in the head with a shotgun – and there was no blood, no brain, only broken shards like volcanic glass – the first time you took your eyes off it, the thing would become whole again. No matter how long you stared at an empty spot where a removed Spectator had been, or kept vigil over a defaced Spectator, they would not take action until you were gone. No one, as far as I knew, had ever actually seen one of them materialize.

I went about my routine. A numbing day at work, and then home again. A microwave dinner – pad thai this time for a taste of the exotic. I resisted as long as I could, but finally, inevitably, my curiosity got the better of me and I went to the room, opened the door and clicked on the overhead light. There it stood, a sentinel guarding the unknown, like a shadow that cast a shadow in the yellow light that reflected off the room's bare black windows. My wife and I had even stripped away our daughter's frilly curtains, leaving only blank white shades that stood half open like the lids of unblinking eyes.

"Enjoy your day?" I asked it. "At least you have a view, huh?" I gestured at one of the windows. Out of spite I considered going to each window and pulling the shade down entirely, but I didn't. Let it have this little bit. I wasn't a sadist. They...they were the sadists, I felt, and what they liked most was watching us squirm. That was the entertainment they sought.

I left the stoic entity, ate my pad thai, read my email (hoping for something from a woman I'd been chatting with...but there was nothing). At last, as if irresistibly drawn to the gravity of a black hole – for there was a profound absence to this being – I returned to the nursery and faced the Spectator again. I shifted side to side but the eyes never followed me.

"So what are you really?" I asked it. "Where do you come from?"

Our government – the governments of every nation – had determined that the creatures meant us no immediate harm. But how could they be sure that one day, maybe in a year, or ten, or maybe a minute from now, every single Spectator wouldn't snap into action simultaneously? And then, kill that person to whom it had been assigned? After which, taking that person's place here on our sad little planet?

Was it an invasion, then? Patient locusts, just waiting to take wing?

The Spectator – my Spectator, my audience of one – was impassive as a sphinx. It revealed nothing.

I watched more TV programs about them, now that I had my own. Heated debates. Maybe they're criminals from…from another planet or dimension, one guest suggested, and they're in exile here, their punishment to be in our company. A female guest proposed, Maybe they find us titillating; maybe they're voyeurs. No, no, someone countered, if that was true they'd all appear in bedrooms – those that do manifest in bedrooms aren't even always facing toward the bed. But the woman retorted, Maybe it isn't just our own sexual activity that excites them…maybe it's simply being in our presence.

Maybe, perhaps, and maybe again. It was like trying to pry one's way inside the skull of God. Who could truly say they understood anything about their motives, their desires, their thoughts?

Maybe the Spectators felt the same way about us. Maybe we were just as mysterious to them. Perhaps. Maybe.

And speaking of God; while some interpreted the Spectators as demons, others believed them to be angels…felt their visitation was a blessing, or that they were here to guide us to paradise when Armageddon came, and actually venerated the unearthly beings.

On Friday night, work finished until Monday, I opened a bottle of bourbon – as had become my weekend habit after my wife had left – and drank it on the rocks while munching chips and lying back in my recliner surfing TV. Soft-core movies, nature programs, crime documentaries, all in a blur after a while, like colored fragments in a churning kaleidoscope. I dozed finally, and dreamed of my daughter. Probably because of the crime programs, I dreamed there was an outline of her body in tape on the floorboards where her crib had been. I woke with a start, got to my feet jerkily, spilling my bowl of chips on the floor.

Without even planning it, I found myself in the nursery with the overhead light turned on. I pointed at the Spectator, and blurted, "Why here, huh? Why are you standing on that spot, of all places? I thought...I thought you things plant yourselves randomly, but this isn't random, you fucker, and you know it!"

The entity looked past me, beyond me, maybe even seeing into its own world at the same time it watched mine.

Tears streamed from my eyes now, and I slid down the wall opposite the Spectator, sat on the floor and wrapped my arms around my legs. My head was pounding from the booze, and I felt like I might vomit. "Why," I sobbed. "Why...you fucking sadist?"

I woke that Saturday morning curled on my side on the chilly floorboards, my headache worse and my body aching. I lifted the ball of fire that was my head and glanced across the room at the Spectator. Slanting rays of golden morning sun sparkled off its glassy black skin. I might have found it beautiful, had it only been a statue.

I'd dreamed again, and as I sat up further some fluttering rags of the dream caught on the edges of my mind and held. I'd dreamed that I'd understood the final stage in the Spectators' plan. Now that they had established themselves here, we humans would vanish by the millions and finally the billions from our world, and take their place in their realm. We would find ourselves frozen like caryatids in the rooms and chambers of their no doubt dark and gloomy domiciles. Freed of their spell, the Spectators would then become animated and move about the Earth as its new inhabitants. And I would stand in the corner of some dank cavern of a room on some other world, or in some other dimension, or in the netherworld itself, unto the end of time.

"There's one thing positive about my baby's death," I said to the entity in a ragged voice. "God forgive me, there's one good thing. And that's that she died before you monsters came. Because I wouldn't want her to have one of you tied to her. Her soul is clean, you fuck…she's gone and she's free."

I had my own "maybe" just then, though I couldn't share it on some talk program. The maybe that occurred to me sitting there on the floor was that these things had been given to us exactly so that we could hate them. Hate them when our jobs were miserable, or we'd been laid off, when our spouses no longer loved us and our parents were eaten by cancer and our children died prematurely. Maybe because of the times we lived in, times of extremis, we'd been given these beings as a gift. A race of whipping boys. Totems upon which we were meant to focus, to direct, all the hatred and anguish that was our lot as humans. They were not here for themselves. They were here for us. Something to help us go on…after we had vented our unhappiness, purged the wastes of our souls, for one more day.

It could be that this interpretation was simply my way of coping with the being's presence, my way of reining in my wild fury and confusion, but after that morning – as if I'd had an epiphany – I saw the being in less of an antagonistic light. If it was here for my benefit, so that I might hate it, ironically it had the opposite effect…by inspiring something almost like goodwill in me. I would talk to it every night after I came home from work. Jokingly, I would pull my wool ski hat onto its head, or tie my necktie around its glossy smooth neck. One evening I placed dark glasses over its eyes, but I took them off again quickly – only a joke; I didn't mean to impede its view. In fact, I opened the shades all the way so it had a better view from my second floor apartment of late winter's bare tree branches and the crawl of drab gray cars in the street below.

I considered making this room my living room, to make more of the Spectator's company, since if I moved it out of the nursery it would simply rematerialize there the next time I was out of the house, or slept. But no, no, I couldn't do that. This was still my daughter's room. So I would simply come in to talk to the Spectator with a glass of bourbon in my hand on the weekend, or with a prudent coffee if it was a weekday, several times each day. My serene and calming companion. I was reminded of people I'd read about, who kept the remains of a dead loved one in the house.

Yes, a dead loved one…I knew why that analogy had

come to me. Because I could almost...almost...make myself believe that this being represented my daughter's soul.

"No," I said to it one Saturday night, close to it and cocking my head to one side as I studied that inscrutable visage. "No...you aren't my baby, are you? You're me. That's why you're here. You're another version of me. Maybe you didn't even plan to come here...maybe it was some kind of cosmic accident. But you're my soul, aren't you? And that's why you're standing in this spot." I nodded. Yes, another moment of revelation. The Spectators only seemed to be standing in random spots. If people would only open themselves to the Spectators instead of hating or fearing them, if they would only see them for the shadows of themselves that they were – with their black skin and silver eyes, like negative photographic images – they would realize that the places where they had stationed themselves held some kind of intimate significance.

"Thank you," I whispered to the Spectator then, without fully understanding why. "Thank you."

The next morning when I went in to see the Spectator with my first coffee of the day in hand, I found the nursery utterly empty. There wasn't even tape on the floor to mark where the Spectator had stood.

Over a course of several weeks, all of the Spectators around the globe would have vanished, without anyone ever having witnessed their disappearance with their own eyes.

So had they all done their job, mission accomplished, and thus gone home? No. Even gone, I could see that many people still hated them vehemently, and most people continued to fear them. Dreaded their return.

But me...no, there was less dread in my life after that day. Less darkness inside me; I could feel it like a lightening of my very body. I was not thoroughly emptied of my anxieties, but things just seemed more bearable. And later that morning I even poured my bottle of bourbon down the kitchen sink.

But at that moment, in the slanting golden rays of the early morning sun, with coffee in hand, I stood on the spot where my daughter's crib had once stood, where the Spectator had stood, and quietly wept.

BAD RECEPTION

The 1954 RCA Craig with its seventeen inch screen had cost Stan a whopping $190. Sometimes he regretted not going for the Barton with a twenty-one inch screen, but that would have been fifty bucks more. He made a fair wage at the vast Plymouth factory on Detroit's Lynch Road, but that didn't mean he could afford to squander it.

He was grateful he had passed the automobile plant's required medical exam. As a Marine, seeking shelter in a trench from North Korean mortar fire, he had sustained a head injury that had required the insertion of a large metal plate in the front of his skull. His head there was markedly depressed. Despite his admission that he suffered chronic headaches, he had passed muster. Furthermore, his supervisor at the auto plant was a World War Two vet, who had taken an immediate liking to him. Maybe it was pity, Stan thought. In any case, he had been working at Plymouth for three months now, his first job since his release from the VA hospital.

Generally Stan was a frugal man, living alone in a small second-floor apartment, eating Swanson TV dinners in front of his new TV, but a television was more than an indulgence these days; it was a necessity. Especially for a man living alone, with no wife and children.

Stan's wife was Lucy Ricardo. His sons were David and Ricky Nelson. His best friend was Joe Friday. His dog was Lassie.

Like any good husband, father, friend, and master, Stan often had to undertake extra efforts to ensure the company of his loved ones...to coax and cajole these cathode ray phantoms into their visitations. In that way, his TV was a modern day ouija board. Though the Craig featured "ROTOMATIC TUNING" to "pin-point your station for you *automatically*," and "MAGIC MONITOR" circuits to "screen out interference," Stan relied on a set of rabbit ears resting atop the box-like TV case, without which he'd be a medium without a planchette. This device consisted of a small black sphere from which sprouted two telescopic "ears," acting as conductors, and between them something like a twisted wire helix. Making adjustments was such a standard routine that Stan barely noticed himself having to set down his TV dinner or bottle of beer to rise from his lumpy armchair and tweak one or other of the antennae just so. One didn't question the limitations of technology when that technology was all one knew.

Stan thought the dipole antenna's black orb with its twin insect feelers resembled the helmet of some outer space monster, poking its head up from behind the TV to gaze back at him as he sat in his otherwise darkened living room with the television's gray illumination fluttering over him. On weekends, and sometimes even during the week, he would fall asleep there in his armchair with a bottle of Schlitz still in hand. He lied to himself that the beer dulled the pain of his headaches, when in fact it only intensified his suffering by leaving him with crippling hangovers. At least it helped wash down the aspirin.

Tonight, while slumped back in his chair, he dreamed he was at the plant – but whereas in his daily work he was on the team that installed the steering column, steering gear mechanism, steering wheel gearshift, and even the rear bumper of fish-faced American cars – in his dream he was instead helping to assemble hulking Sherman tanks of the type that had been used in Korea. In fact, the Plymouth plant had supported war-time efforts in the past by manufacturing trucks for the military, though Stan had never been part of such an operation. He had also learned that in a special clean room at the Plymouth facility, a team of Chrysler engineers had developed a cost-saving process for the military, electroplating steel drums with nickel in order to help refine uranium for the creation of atomic bombs, including the very first atom bomb. But Stan had of course never witnessed this project, either.

Working on the tank assembly, just as in Plymouth's real-life operations, was a mix of men and women, white and black. One of these workers was Alice, a young black woman with warm eyes and a bright easy smile. He had dreamed of Alice before. Standing on the far side of the tank they currently labored over, she looked up and gave him one of those big white smiles. Encouraged by this, Stan overcame his shyness to ask her, "Say, Alice, what are we making all these tanks for, anyway? I thought the war was over."

"There's another one coming, honey," she told him. She called everyone honey, but it made Stan's heart give a little kick every time, even in dreams, as if she only ever said it to him.

"Always is," said Frank, another worker close by. "Another war, that is," he clarified.

"This one's gonna be different," Alice told them both. "Don't know why we're even gonna bother, though. No way we can win this one."

"The USA not winning a war?" Frank said. "You're out of your mind."

"We'll all be out of our minds," Alice said, no longer smiling. "When we see them."

"Who is 'them,' Alice?" Stan asked her.

She turned her now solemn gaze to Stan, and she was so pretty he almost didn't notice the fear in her eyes. "Can't tell you that, honey."

"What's it, a secret?" Frank taunted. "You damn Negros gonna rise up against us, is that it?"

"Can't tell you who they are," Alice repeated, unblinking, not taking her eyes off Stan's. "Couldn't if I tried."

Stan woke from this dream to the Indian Head Test Pattern on his seventeen inch screen, blurred as if it weren't tuned in properly, when in fact the blurring was from the pain that fizzed like static in his skull.

Stan slouched in front of his TV with his third beer in hand. He couldn't be bothered to shove a TV dinner in the oven tonight.

Framed in the Craig's glass screen, a window onto an easy make-believe, the world was all black and white.

Tonight Lucy and Ethel had somehow wound up atop the Empire State Building dressed as Martian invaders, in bizarre costumes with insect-like feelers and wearing prosthetic noses, jabbering in some weird outer space language. The tight costume emphasized Lucy's bust, and Stan found himself becoming aroused, just as he had in that episode when burglars tied Lucy up with rope and put a gag in her mouth. The beer in him made the scene all the more surreal. He was torn between changing the channel to spare his brain – already filled to bursting with agony both literal and figurative – or unzipping his fly to alleviate his frustrations.

He had lost his job today.

He blamed Frank, of course, but he also blamed the pain in his skull. A storm had begun rolling in late in the afternoon, the summer sky weighted with iron gray clouds, and he could swear that changes in barometric pressure, and maybe changes in the air from dry to damp, had an effect on the steel plate in his skull. His headache today had sent spots of burning color swarming across his vision, like weird organisms viewed through a microscope.

He should blame Schlitz, too, because he'd had to endure a hangover at work this morning, but mostly it was Frank.

At work they called Stan the Gorilla. He had overheard it behind his back, but sometimes the other workers like Frank had even teased him to his face. It was not only because Stan was tall and heavy-set, but because the way his metal-patched cranium dipped radically, it gave his head a concave slope like that of a gorilla. He'd tried to ignore these jokes, had even laughed along self-consciously that time he had caught another worker holding a piece of steel up in front of his own forehead and staggering around with a slack expression, like a zombie, while the other men snickered. But today they had gone too far.

Stan had cornered Alice at a time when there was apparently no one else around, just as the workers were returning from lunch break, at her station where she helped assemble instrument panels. He had been summoning the courage to ask her out for weeks, and today he had finally stammered, "Hey, Alice, I was wondering if, uh, you'd like to catch a movie with me sometime. They say *On the Waterfront* is really good. You know...Marlon Brando? Or, um, *The Atomic Kid* with Mickey Rooney sounds fun."

Alice had looked at him with a mix of surprise and

sympathy. Or was it shock and pity? And not without a dash of horror. Stan figured the shock was partly from being asked out by a white man, and mostly from being asked out by a disfigured white man. After a stunned second or two she said, "Aw, honey, I'm sorry but I already have a fella. Thanks for offering, anyway...that's awful sweet of you."

"Yeah, sure," he said, immediately looking away, no longer able to meet her eyes. He shrugged. "I just thought. Anyway...sorry. See ya around." And he had quickly turned to shamble off toward his own work area.

But someone, probably one of the white women Alice worked with, had obviously overheard him...and told others what she'd heard. Because in no time, some of the men in Stan's own area were laughing loudly and gesturing toward him. When Stan looked up from his work, there was Frank in front of him, saying to another worker named Jack, "You see how it is, Jack? If you can't get yourself a nice regular white woman, you go for the next best thing, figuring she ain't gonna be as picky."

"Hey," Mike said, chuckling, "it ain't no surprise the Gorilla would want to go with a monkey."

Stan didn't consider his reaction, and didn't hesitate in acting. He straightened up, took two strides toward the men, clapped each on the side of the head with one of his big hands, and forced their skulls together with a loud thunk. Mike dropped like the proverbial sack of potatoes. Frank managed to shuffle back a few steps, staring at Stan in dazed disbelief, before he went down.

Stan's boss took him aside later and was very stern, though he could have been worse about it, because he told Stan he was sorry when he fired him. Stan didn't see Alice as he was walked out, but he supposed the story would get back to her. He wondered how she'd feel about it. He only hoped she wouldn't be harassed by her coworkers henceforth.

On his way out Frank, now awake and holding a cold wet towel to the side of his head, had shouted after him, "You're crazy, you know that? Battle fatigue, huh, Stanley? Is that it?"

Fred burst into Ricky's living room, wearing a WWI style helmet and carrying a pump-action shotgun, breathlessly warning Ricky that he had heard about an invasion from outer space.

     Outside the twin windows of Stan's living room, in the night, thunder growled as the storm that had been building for the past few hours broke at last. Two things happened at that instant: Stan's TV picture filled with snow, turning Ricky and Fred into grainy shadows – drowning out their voices with static – and unseen knives stabbed Stan in both temples. He actually dropped his mostly empty beer bottle to the floor and hunched forward with his palms pressed to the sides of his head. For an irrational moment he wondered if a bolt of lightning had shot through the nearest window and struck him, attracted to the metal plate under his skin.

     Peripherally he saw another flash of lightning outside his windows. The thunder followed only a second later, indicating the storm was already directly overhead; a massive boom that made the walls vibrate. Stan felt as though he were again ducking down in a steaming trench gouged into that hellish Korean battlefield. He pulled his head into his neck, waiting for the shrapnel to hit him, though the plate in his skull was like shrapnel already, bigger than the chunk that had struck him on the battleground.

     He lurched up from his chair somehow, staggered to one open window and then the other, shutting them just as a torrential rain was unleashed upon the city. Crashing down like a Biblical flood in the making. It slammed his windowpanes as if it were an angry, sentient force demanding admission. Stan pulled the shades down, to further shut out that malignant force, before he turned and fell back into the armchair with a groan.

     When Stan managed to lift his head, which seemed to have tripled in weight as if its entire mass were now made of metal, and focused his watery burning eyes, he saw that horizontal bands were now rolling up his TV screen from bottom to top and the snow had intensified, so that Ricky and Fred were even harder to distinguish. Or was that Lucy and Ethel? The two distorted figures were weirdly elongated, gesturing in dripping blurs, black holes that were probably their mouths stretching wide. Snatches of metallic voices could now be heard through the hissing static, but they were incomprehensible...unless that was Lucy and Ethel imitating Martian talk again.

Another detonation of thunder. The glass in the windows rattled. The plate in his forehead felt like it was rattling in its frame, as well. Stan moaned again.

The tinny, garbled voices were like ice picks in his ears, fingernails on the chalk of his spinal column. He braced his hands on the grips of his armchair and once more shoved himself to his feet. As he stumbled to his TV, the static jumped louder in a crackling burst and the horizontal bands quickened to a flutter. He took hold of the left antenna of the rabbit ears, changing its position slightly. The rasp of static diminished to a milder hiss of white noise, the unsettling voices gone. He nudged the right ear next, and the horizontal bands slowed. As he stepped back to look down at the screen, the horizontal bands stopped altogether and the veil of electromagnetic interference lessened dramatically. Stan realized then that his proximity to the TV made the reception worse, somehow, so he backed away further and reseated himself to gauge the results. Sure enough, the snow cleared to the extent that he could view the television's images pretty clearly, and though there was still no proper sound, the fizzing static was just a whisper, almost lost under the pummeling of the rain outside.

I Love Lucy must have ended, however, and another program begun. Whatever this show was, it was not centered on some cheap interior set, some painted outdoors backdrop. The backdrop appeared to be an actual city, but a city half reduced to its constituent parts, its components, its bricks and blocks. Rubble and rebar, wafting smoke, and Stan was reminded of the destruction in Seoul or Pyongyang or Wonsan. Was it a documentary, then? An exposé on war? But which? Only technology differentiated wars. *His* war? Earlier, maybe...WWII? A lot looked flattened there in the background. Nagasaki, then? Hiroshima? Stan didn't know that this year – the same year the war in Korea had ended – the US had proposed a plan called Operation Vulture, in support of the French in Indochina, that if it hadn't been rejected would have allowed for the use of three atom bombs dropped on Viet Minh positions. Otherwise, he might well have believed this to be the aftermath.

In the middle distance, a dirty white sheet fluttered by on the wind, dragging its tattered ends across the floor of pulverized debris. Or maybe it was a torn-away canvas awning, or a futile white flag of surrender.

Yet another rumble of thunder, like a freight train barreling through the apartment overhead. The plate in his head hummed as though an electric current were being passed straight into it. And – as if the lightning storm, the electrical field of his own body, and the television were all connected – the TV screen went all snowy once more, but this time in a negative image of static: a field of seething black sparkling with glitter, like time-lapse photography of galaxies of stars being born and expiring in the briefest flicker of existence.

When the avalanche roar of thunder had passed, and the vibrating hum in his head had receded, the screen cleared to show a different angle of perhaps the same destroyed city. A church steeple stood in puny defiance, but the rest of it was a carbonized shell. There was still a faint degree of snow to the reception – yet then Stan realized it was not interference, but actual snow drifting down on the blasted city. No...no...not quite. It was a lazy fall of ash, sprinkling across the city from the churning black ceiling of cloud that capped the sky like an encroachment of deep space itself. Inky space pressing down on the atmosphere of the Earth, crushing the air, the friction of these opposing forces burning the oxygen itself into ash.

Several more ragged-ended sheets came fluttering along on the wind, one further in the distance than the other. The funny thing was, the plumes of smoke rising into the air everywhere from the piles of shattered rubble were being carried in the opposite direction.

The scene was depressing Stan on top of his pain, overcoming his curiosity about the nature of the program. He had learned all he wanted to learn about war – any war – firsthand. Before some orphaned tot with her face smeared in soot could stagger dazedly into the frame, Stan took advantage of the abatement of his suffering to get up from the chair yet again and reach out to turn the TV's dial to a different channel.

The next channel revealed a new image, but this image was a third angle of the same demolished city. He clicked to another channel. Another view of the same subject matter. Click...click...click. Only the perspective changed; the annihilation remained the same. In fact, Stan was finding that channels not normally active were receiving the transmission. He made several full circuits of the dial, as if futilely trying to crack a safe, and found that every channel featured the broadcast...only the point of view altering, as if he were receiving live feeds from a dozen or more TV cameras dispersed around the city.

Something of great import had happened, then...but where, exactly? And what, exactly?

When he'd drawn close to the TV to change the channel, his nearness had again caused the reception to grow grainy and noisy with static, but the various city scenes were only obscured, not fully erased. He gave both rabbit ears a few hard, impatient shifts that lessened the video and audio interference, but it wasn't until he retreated to the armchair that the picture was clarified and the sound went mostly quiet. He had settled on one channel arbitrarily: the one that showed the blackened church steeple. He had been tempted to turn the set off altogether, but he had to know what was going on. Whatever it was, it was obviously of profound significance. Would some announcer finally come on to explain what the hell he was witnessing?

Along came yet another bed sheet (had an exploded laundry dispersed its contents across the city?), blowing into the scene, but it stopped in the middle of the street...and hovered there. And hovered there. Hovered there, with its torn ends stirring as if it swam in place. Its surface rippled or pulsed or undulated, and the sheet was not so much dirty white as cloudy gray, with the faintest metallic sheen. As he stared fixedly at it, the floating shroud raised itself up a little, its membrane appearing to stiffen with alertness, and Stan realized then it was not a bed sheet or any other inanimate object, but some kind of living thing, however primitive its protoplasmic ameba's body; a sentience manifested as a raw scrap of primal tissue. And it had stiffened in alertness because, just as Stan had understood on some deep intuitive level what he was seeing, the thing had seemed to understand him as well. It was *seeing* him. Or sensing him, in whatever manner the thing perceived the material world. And even as Stan recognized that it was aware of him, the tattered membrane started moving directly at the camera. Directly toward his screen. Toward *him*.

Stan launched himself forward, thrusting his arm out. The membrane was sailing at him quickly as well, as if trying to intercept him before he could touch the dial. As he came at the screen the reception worsened, but unfortunately it wasn't enough to blot out what he was seeing.

Stan realized he had given out a wild cry, a blurt of panic, but before the thing could reach the thin windowpane of his screen – the flimsy bubble film that separated the two of them – his fingers found the dial and snapped it.

Another channel. On this street, none of those hovering, parachute-like bodies. Blending together, ash and popping electrical bugs filled the smoky air. The static roared like a raging fire.

Stan fell to his knees, his fingers still gripping the dial in case another of the apparitions came out from a shadowed alley of the ruins. He heaved with gasps, shaking badly, feeling as if he had just emerged alive from a firefight...but most of all he felt pierced by the eyeless, faceless creature that had spotted him, as if its awesome sentience had burned a hole straight through him. A lingering aftertaste of that inhuman, alien sentience seemed imprinted on the metal plate in his skull as if it were photographic film. Had the plate attracted that mental force, or had it in fact *shielded* him from it? If not for that little chunk of armor, might the creature have burrowed into his mind to consume it, or replace it with its own?

Through his shell-shocked terror and confusion, Stan belatedly registered a few details about this particular scene that had escaped him on his previous circuits of the dial. Framed within the TV screen was a downed camouflaged helicopter, crumpled by the side of the street. Despite the damage it had sustained, it was clearly unlike any such machine Stan had ever seen; certainly nothing like the choppers he'd known in Korea, such as the Sikorsky H-19. And now he more consciously took in the charred and gutted bodies of cars he'd only noticed peripherally before. Scattered everywhere, often half buried, many crushed, some upside-down – as if they had been borne high aloft on fiery winds before plummeting back to Earth. Despite their deformities, they too were of styles unfamiliar to him. Smaller than any of the big, solid American cars he had helped construct at Plymouth. More compact, more toy-like, more...*futuristic*.

He had another of his strange intuitions. This prescient instinct told him that he wasn't witnessing a catastrophic event occurring now at some distant location of the Earth. He was witnessing a catastrophic event occurring at some as-yet distant location in *time*.

But all these considerations had distracted him. He'd let down his guard. Suddenly, there it was: another of the jellyfish-things, appearing like an extrusion of ectoplasm from behind the crashed helicopter itself. It might even be the same entity that had tried to reach him before.

"I'm going crazy," Stan muttered to himself, quaking all over and close to tears. "It's battle fatigue, that's all. And I drink too much. And that shrapnel scrambled my brains. I'm still watching *I Love Lucy* and I just don't know it."

But he had made a mistake in speaking to himself aloud. The creature had heard him; he could tell by the way it lifted a little and its membrane stretched more taut. It stopped drifting, spun to face him facelessly, and as before began whisking toward him.

Click! The next channel. Stan was whimpering. In this shot, a scorched tank rested in the center of the road. Again, it was some impressive make that had yet to be invented. Not impressive enough, though, to have defended the city from the threat that had come. But where were the bodies of the soldiers, the citizens? *What had they done with the bodies?*

There, at the end of the street: three of the jellyfish glided into view, pale against the black smoke, almost glowing. Now four of the creatures...five. They hadn't noticed him yet.

Stan had seen enough. Enough. He reached his hand to another knob, and turned the RCA Craig's power off.

But the image didn't vanish. The static kept rasping. The only thing he accomplished was to make those five phantoms at the end of the street whirl around in the air to direct their attention his way.

Stan jumped to his feet and darted to the wall near his two windows, where the set's power cord was plugged into an outlet. He jerked it out of the wall socket, then turned and looked back at the screen.

Because he had moved away from the set, the reception had improved. That was the only change. The black and white vision of destruction remained, with the five entities approaching him steadily.

He thought of fetching a hammer and smashing that seventeen inch screen. But what if that only opened the window? Let them into his reality, here in the past?

A flash of light outside his windows, like a bomb igniting. There were several beats of delay before the accompanying peal of thunder. The storm was moving along, then. Good...*good!* It was the storm that had opened the way, wasn't it? Some triangular relationship between the electrical storm, the TV, and the conductive metal hatch bolted so close to his brain. If that triangle could be broken again, *that's* what would really cut the power to his set.

But he was afraid the storm wouldn't pass in time. The five entities would have reached him by then. He had to take more decisive action. He was a *soldier,* damn it. The war was not yet over; hell, it was a long way from beginning. Maybe he could change the outcome – keep the invaders from entering his world right here and now.

So Stan rushed to meet the enemy. Charged his TV as if to hurl himself onto a sprung hand grenade to save his comrades. What he had learned was that he could disrupt the signal; it was probably the steel plate that was doing it. So he snatched up his TV antenna and bent his head forward and pressed his indented cranium against the twisted metal helix that jutted from the black orb between the two rabbit ears.

That did it, all right. The surge in static was almost deafening. The TV screen turned entirely to snow, as if a sandstorm were raging inside that little box. He could not see the creatures, and they could not see him. Right? The snow formed an obstruction, a wall...and blocked this way, the invaders could come no closer.

Right?

He closed his eyes, squeezed them tight, and held his position until the lightning storm could truly pass, to cinch the deal. Held his ground like a good soldier.

Stan opened his eyes at last, and what enfolded before him as his lids lifted was like watching an idle TV power up for the day's first viewing.

Static still sizzled in his ears, but maybe that was flames crackling, because fires still burned here and there all around him, sending smoke twisting into the air. He looked above him, making an inarticulate sound deep in his throat, and saw the black clouds that formed a near-solid cataract across the sky, as if to encase and trap this insignificant little world, an insect preserved in amber. Falling ash alighted on the skin of his upturned face and came to rest delicately on his eyelashes. Was it his imagination that the ashes smelled of death, as if they were the thinnest parings of human flesh?

Looking down again, he whipped around to glance this way, then that. He was standing out in the open in the middle of the street. Then he raised his hands in front of his face and examined them. His skin was utterly colorless. The world here was black and white.

A tiny disturbance in the air like an unheard whisper or rustle reached him, and he whirled again to look down an intersecting street. Hovering toward him was something like a burial shroud, a winding sheet instead of a bed sheet, carried on the wind. But there was no wind.

He spun to look down an alley on his other side, from which two more of the airborne membranes were emerging. The enemy forces were advancing on him from every direction. And that was when Stan had one more of those intuitions that the creatures themselves, perhaps, were putting into his head, with its special receiver. This intuition told him these were not so many individual beings, but individual *cells* – numbering in the millions, the *billions* – that in their totality constituted one great, single entity. God was too small, too humble a word for it.

"I'm going crazy," Stan sobbed loudly, as if protesting to the nearing cells themselves. "It's battle fatigue. And I drink too much. And that shrapnel messed up my brain. I'm still watching *I Love Lucy* but I just...don't...know it!"

He dropped to his knees there in the middle of the street as the circle around him tightened, as if he were the center of some TV test pattern...the hub of a complex geometry...an integral figure to complete an unfathomable equation...a vacuum tube to be inserted into a faulty television set. They had lured him. They needed him. And he would, thankfully, never know why. It was beyond human comprehension.

Stan threw back his head, palms pressed hard to his

temples, and wailed to the crushing sky. The encircling entities converged on him...making it time to cut away for a commercial break.

SUNSET IN MEGALOPOLIS

-1-

The worst part of being held prisoner in the Limbo Field all those millennia was that he badly needed to relieve his bladder. Ultimatum didn't need to eat or drink in order to survive – the manna waves he had been exposed to in 1962 had rendered him immortal – but he still enjoyed eating and drinking nonetheless, and this was how he had come by his uncomfortable situation. He'd had plenty of time to regret his behavior since.

Only minutes before he had been imprisoned in the Limbo Field, like a fly in amber, Ultimatum had at long last discovered the underground laboratory of the heinous Castigator. But the evil scientist had been ready for him; his Limbo Field projector could immobilize even one with the god-like powers of Ultimatum. And since that time, if there was one thing Ultimatum had regretted as much as having drunk a supersized soda at his favorite fast food restaurant shortly before raiding the Castigator's lair beneath the city streets of Megalopolis, it was that he had acted on his discovery immediately instead of waiting for other members of the League of Heroes to back him up. In the early years of his imprisonment – long after the Castigator had fled his headquarters, cackling in triumph – Ultimatum had waited for his teammates to finally uncover his whereabouts and free him. But decades dragged on, then centuries, and Ultimatum had to admit to himself that they would never come. Despite the super powers of several of his fellow Leaguers, none were immortal like he, and they would have long ago died out – no doubt believing he had somehow died before them.

Had they ever caught the Castigator and brought him to

justice? Ultimatum only knew that the Castigator never returned to his subterranean hideout. In fact, in what he judged to be thousands upon thousands of years, no one else had entered that hideout and encountered Ultimatum there, frozen in the middle of bolting down a murky corridor, his face set in a grim and determined expression and his silver cape flowing out behind him.

In all those waiting years – unblinking, not breathing, the only moving aspect of him being the electrical activity of his brain – Ultimatum had staved off madness by reliving again and again the many successes he had enjoyed before his ignominious downfall. The villains he'd defeated and brought to justice, such as the Carcass, Dark Cloud, the Attila Brothers, the Jackanapes crime syndicate, and the Black Russian. He recalled the happier phases of his long, bittersweet love affair with the beautiful Kimberly Kristal, and tried not to dwell on the fact that in his absence she must have eventually turned her affections to another man. And that she would have passed away a long, long time ago.

He reflected repeatedly on the events that had led to his fateful mutation – when he had been a brash young scientist developing a controversial invention of his own design, a device that would project what he had dubbed the manna ray, which was intended to increase the size of livestock and poultry so as to better feed the Earth's poor. But an accident in which he himself had been exposed to a mega-dose of manna rays had enhanced his own body in ways he had never foreseen.

He tried to remember scene-by-scene every movie he had ever watched (including a few based on his own adventures), ran every song he had ever loved through his head *ad nauseum*, but his restlessness was as difficult to rein in as his sanity. Ultimately, he was able to will himself asleep for long periods. For unbroken centuries at a time, in fact, even with his eyes open. It was a kind of self-hypnotism, a way of putting his mind into suspended animation along with his body.

But he was awake the day that he was freed at last from the Limbo Field. So it was that he saw the beings who liberated him, and saw that they were not human.

There were two of them, and Ultimatum could see them clearly because of his enhanced vision. How they could see down here, however, he couldn't tell; they carried no artificial light source, and the bulbs in the hallways of the Castigator's former hideaway but burnt out untold ages ago.

If his mind was in a subdued state, the appearance of the pair of creatures roused him to acute interest – and wariness. Surely the Earth had been invaded during his interment. These entities were less than four feet in height, looked like bluish-gray lollipops maneuvering on limbs like those of a walking stick insect. The flat, circular heads bore no features other than one black, unblinking orb in the center that might be an eye. These two made no sound as they approached him slowly, leerily, except for the scratching of their appendages on the dusty cement floor.

The Limbo Field projector caught their interest, resting as it did on the floor of the hallway where the Castigator had left it. It had never run down, ingeniously powered as it was by the super-charged emanations of Ultimatum's own body (if this were not the case, the device would never have had the capacity to overwhelm him). If his breathing were not already suspended, Ultimatum would have held his breath in anticipation as he watched the bizarre duo take to tinkering with the projector. In his observation of them, it was difficult for Ultimatum to determine if they were sophisticated beings, mere children of their kind, or dumb animals acting on primitive curiosity.

Whatever the case, within moments of their investigation there was a loud beep that startled both creatures into panicky flight, back down the corridor the way they had come. A green light on the side of the projector had turned red, and at long last the Limbo Field was extinguished. Ultimatum's forward momentum was spent, and he crashed forward onto hands and knees, panting furiously as if he had been submerged underwater all this time.

After this momentary lapse he regained his strength and coordination, rose to his feet, and went in search of a restroom. He found what he believed to be a bathroom, but the ceiling in this section had partially collapsed and he was afraid of creating a greater disaster by clearing the rubble away. Though it hardly seemed dignified behavior for a member of the League of Heroes, he opened up his costume enough to permit him to urinate on the wall of the hallway itself. Meanwhile, he kept an eye out for those strange beings, lest their curiosity compel them to return. But they did not, and when Ultimatum had finally emptied his bladder (he resisted giving out a great moan of relief that might attract hostiles), he followed the same path the creatures had taken when they'd fled in alarm from the field projector.

As he stalked what was left of the darkened labyrinth (having to double back and take alternate off-branching corridors a few times due to further cave ins), Ultimatum wondered if these unearthly creatures might even be mutants of the Castigator's own making, a race of guardians bioengineered to watch over Ultimatum lest he ever escape the trap that had been laid for him. But if that were the case, he reminded himself, it was unlikely he wouldn't have seen them much earlier...or that they'd free him, however inadvertently.

Ultimatum didn't reencounter the pair that had liberated him, but he did stumble upon an unobstructed flight of cement stairs that carried him up into the light – and the open air of Megalopolis.

What had once been the city of Megalopolis.

-2-

Ultimatum had been on the scene only moments after the 110 storey tall Megalopolis Business Hub collapsed as a result of bombs planted by Middle Eastern terrorists. For all the crime the great city had known since its inception, this was an act of unprecedented savagery, and Ultimatum would never forget that even the notorious criminals Foul Ball and the Reamer had lent their super powers to searching for and digging out the bombing's victims. Villains like them had still held to old standards of fair play, a kind of criminal code of honor which on that terrible day proved itself to be an artifact of a time that would never be seen again.

Now to Ultimatum's crushing despair, instead of finding an even more awe-inspiring, futuristic update of Megalopolis, what he encountered was a city which in its entirety resembled the aftermath of the Business Hub bombing. Half of the city's skyscrapers had been flattened, and those that remained did so only in part. An invasion by an otherworldly enemy, surely, and one that had succeeded a long time ago: vegetation had run

Each landmark he recognized, like the Megalopolis Public Library or the Gallerium Mall – crumbling and half assimilated by plant life – was a fresh stab to the heart, like seeing a loved one in the hospital, wasted away and at death's door.

With the vivid green light of the declining sun still casting its long shadows, Ultimatum had worked his way deeper into Megalopolis, which reared from the forest like a titan graveyard to forgotten gods. He had come upon more and more of the simply rendered stick figures, frolicking amongst the trees and shattered shells of ancient structures. His theory about three color-coded sexes (a single gray/blue "female" designation, and two "males" of orange and yellow) was dashed when he encountered purple creatures, orange, emerald green, sapphire blue, jet black, pure white, and even mottled specimens. None of the little entities moved to attack him, nor did they outright flee from him, but they did keep a wary distance. Other than that they didn't seem to pay him much heed, so absorbed were they in doing nothing. Nothing, that is, except pluck wildflowers and throw handfuls of petals at each other, chase each other about like school children at recess, or engage in incomprehensible orgies of three to six participants. The petal-throwers would leap over these squirming tangles where they lay, and the air was full of those wild monkey-like cries of pleasure Ultimatum had earlier misinterpreted.

His body didn't require rest, but his mind did, so at last he sat down on the granite front steps of MegaBank Savings and Loan, reminisced about thwarting Yellow Menace's attempt to rob it – how he, Ultimatum, had appeared on the front page of newspapers across the country after rescuing that villain's grateful hostages.

The more he observed these primitive beings at play, the less he believed them hostile aliens capable of bringing the Earth to this state. Even considering that they were the more peaceful descendants of such aliens. He supposed they might represent the evolutionary ascendancy of an animal species – such as insects – to a sentient, dominant race in the absence of humans. But his gut told him these *were* humans – what humans had become in his own absence, either through an evolutionary decline or perhaps, even, an evolutionary *perfection* to a less complex, less fallible configuration. Might even the green cast of the sun be a natural phenomenon, and might Megalopolis' condition not signify a devastating war, but simply an abandonment? Could the city have simply become obsolete, as had his own body?

Well, his own pre-superhuman body.

Night fell, and the stick figures all settled down to sleep (or to even larger, more complex orgies as a precursor to sleep), without lighting any fires, and they apparently utilized no technology so there was no artificial light. Ultimatum could see perfectly well, however, by merely the light of unfamiliar constellations. And no stars had ever appeared so bright, so unobstructed above Megalopolis before.

Haunted, perplexed, conflicted, Ultimatum sat on those steps throughout the night, simply watching the dozing creatures. He didn't budge through the long hours, as if he were a statue erected to his own memory, but his millennia in the Limbo Field had taught him patience no mortal man had ever needed to learn.

At last, though, toward dawn he did doze off for a while, because it was the first time in countless centuries that he had had the luxury of sleeping with his eyes closed.

A commotion awoke him, with the green rays of dawn scattered and splintered by the canopy of leaves overhead. Ultimatum launched to his feet, looking sharply toward the source of the uproar. At last, the sound of discord. It gave him a guilty feeling of satisfaction.

He leapt from the steps of the bank, raced toward the mad cacophony, and found a sizable crowd of the many-colored beings gathered around the trunk of a particularly large tree, into the bark of which strange symbols had been etched a long time ago. An immature stick figure, slighter than the skeleton of a spider monkey, clung to a high branch, while an adult creature of a devil red hue stood on a lower bough, brandishing a stick at the child. A parent attempting to discipline an errant son or daughter or what have you? It looked to Ultimatum more threatening than that, and why then the agitated crowd? Without wasting any further time on speculation, lest the adult reach the child or the child lose its footing, Ultimatum surged forward into action. A few bounding steps, and he was airborne – flying toward the tree with his metallic silver cape snapping in the air behind him.

Recalling the fragility of the two beings he had accidentally killed, Ultimatum decided at this point simply to rescue the child from its precarious perch, and then to gauge the reaction of his pursuer. If the stick-wielder backed off, he wouldn't need to use potentially lethal violence. But if the thing was foolish enough to press him, well then he'd have no choice.

And so Ultimatum alighted on a sturdier branch below the child, just long enough to reach up and delicately close his hands around the creature's middle. Perhaps not trusting this huge but lighter-than-air alien, the child clung to some twigs and resisted at first, but pulled away handfuls of leaves as Ultimatum gently persisted. Gracefully, he floated to the ground with the bug-like child in his hands, and set it down safely on the grass.

The crowd gathered around the base of the inscribed tree had turned to him, and in unison started up a hissing sound, maybe issuing from the orifice on the flipside of their flat lollipop heads. Many of them began shaking one twig-thin arm above their heads. Still up in the tree, the red-hued creature shook its stick above its own head and joined in the chorus of hissing.

As before, Ultimatum backed off and lifted his empty palms in a passive gesture. "What now?" he asked them. "I didn't hurt him, did I?"

The red-colored being scrambled down the tree, and the crowd parted to let it pass through, none of them attempting to seize or berate the creature. Now the child turned and ran through the gap in the crowd, hooked its barbed appendages in the carven trunk and commenced climbing back up into the tree. The red entity chased after the child, shaking its stick again as it climbed. The group closed around the tree once more, many of the beings casting looks over their shoulders at Ultimatum. Despite their lack of features, he distinctly felt their scathing disapproval.

He sighed, retreated to a moss-covered fallen tree trunk and sat there to study them. He deduced, ultimately, that this was some religious or coming-of-age ritual. Driven on – apparently only symbolically – by the red being, the child continued higher until it broke off a thin branch of its own close to the tree's summit. Then, both the red-colored entity and the child descended. The child stripped the leaves from its branch, then it and the red being shook their branches above their heads while from the crowd around them arose a more approving chorus of buzzing monkey shrieks.

For the next few days, Ultimatum followed this or that group of the stick beings, watching for conditions of peril that never came. Once, a large animal resembling a praying mantis with the skull of a triceratops came crashing out of the foliage, charging a group of children. They scattered from the beast, and Ultimatum leapt up from the block of concrete he'd been sitting on and dashed after the nightmarish animal. Once he'd tackled it and smartly twisted its huge head off its bony frame, the children all turned and made a shrill whistling noise. When the adults gathered and began comforting their offspring, Ultimatum realized he'd just killed the tribe's pet or mascot. The parents looked up at him with those impenetrable black Cyclops eyes, and he wanted to hide the big dinosaur skull behind his back. Instead, he set it down gently in the grass, raised his empty hands and backed off. "Sorry about that, kids," he sighed.

-4-

Another night was falling, a last smudge of green on the horizon – where buildings and trees blended into a serrated edge of silhouettes. Ultimatum crouched on a projecting piece of ledge, several stories above ground level. Perched there like a gargoyle, an ugly and incomprehensible monster to the little stick people below him as they settled in for another round of orgies before sleep came.

Maybe the whole world wasn't like this, he considered. He could take to the air, fly anywhere and explore – perhaps find others like him who had cheated time, or races of humans who had not evolved so radically. But he knew he was deluding himself. Anyway...he was Ultimatum. Everyone knew – or, everyone had once known – that Megalopolis was his home.

His super-sensitive ears picked up a tiny, stealthy crunching sound somewhere behind him. He guessed, on the shattered stairs he had used to mount this ruin. He turned casually, staring into this level's shadowed interior. He smiled to himself thinly when he detected two creeping stick figures; he could see them even through several intervening walls. They couldn't see him yet, but they knew he was here.

So...at last, even as infuriatingly peaceful as they were, they had had enough. He didn't blame them for it. The fact that he found their blissful, innocent existence infuriating told him well enough that they did not need this hero.

A primal survival instinct urged him to fire heat rays from his eyes. Even through those intervening walls, he could turn the two flimsy gray/blue critters – and the machine they carried between them – to ash. But he stilled such thoughts. Turned forward again and closed his eyes.

He did not want to see them come, lest the heat rays beam from his eyes on an unconscious impulse before he could contain them.

But more importantly, this time when the Limbo Field enveloped him, he wanted his eyes to be shut. This time, he wanted to be able to truly find sleep.

PORTENTS OF PAST FUTURES

The vacant lot was positioned at a street corner, so it was open to the sidewalk along two sides. Its left-hand border was demarcated by a chain link fence, while the rear of the lot was shadowed by a high concrete wall covered in artwork. Dill didn't know whether to classify this art as a mural, despite its consisting of a row of unrelated images, or graffiti. Since the painting was composed of images rather than gang-style tagging, he was leaning toward mural. The images included: a fish bowl occupied by a goldfish skeleton, which regardless of being picked clean sported big blue eyes with curly lashes and puckered crimson lips...a dark-skinned old woman in an armchair with a TV for her head, its screen shattered...a sandwich lying on the ground being dismantled by cranes and steam shovels, the ant construction workers wearing yellow hardhats...and a little red devil in diapers pointing his pitchfork and announcing in a word balloon: "Art is dead!"

Perusing the wall with hands on hips and wagging his head in disgust, Dill's partner Sloane remarked, "I wish."

"Different," was all Dill opined.

"Doesn't look like gang art. Must be druggies." Sloane shambled his bulk around in a little circle, scowling at the buildings that flanked this convergence of sun-blanched streets, as if he might catch glimpse of the artists peeking down at them around the edges of window curtains.

"There's a high school just a block over," Dill said in his laconic tone, pointing with his chin. "Maybe students did that. Art students."

"Druggie art students."

Dill gestured at the body splayed in an X at their feet, as if they had been putting off this part. "What about her?"

The uniformed cops who had been the first to respond

now deferred to the two plainclothes detectives, having withdrawn from the crime scene to regroup in front of their cars, which lined the curb as if to block the scene from the public. Neighborhood people had been drawn to the scene nevertheless, but hung back in little knots and clusters behind the yellow tape that had been strung like party bunting. The locals seemed to know the drill, as if they had been through this as many times as the police officers. They were all assuming their roles, right down to the forensic team as they unpacked equipment from their own vehicle. Even the spread-eagled victim played her part, the focal point, X marks the spot.

The hair of the young Jane Doe was long, black, and soaked wet – plastered to her pallid face like streamers of seaweed. Her lips were parted slightly, and bluish. The lid of her right eye was at half-mast, open just enough for Dill to see that the iris of her glazed eye was a pretty blue. Her left eye was swollen nearly shut, however, obviously from a blow.

The body lay immodestly with all four limbs flung wide, completely unclothed, the woman's grayish nipples looking hard as if she were cold despite the sun's hard glare. Dill's gaze tracked the progress of two ants as they scampered along the woman's paper-white thigh, making a run for cover in her sodden mass of pubic hair.

When he lost sight of the insects in the glistening underbrush, he lifted his eyes to the mural on the wall at the back of the lot. The ants wearing hardhats, demolishing a gigantic sandwich, carting tasty morsels toward the opening of their underground lair.

"It sure as hell hasn't rained lately," Sloane stated. "Killer must have given her a bath to wash away evidence. Or blood."

"I don't see any wounds," Dill said. "Aside from the contused eye."

"Maybe on her back. We'll see when Ken flips her over." As he said this Sloane nodded in greeting to Asamatsu, the lead forensic identification specialist, as he approached them carrying his field gear.

Dill conjured a mental image of a man with an indistinct face washing Jane Doe's slack, dead body in a bathtub. It wasn't his method, though, to limit his thinking to the obvious. What alternative causes might there be for the woman's drenched state? He began turning slowly in a circle, as his older partner had done, but not so much looking at the drab buildings as through and beyond them. The Pacific Ocean was close, but not *that* close, and would a blighted neighborhood like this feature any community swimming pools? And if it did, how easily could a body be brought here from there, even under cover of darkness – let alone the killer having access to that pool off-hours?

Dissatisfied, he returned to Sloane's suggestion of a bathtub. But this time he pictured that faceless figure holding the young woman's thrashing, *living* body under the water.

He didn't have to voice his opinion on the manner of Jane Doe's death, however, because the moment Asamatsu stood over the naked corpse he remarked, "This woman was drowned."

"Well, ain't you young and good-looking for a policeman," the elderly black woman noted after opening her door.

"Thanks," said Sloane, squeezing into the apartment ahead of Dill.

"Wasn't talking to you," the woman muttered.

"I know that," Sloane said.

She motioned for them to enter her dark, cluttered parlor. Atop tables and bureaus, potted plants abounded. Half of these were brittle and brown, long-dead, though she seemed not to have noticed. Her TV was on, playing a soap opera. The reception was terrible. Dill figured she didn't even have cable.

After introducing himself and his partner, Dill said, "Mrs. Otis, you called our office and said you had something to tell us about the girl they found in the lot across the street?"

"Yes sir I do," the old woman said. "Can I get you boys some coffee? You policeman sure do like your coffee, don't you?"

"We're all set with the coffee," Sloane said, glancing around dubiously at the apartment's dusty, grimy state. The chairs had thick layers of newspapers spread across their seat cushions as if to absorb stains. Sloane opted to remain standing.

"Please sit down, Mrs. Otis," Dill prompted, "and tell us what you know about that girl."

Mrs. Otis lowered herself onto one of the yellowed mats of newspaper, her arms shaking as she gripped the chair's armrests. "Don't know nothing about the girl," she told them. "I never seen her before." She looked up at one man, then the other. "Do you know the poor girl's name yet?"

"No ma'am," Sloane replied, "we don't. She's still unidentified."

Dill stepped nearer to a window with dingy lace curtains, and brushed one aside with the back of his hand, gazing down into the street. On the corner: the vacant lot, strewn with the flotsam and jetsam he and Sloane had poked through extensively yesterday. Used condoms like shed snake skins, cigarette cartons, candy wrappers, iridescent shards of CDs. Like an archaeological dig, and these the items that had been unearthed, to represent some extinct and poorly-understood culture.

"Did you see the men from here, Mrs. Otis?"

"Men?" she said.

"They told us you said you saw men...leaving the girl's body in the lot."

"That's why we're here," Sloane told her. "Remember?"

She glared at Sloane. "I remember why you're here, detective. But I didn't see those...people from my window. I saw them *there*."

The investigators both followed the woman's pointing finger. She was indicating her outdated television set.

"Come again?" Sloane said.

"I can only get a few channels, and they don't come in so good," she explained. "Some nights I'm seeing two shows at once...one on top of the other. But last night I lost my show entirely, right in the middle...got more and more snow 'til I couldn't see or hear nothing. But then I started to see people moving around behind the snow."

"Snow...on the screen."

"Yes, on the screen! You think I mean snow for real in L.A.? You think I got Oldtimer's Disease or something?"

"No, ma'am," Sloane sighed patiently. "Please go on."

"Well...the picture eventually got clearer, so I could see

it better, but I still couldn't hear nothing."

"And you saw..."

"Three people all dressed in black. They were carrying a woman's body, and she didn't have a stitch on. They laid her down on the ground in that lot...and I knew it was the same lot across the street, 'cause I could see that wall behind them, with the crazy paintings on it. It was only a few seconds, then the snow came back and everything disappeared...but my damn show didn't come back for a whole half hour, and by then it was at the end!"

"So just to clarify again...you saw this on TV. Not from the window."

"Yes! But let me finish! There was something wrong with the people's heads...all three of them. Looked like...well, when my kids were little they used to play with that Play-Doh, and my son used to tease my poor daughter by putting the Play-Doh on her dolls' heads and shaping scary faces on them, then he'd leave the dolls around for her to find."

Sloane barked a single, loud laugh. "Oh wow...that's sick!"

Seeing the old woman glower at Sloane again, Dill urged her, "Yes, Mrs. Otis?"

"Well, these people looked like that. Like somebody covered their heads in white Play-Doh, with just some holes for their eyes...maybe the mouth, too."

"So they were wearing masks, then. To prevent people from recognizing them when they left the girl in the lot."

"Weren't no masks!" Mrs. Otis blurted, squeezing the armrests of her chair. "That was their *faces!*"

Sloane shuffled a little closer toward the doorway to the next room, and thus the apartment's exit. "Okay, Mrs. Otis, then we'll be on the lookout for three deformed men in the neighborhood. Maybe someone else has seen them; they should be easy to remember."

"Do you boys believe in devils?" the old woman asked, her ivory-stained eyes gone wide and unblinking. "I bet you don't! That'll be the downfall of this world...that's what makes them strong! The less we believe, the more real they get! And nobody thinks about it, but Hell is down there deeper than the oceans...and if the devils ever want to come up here, they'd have to come through all that water! So it's no wonder that girl they brought with them was all wet – is it?"

Dill and Sloane turned to face each other silently.

Outside, on the hot skillet of the sidewalk – across the street from the vacant lot – Sloane said, "Well that was a waste of time. Loony old lady."

"Fred, I think she did see something," Dill said. "She's just confused about where she really saw it, and the details."

"Yeah – details like three mutants with Play-Doh heads?"

"Masks."

"Maybe they were aliens, huh? Getting rid of their abducted experiment? Dressed all in black, too...so maybe they were Men in Black."

"You heard what she said as well as I did. She said the girl was all wet. We haven't released that detail to the public, so how could she know?"

Sloane chuckled. "Daaamn...come on. Yeah, at first that gave me pause, too, but think about it – how many people saw her body lying there yesterday? A bunch. And if you were up close it was clear she was wet...just seeing her hair alone. So this old lady obviously just heard it through neighborhood gossip. Either she's getting that mixed up with her delusions, or she's just pulling our leg for a little attention."

Dill sighed, opened his mouth to protest, but found that he couldn't defend his intuition that the old woman had seen *something* legitimate.

As if he felt his partner looked dejected, Sloane stepped forward and slapped him on the arm. "Come on; let's get our asses over to Bob's Big Boy for some lunch, huh? I always think better on a sugar rush, and I need my daily shake."

Dill sat with a black coffee in front of him, watching Sloane talk on his radio and jot notes in his spiral pad. Beside that, Sloane's chocolate milkshake stood half finished. Or half unfinished, Dill thought.

When Sloane set down the radio, he grinned proudly at the younger detective – as if he himself had uncovered what he was about to reveal – and said, "We have an ID on our girl who drowned in a vacant lot. Angela Renee Turner...a runaway from Philadelphia. Arrested at seventeen-years-old for drugs and theft, then ran away from the rehab center they had her in."

"Ran away when?"

"Four years ago."

"Whoa; four years. Well, looks like we better talk to people in Philly...see if anybody knew she was heading to Los Angeles, and if so, where she might have been staying. Who she knew out here."

"Too bad for the parents, when they hear about this."

Dill lifted his coffee mug for a sip. "Yup."

"But we'll need to contact her folks, see what they might tell us."

"I want to speak to somebody at that rehab center, too, and find out what they knew about her."

"Well, if it was drugs that got her in trouble in Philly, then I reckon it was drugs got her in trouble here."

"That's a fair bet. Got in with the wrong crowd."

Sloane snickered. "Yeah...apparently a gang of drug dealers who snort Play-Doh."

Afternoon was winding down and Sloane was on the phone with yet another person in Philadelphia, so it was Dill who took the call about Phyllis Otis – the elderly woman they had interviewed that morning.

"What's going on, Terry?" Dill asked.

"Thought you guys might want to know: that possible witness you interviewed today is dead."

"*Dead?*" Dill hissed. "Who found her?" He had been under the impression she lived in her apartment alone.

"Some kids walking down the street. She was lying there in that same lot where your former Jane Doe got dumped."

Dill didn't want to interrupt his partner...nor be

discouraged by him...so the moment he got off the phone he grabbed his jacket and strode for the door.

Dill learned the woman's body had already been removed, but when he heard a few details about the scene he stayed on course for the lot to see for himself. While driving, he asked into his radio, "Is it looking like foul play, Terry?"

"Nope," was the reply. "What they're saying is heat stroke."

"Her body wasn't...she wasn't wet, was she? Like she'd been submerged in water?"

"*What?* No, I didn't hear anything like that."

"Okay...okay...I'm coming up on the scene now. Thanks." And Dill set his radio down on the passenger seat as he pulled his car up to one of the two curbs that bordered the front of the empty lot.

In spite of the recent activity in the lot, Dill was alone here now. Even the yellow crime scene tape had already been torn down. He stamped across the dusty grass, kicking up scraps of litter, until he neared the high concrete wall that formed the lot's rear boundary. Even before he reached it, however, he could smell the fresh paint...and see the damage Phyllis Otis had done to the colorful mural.

The old woman hadn't been tall in life, so she hadn't been able to reach the tops of several of the painted images, but she had still covered up much of what had been there. A bucket of white latex paint and a paint roller pan rested in the scrubby grass, while a paint roller lay where it had apparently been dropped in mid-stroke. Even with evening approaching, the air was still baking hot. The paint was already nearly dry, even though she had applied multiple layers in irregular areas. Some of the images beneath were entirely hidden behind this snowy expanse, while elsewhere ghostly glimpses still peered through. She had worked from left to right, and must have become overwhelmed by the heat and dropped while painting over the diminutive, cherubic devil in his diaper. He was partly effaced but his eyes still gleamed through a white fog, and she hadn't yet touched the word balloon that said: "Art is dead!"

Staring at the word balloon, Dill said aloud, "Art. *Art is* dead."

He turned to stare across the street, settling on the third floor window where he himself had stood gazing out that morning. Might an echo of himself, a lingering shadow, be standing just behind that curtain even now, his past self watching for his future self down in this lot...waiting for the two of them to converge in revelation?

"Angela...Renee...Turner," he muttered to himself. "Is dead."

She had left her apartment unlocked before going downstairs and across the street to paint the concrete wall.

Dill had washed out the coffee maker's glass pot, plus one mug for himself, and while fresh coffee brewed he spoke with Sloane on his radio, peering through the parlor window at his car parked and locked at the curb.

"So where are you now, man?" Sloane asked him.

"After I took a look at where they found Mrs. Otis I headed home," Dill said. He wasn't lying...it just wasn't *his* home. "Pretty bad headache."

"I can relate. Anyway, I told you that poor old lady was a loony. Painting over that graffiti...not that I blame her. It's not connected, buddy – let it go. Let me tell you what I found out after you left."

"Shoot." Dill wandered back to the kitchen and poured himself some black coffee. He wanted to be sure to stay awake through the night.

"Didn't talk with them myself, but I'm told Mom and Dad are both pretty shaken up; they were under the impression she was dead these past four years. They never heard a peep from her after she vanished from the rehab center."

"Huh," Dill said. "Well, at least now they have some closure." He hated using that inadequate cliché, but he was at a loss as to what else to say.

"As for the rehab center, as far as the staff knows our girl never told anybody she planned to escape, let alone run off to California. But they remember something funny."

"Which is?"

"They had this therapy program, encouraging the kids to vent all their inner demons through art. Well, sometime during the night, right before Turner ran off from the place, she painted a mural on the wall of her room. She shared the room with another girl, and that kid left the place legitimately a long time ago so I didn't talk to her, but the staff swears the roommate slept through the whole thing – never saw the mural or discovered Turner was missing until she woke up the next morning."

"What was it Angela painted?" Dill asked in a quiet voice. Why did he want to ask if what she had painted was a door? What would make the image of a doorway paint itself in his mind?

"A fish bowl...one goldfish inside. Blue eyes, long eyelashes, lipstick on its lips."

"A skeleton? Like the mural at the lot?"

"Nope. Scaly. This one was supposed to look alive," Sloane replied. "Before and after, I guess."

"I guess."

"The fish had a word balloon, too. It was saying: 'Art is Free!' You see that? She's obviously the one who painted that stuff in the lot."

"Mm," Dill grunted noncommittally.

"One more funny thing. Apparently what set the girl off so she wanted to run away that night was she got in a big fistfight with another kid in the cafeteria. The staff says she ended up with a real shiner."

"Left eye?" Dill asked.

"They didn't specify which eye. But that has to be a coincidence, my friend. It's not like our girl would have a black eye for four years, is it?"

Dill had turned off all the lights in the parlor, except for the ghostly blue cathode glow cast by the television set, which he sat in front of in Mrs. Otis's old armchair, a coffee cup in one hand.

He had no wife to go home to, and so he sat for hours,

getting up only to pour more coffee or use the bathroom. Mrs. Otis hadn't specified which channel she had been viewing when her program had been interrupted, so he pointed the remote and changed channels every so often between the few that offered halfway decent reception. The others were nothing but solid, hissing static.

Despite his efforts, despite the coffee, he woke with a startled jolt in the early hours of the morning with the realization that he had dozed off at some point.

He wasn't sure what had awakened him. Maybe it was the silence of the TV, replacing its incessant chatter. Maybe an intuition in his very nerves.

Whatever it was, when he straightened up in the chair and focused on the TV screen, he saw three indistinct figures behind a layer of grainy snow...like a trio of portraits that had been obscured under a thin layer of paint.

The figures were garbed in black uniforms or jumpsuits, but more striking was their hairless, lumpy white heads. These heads looked formed from some raw matter, like virgin protoplasm. The eyes were mere punch-holes, and yet Dill felt their stare penetrate him. For all three figures had been studying him while he slept, and continued to study him now that he was awake. Gazing at him not as if they were enclosed in the TV on the other side of its glass, but as if he were the one enclosed...imprisoned like a fish in an aquarium.

Dill's fingers dug into the chair's armrests like claws. But then he thought of the remote on the little table beside him, on which also rested his coffee cup. He shot his hand out for it, knocking over his cup and spilling its dregs of coffee in the process. Jumping up from the chair and backing away from the TV a few steps, he pointed the remote at the screen like a gun and thumbed the OFF button.

The image of the three obscure figures flashed to darkness. Now in the screen he saw only his own reflection, but even that shadow being's face with its crazed expression unnerved him.

In a lower kitchen cabinet he found a toolbox with a hammer in it, and another can of white interior house paint.

He used the hammer to smash in the television's screen.

That morning, people driving or walking past the street corner on their way to work or school glanced over into the vacant lot where that young woman had been found murdered, and where their neighbor Mrs. Otis had dropped dead from the heat...a little perplexed to see a man standing in front of the high concrete wall at the back, his arm pumping fiercely as he finished what the old woman had started: covering over the colorful mural completely.

THOSE ABOVE

Home from the night shift at the factory, Hind looked in on his children before joining his wife in his own bedroom. There were two bedrooms in their chilly little flat, his two sons sharing one of them. Five-year-old Jude lay stiffly on his back in his cot by the door. Eight-year-old Alec was by the single window. The older boy had the quiet handsomeness and straw-colored hair of his father, while Jude possessed his mother's dark hair and eyes and rounder face. But Hind knew these details by heart more than he actually observed them now. With the boys' heads inserted into grayish blocks of gelatin, their features were presently hard to discern.

Hind moved on to his bedroom, treading lightly on the creaking floorboards of the hallway as he thumbed off his suspenders. While stripping off his black trousers and white shirt to the dingy long johns beneath, he stared down at his sleeping wife. Netty's pretty face, too, was indistinct in its pillow of gelatin. It was Netty who set out these large cubes each night, as they could only be used once. A blunt-tipped metal probe was inserted into the block, attached to a thick black wire that ran to a brass mechanism on a cart beside the bed. Idly, Hind shifted closer to this heavy device to confirm that it was functioning properly, as he had done in his sons' room. Gears delicate as snowflakes whirred almost silently inside it, and there was a faint ghostly sound of scribbling as a graphite needle traced an ever-unfolding landscape of peaks and valleys upon a slowly unspooling roll of paper. It wasn't really necessary for him to check on the machine, however. If any of these peaks or valleys extended beyond their safe parameters, a brass bell would ring and the sleeper would be awakened to recalibrate the device.

Clever machines, they were – the height of technology.

Due to the gelatin's conductivity, the machines were powered by the brain's own electrical output. But they were not meant as batteries to harness such energy, though Hind had read in the newspaper that there were scientists studying how the electrical output of human minds might be utilized to power whole cities, replacing steam-driven thermal power. No, the function of the gelatin and the apparatus on its wheeled metal cart was to suppress dreams.

He noted that the peaks and valleys were all of proper height and depth. No dreams had insinuated their tendrils into Netty's sleep. She was, thankfully, as empty of thought as the corpse she so resembled lying there flat upon her back.

Hind slipped under the blankets beside her. It was warm within their envelope, warm from her body heat, but he shivered as he pressed his head into the cool block of gelatin that Netty had positioned on his side of the bed.

He stared up through its smoke-tinted substance at the ceiling, waiting for sleep to close around him as the gelatin had. Though the pressure of the substance was little more than that of the air, he kept his lips pressed in a small thin line against it.

Hind didn't want to turn his head and stress the material, but he did shift his eyes to glance over at the bedroom window. The curtains hung to the sides of it like a pair of specters stealing a glimpse of the street below, as silent as a street in an abandoned city. He wished he had closed the curtains before climbing into bed, but he couldn't withdraw now. He wouldn't leave the bed again until that same bell rang in the morning, announcing it was time for the children to be up and preparing for school.

Yet it still bothered him, those parted curtains, as if the night sky overspreading the jumbled rooftops and sentinel chimneys might be gazing in at him while he lay vulnerable like a frog awaiting dissection.

Ha, he thought…as if those gauzy veils, even if he had drawn them together, could keep out the icy scrutiny of the sky.

The start of his shift, and Hind stood outdoors on the

broad loading dock smoking his pipe amongst a cluster of other laborers, all of them shivering against the golden afternoon cold as they watched a team of burly dray horses pull a long wagon up the street toward the factory – the street with its flagstones like the scales of some immense dragon on whose body they all dwelt as precariously as parasites.

Some workers balanced hooked iron pikes across their shoulders. Some held long saws or other carving instruments. In a leather pouch on his belt, less ominously, Hind carried measuring tape, sets of calipers, his pad and stub of pencil. But they all waited the same, like dogs for their dinner scraps.

The Chief Engineer, Tweed, had come to stand beside Hind. Other workers had warned Hind that this man preferred the company of his own sex to that of women, had joked that Hind's handsomeness always seemed to draw the older man to his proximity, but it wasn't this that made Hind uncomfortable around him. Rather, it was the funny tremble in Tweed's lips on those infrequent occasions when he spoke openly of Those Above, and the way he always seemed to be keeping half of what he knew to himself when he did speak of them. Hind could see it in his wide, wet eyes.

"The cartilage doesn't look right," Tweed muttered to him, even with the horse-drawn wagon some distance away. He pointed with his own aromatic pipe. "There's too much cartilage. See there? Its almost pushing right through."

Hind glanced at Tweed and saw that his lower lip was quivering in that funny way, as if he might cry, then returned his gaze to the approaching wagon.

A huge, shapeless mass was being borne along on the wagon, resembling a whale half-turned to ghost. Hind hadn't as yet heard where it had fallen. Hopefully in a field or pasture or by the side of the lake, and not upon someone's farmhouse or, even worse, a tenement building full of families crowded like mice. A few canvas tarps were thrown over it, roped to cleats in the wagon's sides, but enough of the mass showed through. Gray, translucent, amorphous. As Tweed had indicated, indistinctly visible within it was a chaotic network of thin white structures of a more solid constitution. Hind thought of leafless birch trees.

Listening to the hooves and wheels clatter solidly upon the flagstones, but with his mind drawn away to more celestial matters, Hind tilted back his head to stare up at the heavens.

The sky was a mass of colossal extrusions, boneless appendages perhaps, tangled and interwoven. They put Hind in mind of a bucketful of earthworms, except that their squirming was almost imperceptibly slow – slower than the movement of the clouds that Those Above had replaced over two decades earlier, though Hind still remembered clouds from his youth. Sometimes, though, they reminded him more of a great pile of glistening intestines. The extrusions were misty with distance, but that in itself didn't entirely account for their partly-insubstantial aspect. They seemed...*blurred*. Hind thought of a photograph he had once seen of a crowd of people moving about a square and climbing a set of steps in the foreground. The long exposure time had left the buildings looking quite solid, but had turned the people to a sea of ghosts. The sky was like a sea of ghosts, then – but the ghosts of what, he couldn't quite say. If anyone truly knew the full nature of Those Above, they hadn't shared that knowledge with the common masses. Whatever the case, the sky appeared the same no matter where one stood upon this globe. The sun barely glowed through the overcast gray of bloated coils, and at night the sky was utterly black. The stars might as well have been swallowed and extinguished. At best, one might witness the pallid smudge of a full moon, walled off from those below.

"No, no," Tweed repeated, shaking his head as the wagon finally drew close to the factory, "the cartilage is too dense."

Hind had tried ignoring the Chief Engineer, not wanting to enter into conversation – and to be fair, he was not a talkative sort no matter who the other person might be – but he replied, "That's why these chunks fall, isn't it? They calcify inside. It makes them heavy."

"Yes, but this is too much, my dear boy. This blubber will be a poor harvest. And there might be other trouble."

Hind didn't need to ask the older man to elaborate. He had seen trouble of the type Tweed alluded to, in the past.

A peripheral presence tugged at the tail of Hind's eye. Turning, in back of the small group of harvesters in their black rubber overalls he spied the factory's Masters, Alastair and Abraham Stoke. Twins, they wore identical black overcoats and black top hats. No one seemed to know which was Alastair and which was Abraham and it didn't seem to matter, anyway.

In unison, apparently sensing his gaze, both brothers turned their heads to regard him. They nodded solemnly. Hind nodded back, then looked away. The brothers knew him by name, had once approached him specifically to commend him on his work. Either Alastair or Abraham had said, "Good man, Hind, good man. You get your work done and don't waggle your tongue like most of your fellows are wont to do. It isn't good, gossip and speculation, fretting and fear-mongering. It's counterproductive. Not good for the Factory, nor for Society, is it?" The way they said such words demanded the use of capitals.

"Yes, sir," Hind had replied to whichever of them had spoken.

The horses had come to a halt, snorting plumes of steam into the air. The wagon was aligned with the edge of the loading dock, and men were already clambering up onto both like a horde of purposeful ants, to unhook the ropes, drag away the tarps, and begin hacking the "blubber," as it was called at this stage, into more manageable chunks to be placed upon carts and brought into the factory.

Within, Hind and the others in his department would set to work treating the hunks of blubber in various chemical baths, subjecting them to electrical charges, and then finally slicing the blubber into smaller, neater blocks. Cubes of what was now termed "gelatin."

It was ironic, Hind had often reflected – or perhaps it was simply apt – that it was the very matter of which Those Above were composed that was used to suppress the dreaming of humans. For they spoke to the dreaming mind, did Those Above. That was how they had pushed through the sky initially, more than twenty years earlier. They had latched on invisibly to the collected dreaming minds of the world, to hoist themselves into this reality, presumably to envelope the globe like a pearl in the gut of an oyster. But humans, however insect-like, had risen to the threat, had used their ingenuity to stave off the entities (or was it *entity*?) – by utilizing the discarded matter of Those Above to insulate their vulnerable, sleeping minds.

Still, despite this success in preventing Those Above from completing their manifestation, Hind's sons had never seen the naked sun or moon. Further, Alec and Jude had never experienced the transporting delirium and magic of dreams. Having never known anything but the oppressive ceiling that forever ground them all down with its unfelt weight, its gravity from above, the children could not mourn lost things as their father did.

Hind released a fatalistic sigh, ready to retreat to the sprawling brick factory and give himself over to the long shift ahead, but he first tipped back his head to once more scan the glacier-slow writhing of the living sky, knotted and coiled like the tissues of an impossibly vast brain. Whatever fragments of Those Above were close to sloughing away and falling, under the weight of the "cartilage" inside as it was nicknamed, from this great distance he couldn't tell. Even the largest chunks when they tore free were tiny, like his own shed skin cells, in comparison to the whole.

A commotion caused him to yank his eyes free of the mesmerizing vision.

The harvesting team had begun applying their various blades to the mass on the wagon, in preparation for breaking it down and transporting it inside in pieces, but something within was cutting its own way out. Workers shouted and backed off, their tools now held as weapons before them, as several white spikes stabbed out of the glossy gray blubber. More of these ivory appendages, like gigantic finger bones, jabbed outward and ripped the translucent matter. An awakened skeletal form rose up inside and in one burst tore its body free of the enclosing membrane altogether – if body this chaotic shape could be called.

"I knew it," Tweed hissed beside him, catching hold of Hind's sleeve as if he hadn't noticed what was transpiring. "You see?"

"The ganglia, boys!" one of the Stoke brothers called, thrusting out his arm to point. "Get in there and strike the ganglia! You know what to do!"

The inner growth Tweed called cartilage, and which Hind had compared to leafless birch branches, loomed above the split cocoon of blubber like a horde of giant albino spiders fused together in such an anarchy of form that it hurt the eyes to try to sort it out. However, here and there in the lattice of interconnected twig-like limbs were thick nodes or nexus points, and these were what the Stoke brother had referred to as ganglia.

The great figure reached out in every direction at once, and so it went nowhere, as if those multiple ganglia were numerous conflicted brains. It made no conscious attacks on the workers, though its erratic movements could easily injure or even kill a man accidentally if he wasn't careful when he moved in close. This had happened before. But as Stoke said, the workers knew what to do. They darted in, swung axes or thrust their hooked pikes, in an effort to reach those scattered nodules.

"Not sentient," Tweed jabbered beside Hind. "Just like a small bit of nerves jumping about...chicken with its head lopped off. No, they aren't sentient like Those Above."

"And just how sentient do you think *they* are?" Hind asked before he could stop himself, as together they watched a worker trip and fall onto his back after lunging in with a hatchet. Fortunately, another man grabbed hold of him and dragged him a safe distance away before he could be trampled by the thing's unthinking, convulsive dance. Sections of it had already become immobile, however, owing to successful attacks upon the ganglia.

Tweed turned to Hind with a face gone slack, apparently shocked or horrified that Hind would openly ask such a question about Those Above. But then, as if he too couldn't restrain himself, Tweed stepped very close to Hind and in a low voice said, "Their sentience is so far-reaching, so complex, so unfathomable, that it is as though we are without sentience by comparison."

"You know things about them, being a Chief Engineer," Hind stated. "Things the rest of us don't."

"I can't speak of such things, my dear boy," Tweed said. "Not here, anyway. But...I've been watching you. You have a quick mind, Mr. Hind, and I see an inquisitive nature. Perhaps you're ready for promotion. I could use an extra pair of hands...if the Masters Stoke consent, of course. Look here – tomorrow afternoon before your shift begins, join me in my office for a cup of tea. We'll talk."

A promotion? Hind had not been thinking of promotions. He had been thinking of the sun, the moon, and dreams. But he stared into Tweed's wet eyes for several moments and at last said, "Yes sir...I'll do that, sir. Thank you."

The uproar had settled down; Hind saw Tweed looking past him toward the wagon and loading dock, and so he turned around to gaze that way himself. And indeed, the monstrosity woven of branches had been stilled. It too would be broken to pieces, but the factory had no use for its material and it would simply be incinerated.

Yet it wasn't the configuration of cartilage Tweed had been staring at over his shoulder, Hind realized. Both Stoke brothers were looking their way, as if even from this remove they had been listening in on their conversation. As before, the twins nodded to Hind in unison. Once more, he nodded back to them – as if some secret had passed unspoken between them.

"Poor old fool," Hind muttered, standing at his bedroom window, peering down into the narrow flagstone street below. Two constables had the arms of a disheveled old man with long white hair and beard. The constables themselves wore leather masks with brass-rimmed goggles, and iron breastplates under their flowing leather coats, which were as black as their tall felt-covered helmets. In their free hands they both carried a metal truncheon, hollow and with a powerful spring inside to drive a bolt from the tip if circumstances required.

"They're coming!" the old man cried, struggling ineffectually as the constables walked him toward their horse-drawn iron wagon. "Slow…slow-like…but they're still coming!"

"What is it, darling?" Netty asked absentmindedly as she collected up their partially collapsed gelatin blocks, to be disposed of in the trash bin.

"That old man we hear screaming sometimes at night, in the lodging house on the corner."

"Oh! Poor man. But he really should have known better. What do you think they'll do with him?"

"I have no idea," Hind said, partially obscured behind one of the gauzy curtains as if afraid the constables might suddenly lift their gaze and catch sight of him there. "But you know how they say people who make too much noise about

Those Above just disappear. To keep from agitating others. Who knows…into prisons? Mad houses?"

Netty looked up at him, smiling prettily, her curly dark hair pinned up in an unruly bun. "Oh, but don't you think those are just stories to frighten children into behaving, darling?"

"I think in that regard," Hind said, "they see us all as children."

Hind was not troubled by the taunts of other workers who suggested he had become Tweed's new pet. Though the tall, slender Hind was reserved in disposition, these coworkers knew he was strong in every sense and hence kept their comments joking rather than accusatory. Anyway, even if their accusations had been real, Hind couldn't have turned down the additional money that enabled him to buy new clothing for his family, more and better food to stock their cupboards. He and Netty had even discussed the possibility of moving to a larger, warmer apartment in another neighborhood. And then there was the fact that Hind now worked in the day, rather than on the second shift, and therefore had more time to spend with his family. All in all, he felt very fortunate for this unforeseen turn of events.

"Engineer is but an easy title to encompass all we do here, Mr. Hind," said another of Tweed's small crew, a man named Quince, as he poured a powdered chemical into a solution bubbling in a large copper vat over a gas jet. Hind stood at his side, observing. Quince went on, "Yes, we ensure that the many varied apparatuses throughout this plant are operating smoothly, and thus we work closely with the mechanics. But we are also chemists, as you can see, for as you well know the blubber has to be treated. We are researchers and inventors, forever working toward perfecting the processes we employ here. Which leads to what you are observing now. We are undergoing experiments to see if we might prolong the use of a finished gelatin cube, so that it might not need to be discarded after a single use. Very wasteful, considering all that goes into rendering them. We need a gelatin that is not damaged by insertion of one's head, that can perfectly resume its previous form, yet still retain its light properties so as not to discomfort the sleeper."

"That would save a lot of trouble," Hind agreed, "for a family like mine. Acquiring new cubes every day, disposing of them the next day…"

"Indeed." Quince stirred his steaming gray broth. "And in fact, it seems that this has been achieved in a few other countries already, though the bastards have as yet not shared their secrets with us. How foolish. We're all working toward the same end. We have to keep the greater good in mind, not the petty competitions and concerns of the common man. The common man is nothing. We must remain humble, Mr. Hind, mustn't we?"

"Mm," Hind grunted.

Quince stepped back from the vat, clapping chemical dust from his palms. "Very good, then."

As his trainer adjusted a valve beside the gas jet, Hind turned and glanced down at an open notebook on the workbench beside them. Quince's notes were in a near-illegible scrawl, but Hind thought he could read the underlined heading on the open page. Did it indeed say, "Dream Enhancement"?

Quince turned his attention to Hind, saw him looking down at the notebook. He stepped forward, closed the book, tucked it under his arm. "In time, Mr. Hind, you will be taught everything. It's still early yet."

In the observation and charting room on the factory's top floor, a single great loft-like chamber with windows that ran the length of every wall, Hind watched as Tweed tinkered with the focusing mechanism of a large, complex brass telescope. The viewer would sit in a leather chair incorporated into the base of the telescope, while an assistant turned a wheel to position the whole device at any desired point along a track that ran the circumference of the room.

"Never seen this beauty before?" Tweed asked while bent over an opened panel, exposing the system of gears within. He squinted through magnifying lenses attached to his spectacles by hinges; there were several sets of such lenses, some of them in colored tints.

"No, sir," Hind replied.

"This is of course how we can predict where the next fall of blubber will be, so we get there quickly before it's disturbed by locals. And do you know dogs and wild animals will actually eat the stuff?" He looked up, his lips trembling in a smile as if his nerves couldn't quite support it. "It's true. But you should see the beasts afterwards – they go quite mad."

"I have heard that," Hind admitted. "As though rabid."

"Precisely."

Tweed reached into his tool cart for a replacement gear, and Hind's gaze lingered on the cart after the engineer had turned back to his work. The handsome wooden cart, resting on casters to make it mobile, possessed a series of drawers and a hinged top – currently open to display an array of small machine parts resting in felt-lined hollows. One of these parts drew Hind's attention, and he reached in to lift it out and bring it closer to his eyes. It was metal, the length of a pencil, one end threaded and the middle mostly encased inside a porcelain insulated housing. It was funny; to him, the piece resembled a miniature of four tall structures – one at each corner – that stood on the flat roof of the building that housed this city's governing body. Hind had heard varying explanations for their purpose, all of them vague; most people dismissed the spires as purely decorative, evoking this age of industry and technology. Those four constructions had always reminded him, in turn, of the twelve even larger spires that had been added to the roof of the House of Parliament, in the capital, during the great renovations to that structure nearly two decades ago.

"Sir," Hind inquired, holding up the object, "what is this?"

Preoccupied, Tweed glanced over his shoulder and stated, "Transmission amplifier." He focused on his repairs again for a few moments, abruptly stopped, and looked around at Hind more lingeringly. "You're not quite ready for that, Mr. Hind. All in good time."

Not that again. Hind sighed inwardly, his pride a bit wounded; did Tweed and Quince think he was dense? But he said, "Very well, sir," and replaced the so-called transmission amplifier into its niche as if slotting it into a machine, the function of which he couldn't comprehend.

Tweed shut the panel in the base of the telescope and secured it place with a screw. "Here...have a look through for yourself. It gives one quite another perspective."

Tweed shifted aside, sweeping an arm toward the upholstered chair. Hind bent forward and slipped into the seat, positioning himself behind the eyepiece of the telescope. Tweed leaned in close beside him to show what knobs and levers Hind could use to adjust the magnification and focus of the image, and when Hind announced his readiness Tweed turned several cranks to bring Hind in his chair more in alignment with the eyepiece.

"Good God," Hind said involuntarily. The focus was already perfect, and he had all he could do to prevent himself from recoiling from the lens with a jolt.

From afar, he had compared the weave of Those Above to earthworms, intestines, the convolutions of a brain...but up close, earthly analogies failed him. One section of a single tubular extrusion filled his view, unthinkably enormous. Through its gray tissue he could see pale branches like petrified veins, some moving in erratic scrambling spasms. A few of these many-limbed growths had even escaped from within, somehow, and clung to the outside. And a portion of the extrusion within his view was slowly tearing away, would ultimately plummet to the earth below. Already one end of the peeling wedge of flesh was merely tethered by long gummy strings.

Aware of Hind's awe, Tweed reflected, "They define us now, Those Above. They have impacted our world, my boy. Redefined our age. Our culture, society – even, for many, our religious beliefs. There is the time Before They Came, and the time After They Came. There is no denying or undoing it – we are too small, too inconsequential, incapable. And so we have learned how to live in the world they have reconfigured for us. But we aren't to hate them, Hind, are we? Any more than we are to hate other forces greater than ourselves. A mountain, an ocean. Weather. The sun we still revolve around."

"What would they really have done to us if we hadn't stopped their materialization?" Hind asked, not taking his eye from the lens, even though he was leaning into it with such intensity that it hurt the skin across his cheekbone.

"We can't be wholly sure," Tweed said, glancing behind him at the door as if afraid to find it open, with the Brothers Stoke standing just outside glowering in at him. "It's safe to assume most humans would be destroyed...that is to say, absorbed. But be assured they would not do away with all of us. They are not corporeal in the same sense we are. On our plane, they would still need a trusted minority as useful servants. That doesn't mean they would love us, but they would take care of us, as a mechanic cares for his tools."

"How do you know all that?" Hind asked, removing his eye from the lens at last and turning toward Tweed in his creaking leather seat. There was a pink depression on his cheek like the mark of a giant suction cup.

Tweed only blinked back at him, his lips in a smile that flickered spasmodically.

The brass bell awoke his sons, so loud that it roused Hind and his wife as well. They rushed to the boys' bedroom to find them awake and wide-eyed, but as if they lay paralyzed the brothers hadn't withdrawn their heads from their blocks of gelatin, afraid to ruin them needlessly and be scolded. Yet Netty helped pull the boys out of the gelatin and smoothed their moist hair, while Hind bent over the dream suppressor on its wheeled cart.

"Netty," he said, "let's switch our cart with theirs so they can go back to sleep. Fetch them new cubes. I'll take this into our room and make whatever adjustment it needs."

"A good idea, dear."

And so, while Netty helped the boys prepare to return to bed, Hind sat on the edge of the bed in his own room, hunched forward with a side panel of the brass machine removed, exposing its clockwork innards. He turned a few knobs inside, hoping that would rectify the problem. If not, then he and Netty would have no choice but to sleep that night with their heads in new blocks of gelatin but without a connection to the machine. It was frowned upon to do so, but sometimes unavoidable until a trained repairman could have a look.

Lately Hind's own mechanical skills had been broadened, however, so instead of screwing the panel back in place he looked more closely inside the device, curious to see if he could detect a problem that might still prevent the dream suppressor from working properly. If the warning bell rang again, and they once more had to withdraw from the gelatin to make further adjustments, he knew they would have exhausted the last of their gelatin cubes until they could acquire more in the morning.

Toward the back of the case, mostly obscured by a number of large meshed gears, Hind spied something curious. He tried to squeeze his hand in past the gears but only succeeded in scraping his wrist and smudging grease on his knuckles. Rather than give up, however, he used his tools to unfasten and remove those gears that blocked his way...exposing the object he had glimpsed, and confirming his suspicion. Not that he was any less confused for that confirmation.

He unscrewed the threaded end of the object from its base, withdrew it and held it before his eyes. It was smaller than the version he had found in Tweed's tool box, but otherwise identical.

"Transmission amplifier," Hind echoed in a barely audible voice.

The observation and charting room had determined that a fragment of Those Above would drop into a crowded slum that day, and so constables had been alerted to go into that impoverished neighborhood and advise people to leave their homes until the threat was over. Despite this, when the dray horses hauled their load to the factory that afternoon, there was a woman imbedded inside the blubber. Two more horses followed, pulling an ambulance carriage. And catching up behind that was a funeral director in black top hat astride a black horse, breathless from having rushed to join the procession.

Though he no longer took part in the dismantling and treating of the blubber, Hind had still wandered out onto the loading dock to smoke his pipe and watch. He had caught word of the trapped victim before the wagon drew up flush against the loading dock.

"Is she alive?" people were either murmuring to each other or else shouting over the heads of others.

Workers in black rubber overalls moved forward with their cutting implements and set to work. Hind moved closer in an attempt to see, but for now the harvesters blocked his view. Two men in white uniforms from the ambulance passed a stretcher up to the dock, and Hind rushed over to help hoist it up.

He had just set down his end of the stretcher when the crew of workers parted and several of them surged toward him, carrying a figure between them. Hind looked up, sprang to his feet and backed away a few steps to make room for the ambulance men as they vaulted up onto the dock. But more than that, he had recoiled out of revulsion.

The woman's arms were extended and stiff as if with rigor mortis, fingers gnarled as though she had been trying to claw her way out of the membrane that had swallowed her. Both her dress and her skin had been bleached as white as paper, and all her hair had slid out of her scalp, leaving her head agleam like an ivory doorknob. Her eyes, too, had gone entirely white. And yet she was talking...gurgling a stream of words in a liquid voice.

"...still coming...still coming...closer every day...you'll see..."

"Shh," one of the ambulance men tried to calm her, as he lifted one end of the stretcher upon which the harvesters had rested her rigid form. "We'll put you in a special bath, dear...we'll wash this stuff off you soon enough."

"Too late for a counter-solution," snorted a coworker standing close to Hind. "Within the hour she'll be a statue."

"Calcified," said another worker nearby. "Just like those coral things that grow inside them."

But the woman could still roll her head from side-to-side, and she had not stopped babbling.

"...they're far away yet, so you can't tell so much...but you'll see...you'll see...every day just a little bit closer..."

The woman's head suddenly stopped whipping and her empty orbs seemed to lock right onto Hind. Without realizing he'd made the decision to speak, he raised his voice above the clamor and asked her, "How do you know they're still coming?"

She had not stopped thrashing her head because she had met his particular gaze, however, but because the paralysis had spread upward. And yet, hearing his words, she still managed to croak one last utterance.

"Inside them…we are one."

"Why don't you come to bed, dear?" Netty said, dressed in her nightgown with her long hair hanging loose as she stood framed in the threshold to their small parlor. Hind sat in his worn leather chair smoking his pipe, staring across the room at its twin windows. He had drawn the curtains of them both, however, against the blackness that curtained the heavens.

"You go without me," Hind mumbled without looking around. "I'll join you soon."

He sensed her reluctance as she turned away.

Some time later he crept in to stare down at his sons, their heads submerged in blocks of gray jelly, before creeping into his own bedroom to stand over his slumbering wife. He watched her a long time, saw that her eyes shifted back and forth in an almost regular rhythm beneath their thin lids, like a restless sleeper tossing beneath her blankets.

"You're *dreaming*," he whispered to her. "What are you dreaming, my love?"

In the morning, after discovering his gelatin cube undisturbed beside her own, Netty found her husband in his chair in the parlor. "Darling!" she cried, her pretty face alarmed, thinking that he had dozed off here although he hadn't slumbered for a minute. "Darling, you slept here all night! You know you can't do that!"

But he only gazed up at her mutely, his face as pale and unshaven as one of those poor blighted madmen who lived in the city's streets begging passersby for change.

"My dear boy," Tweed said when Hind entered his office that morning. "Look at you – are you ill?"

After closing the door Hind stood silently for a few moments, unable to formulate words, but then his eyes wandered from the Chief Engineer seated behind his cluttered desk to his mobile tool cart nearby. Hind moved toward this, opened its hinged lid roughly, and withdrew the porcelain-insulated object he had recently handled. Holding it aloft, shaking it, in a hoarse voice he said, "Transmission amplifier? Transmitting what?"

"What's wrong, Mr. Hind?" Tweed said, leaning back warily in his chair.

"Transmitting *what*, Tweed?" Hind took a step nearer to the desk. "*Dreams*, isn't it? Dream amplification. Dream enhancement. That's what's happening, isn't it? That *flesh* we stick our heads into each night…that unholy communion…those cubes aren't suppressing our dreams at all! It's exactly the opposite!" His eyes bulged in their purple hollows. "Every night we're calling them down!"

"Hind," Tweed sighed, smiling tiredly, lower lip shivering, "I told you, you weren't ready to know everything just yet."

"Oh no…none of us are ready to know the truth, are we? How could I possibly ever be *ready* to know that Those Above are being summoned down here to extinguish us all? Oh…but not all, right Tweed? That's what you said – that they'll still need their servants when they come."

"Yes, Hind!" Tweed said brightly, as if seeing an opportunity to calm the younger man. "Precisely! The ones who were loyal, who were faithful and helpful, will be spared and utilized!"

"And I'm to believe I will be one of them?" Hind shouted, his whole frame shaking. "Or the question is, do you really believe *you* will be one of them? One engineer in one city in the whole of this world? How many of us do you really expect they'll need? Wake up, Tweed – this is madness! It has to be stopped, for all of us!"

"Hind," Tweed said, rising and coming out from

behind his desk, "please keep your voice down. Panicking others will do no one any good."

"Yes, yes, it's all about keeping the sheep ignorant. But that can't go on any longer! We need to do what we thought we were doing all along – we need to suppress our dreams to stop them from coming!"

"My boy," Tweed sighed again, wagging his head sadly as if talking to a child, "that was just a story. Don't you see, now? It's never been possible for us to keep them out of our dreams."

Hind stood gaping. "Good God," he hissed.

"Why do you think our leaders cooperate? Because we have no choice...we have no power against them. It is inevitable that ultimately they will fully materialize. Therefore, the best we can hope for is to curry their favor, so that at least some of us will be saved."

"We must still *try* to fight them!"

"I tell you, it's impossible." Tweed shuffled closer, extended a hand with the palm turned up – either asking Hind to give him the transmission amplifier, or to take his hand both literally and figuratively. "Look at it this way, my friend. It will take so long for them to fully manifest in our realm that it probably won't even happen in our lifetime."

"But it will in my *children's* lifetime, won't it?" Hind bellowed.

"There's nothing that can be done about that. If it's any consolation, those who are assimilated become part of their essence. It might even be a blessing...to become one with something infinitely greater than ourselves."

"My children would be *blessed* to be absorbed by those things?"

"Let me ask you, what kind of life would they live in any other world? Toiling like insects for a handful of decades before they return to clay? At least now they'll have a kind of immortality."

"No!" Hind roared, lunging forward. He swung the clenched transmission amplifier in an overhead arc as if plunging a dagger.

Tweed staggered backwards, howling, his dislodged spectacles hanging off one ear. The transmission amplifier protruded from his left eye socket, a red wave flowing down half his face. The imbedded mechanical part looked like a miniature telescope, implanted in his skull to enable him to view a new universe of pain.

The two tall constables who had hold of Hind's arms – his wrists shackled behind him – walked him down a series of narrow metal staircases, in a brick-walled back stairwell of the factory he had never seen before. Along the way from Tweed's office to the locked door of the stairwell, through a string of hallways and open rooms, he had shouted to a number of other workers that Those Above were still descending...that the dream suppressors did not prohibit dreaming, but magnified it...and so he guessed they were removing him from the building by an obscure route so that he might not be exposed to any more of the factory's employees than was necessary.

The pair of constables who had been summoned to the factory (along with an ambulance to cart Tweed away) did not speak to Hind no matter how much he ranted to them. He told them, too, about the dream suppressors summoning Those Above. About the truth behind the twelve towers atop the House of Parliament. They did not respond. Nor did they answer when he demanded, "What will you do with me? Where is the prison you'll be taking me?" His rage crumbled into grief and he sobbed, "I have a family! I want to see my family, damn you!"

But there was still no reaction from the masked peacekeepers. Only the clanging of their boots on the metal steps. The hissing of the gas jets that fed the lamps set into the stairwell's walls. The deep, ominous rumbling of boilers and external combustion engines on the other side of the brick walls, like the laboring organs of a titanic mechanical entity.

At the bottom of the stairwell he noted two identical metal doors. Just as the three of them descended the last of the steps, one of these doors was loudly unlocked, squealed open, and through it into the stairwell stepped the brothers Alastair and Abraham Stoke. Against the stairwell's chilly air, for Hind could see his breath misting, the factory's Masters wore their long black overcoats, though they were without their customary top hats.

"Tsk tsk, Mr. Hind," said one of them. As usual, Hind could not tell which. "And you had showed such promise."

"Promise for what? Furthering your lies?" he cried, starting toward the twins. The constables gripped his arms more tightly. "Promise for bringing about the annihilation of life on our world that much faster?"

"This is what has always stood in the way of any kind of progress," the Stoke brother said, with the philosophical weariness of the enlightened. "Little men who fail to see the big picture. What are you, in whole of the black cosmos?"

"And what are you?"

"Part of it, Mr. Hind." The man smiled, and at the same time so did his double. "Part of it. But there may yet be hope for you in that regard. Hope for you whether you welcome and understand it, or not."

This Stoke turned to the other of the pair of metal doors, and slipped a key into its lock. The resounding clunk of a bolt being withdrawn, and then he pulled the door open and stepped over its threshold. After his brother had followed, the constables pushed Hind through.

When he saw what lay beyond, he said, "*No.*" But that tiny word was inadequate in expressing his awe. His horror...and terror.

They were in a basement level, well below the factory. In fact, its subterranean area was so great that he realized it must extend beyond the borders of the factory property. It spread away as far as the eye could see, its limits lost in the darkness of distance. A great cavern, partly natural and partly man-made, its ceiling supported by countless columns – some shaped from stone or built with bricks, others being iron girders. And this cavern contained a sea...a sea of gray, gelatinous flesh, more or less level in a convoluted topography, though composed of knotted coils thicker in girth than the greatest whale. The flesh shined glossily where the meager glow of gas lamps reached it. If one stared long enough, one might detect that the gargantuan extrusions slithered across each other. This accounted for the almost subliminal hissing or rasping sound that filled the cavern, like the rustling of a distant surf.

Part of that rustling, though, had to be from the restless skeletal forms secreted within the ash-colored flesh. In some places, white spines had punched through the outer membrane, while elsewhere the calcified growths had emerged from the jelly entirely, to perch atop the coils and spasm in what looked like feverish dances.

"There are Those Above," said one of the Stokes, "and Those Below. Rising from the dark places…not so much places within our world, as portals to their world. A tide rising a little bit higher every day."

"When the two forces meet, like great hands coming together," said the other brother rapturously, "then we will know the true God."

Here and there the tapered end of a fat tubular limb had wound itself around a pillar, as if the seemingly infinite mass were using these to hoist itself up from below.

The party of men stood on a stone platform, elevated like a little cliff above this ponderously churning expanse. Hind stood with hot tears streaming down his cheeks, like the blood that had flowed down Tweed's face. He even wondered if what he felt on his skin was blood, not water, as his blasted eyes took in this scene. He had stopped struggling in the grip of the constables. He had quit ranting. In the face of this revelation, all the strength had gone out of him. The last spark of rebellion.

It wasn't acceptance, however. It wasn't a hope for conversion. He did not see the hands of God coming together to cup his world between them like a precious egg. He saw two hands coming together to crush that egg out of existence.

If he had any hope at all now, it was that he and his family would not become one with this deity and thus live on in a unified, transfigured state. His hope was that existence would indeed end for them, utterly.

And so it was, that when the constables urged him to walk forward between them – toward the edge of the stone platform – he walked along freely, without protest and without prayer.

THE INDIVIDUAL IN
QUESTION

The individual in question gave me his consent to interview him, regarding tonight's occurrences, in the hotel room that he believes is his own. He cannot say with absolute certainty that it is in fact the room he rented, but he found the door left open when he returned from the event. He reports that the door to the next room was also standing partly open, and in that room as he passed it he heard a woman apparently speaking on the phone in a very agitated manner, while sobbing.

The subject of my interview relates that he feels it is surprising enough that he was able to locate his hotel at all, considering the state he was in, if this is indeed the same hotel in which he rented a room. There are several hotels in the vicinity of the outdoor activity or performance he attended, though he can't now recall what the nature of that activity or performance was. He seems to feel it was a large-scale magic act or fireworks display gone awry, and vaguely recollects a huge shape looming out of a strobe-lit fog that put him in mind of the brontosaurus balloon named Dino that as a child in the 1960s he looked forward to seeing on TV during the Macy's Thanksgiving Day Parade. He also references a giant floating pig he once saw at a concert by the music group Pink Floyd, but he stresses the shape in question was not a brontosaurus or pig.

As I interview the person I'm facing it's hard to believe he can actually see me, and yet he moves his head to follow me as if maintaining eye contact. Brimming from both his eye sockets are thick clusters of long crystals like quartz, but black like obsidian. The whole of my subject's head, face, and hands appears to be badly burned, with all traces of hair gone from his head, all his exposed skin being charred black and yet also with a strangely metallic aspect, giving his skin the effect of crumpled aluminum foil blackened by fire. Strangely, his clothing is entirely undamaged. The interviewee recounts that as he was ascending to this floor in the elevator, another hotel guest who was attending the same convention that the subject believes he was attending – though he cannot at present confirm that he was in this city for that purpose – asked the interviewee, "So what are you supposed to be?"

To which my subject replied, "I'm supposed to be a man."

Given the unknown nature of the injuries both physical and psychological sustained by the interviewee in the course of tonight's events, he cannot offer an opinion on his chances for recovery. On a positive note, however, he reports that he is not in any pain, only experiencing a profound disorientation. But even this he says is more in the nature of a stunned euphoria than involving any degree of anxiety. Though he can't explain why this might be so, he says that he feels he is now perhaps "better configured for the future."

I'm not sure I share his sentiments, myself – though as I turn away from the wretched figure in the bathroom mirror, my interview with the individual in question completed, I am surprised that I too can see perfectly well through the black crystals that have sprouted where I once had eyes.

In fact, I feel I can see *too* well.

As if from a vantage point in space, I see a reconfigured Earth, in some unknown future epoch, crumpled like a ball of aluminum foil blackened by fire.

THE RED MACHINE

Leslie was a stripper. A commercial stripper, to be more precise – as opposed to a social stripper. The printing company for which she'd been working for three and a half years divided its work thus: social work meant personal stationery, wedding or party invitations, birth announcements and the like...commercial work being business letterheads and envelopes, and business cards. As a stripper, she "stripped" the negatives from which the plates would be made for the presses; that is, she positioned the negatives on graph-lined sheets of paper with the use of a light table. She had once been a plate burner, the one who transferred the negative's image onto the plate, but she had grown restless and her supervisor had made her a stripper to "make better use of her artistic talents."

Positioning negatives on yellow paper sheets and cutting out the areas to be exposed with an X-Acto knife was little more artistic to Leslie than would be stuffing the red pimento in olives. She wondered if her boss really believed that she felt artistically fulfilled simply because she occasionally had to use a cheap watercolor brush to dab opaque brown paint on the scratches and dust spots on the negatives.

Her boss, who acted as though he were encouraging her talent, was the one who had told her not to pin so many of her drawings on her section of the cork bulletin board which entirely encircled the commercial stripping room. Some people had found the cartoons offensive, he explained a little bashfully – naturally he himself admired her talent. She had taken everything down the first time, but slowly new ones returned in their place, finally in greater profusion. One series, though drawn in black pen, utilized a lot of red marker blood.

Her boss asked her again to refrain...couldn't she just hang one picture, and change that from time to time? People would think all she did was draw instead of work, he said (the evidence of her rate sheet aside). She did hang only one picture. For Thanksgiving she drew a rotting turkey carcass buzzing with flies, with the caption, "What do you want for meat – white, dark, or green?" A white sheet of paper hung from the bulletin board, with the words "Don't Look" on it. If flipped open it revealed the bloody series of sardonic cartoons. Those easily offended didn't have to look if they didn't want to, did they?

Anyway, other strippers displayed the photos of their insipidly grinning boyfriends, of their cars (!), sexy postcards from vacation cruises, calendars of oiled tanned hunks. Leslie found these things offensive, but she didn't try forcing her sense of aesthetics and values onto others. She had as much right to express herself as they, she felt.

A lot of people did compliment her on her drawings. "What are you doing working here?" had been the words most directed to her over the past three and a half years. Followed closely, however – with chuckles and wagging heads – by something like, "You're *sick*."

"What do you call that, H. R. Giger meets Georgia O'Keefe?" said Aileen.

Leslie had sent away for the cattle skull from a mail order house specializing in replica weapons and authentic war memorabilia. Once painted a fake bleached white, it was now a glossy inner sea shell pink, resting on newspapers spread on Leslie's work table. The entire surface of the skull, before painting, had been covered with plastic pieces snipped from tank and car models, little oddly shaped pieces of metal she'd collected, and sanded chicken bones, all super-glued in place. Only the horns were a glossy black, and smooth.

"I call it *Icon*...and I've never seen anything like it," Leslie mumbled, folding clothes.

Aileen, tea in hand, smirked. "Oh, come *on*, Les. I know how much you love Giger and O'Keefe."

"Everything resembles something. Everything's been done before. There are only new approaches and combinations, and I've never seen a combination just like this before."

"Well, I'm your sister – I can trace it pretty easily. I mean, it's *good*...I can see a lot of work went into it. But what does it do? You're obviously just out to shock people again. Shock can be good, but shock can really put people off. Have you ever thought of *seduction* instead?" Aileen was, of course, referring to the approach of her own art. She was now exhibiting fourteen of her erotic acrylics at one of the galleries along Boston's Newbury Street. She'd invited Leslie to the opening night party but she'd declined, reminding Aileen that she worked second shift. "You should really *try* something other than shocking people. I swear you want revenge instead of attention."

"It has meaning," Leslie said, her back to Aileen as she slid open a bureau drawer. "It's an updated tribal icon, a modern...interpretation of ancient magic. It has mythic resonance."

Aileen laughed hard, almost sloshing tea to the floor. "Did you rehearse that line in an imaginary talk show in your head? Les, that thing is just another version of that fetus in the fridge." Aileen was referring to a mutant embryo Leslie had made of clay painted over with latex rubber she'd ordered from a theatrical supply house, the sculpture kept in an old pickle jar in the refrigerator. It was labeled *Unwanted Child* and Leslie had been tempted to leave it in the refrigerator at work. She considered defending the meaning of that piece, but remembering her temptation to bring it to work, Leslie wondered, as she often did, if her sister were a little – or a lot – correct.

All of the clothes Leslie folded away in the drawer were white. She hadn't worn so much as a colored pair of panties for eight months now, and had worn primarily white for months before that. Leslie expected Aileen to comment on this at any minute, with the drawers opening under her nose, looking as if they were full of nurse's uniforms. She didn't. What could she say, anyway, Leslie thought. All Aileen had been wearing for the past year, it seemed, like all the people down on Newbury Street, was black.

Aileen was no prettier, really...even Leslie had to admit. Bustier, a rounder bottom and hips, but Aileen had professed to envy Leslie's slenderness instead. They both were very pale and clear-complexioned, and both had striking acetylene blue eyes, but Aileen had a tangled mass of black curls (she joked to Leslie she was trying to look Jewish) and Leslie had a choppy, boyishly short cut, dyed a bright blond. She turned heads, particularly back in summer in her white dresses, low cut and with thin shoulder straps, for it seemed the only real color on her was her pale pink lips and the startling blue of her eyes.

Even now at work men eyed her constantly but none had asked her out for a long time. She'd reluctantly accepted a few first dates, but no seconds. One pressman had given her flowers at work in front of everyone on the night of their first date. Now he no longer even talked to her. Sometimes Leslie felt that she *radiated* too strongly, in white, with her dyed hair, would have liked to hide in black, trap light instead. But she couldn't. Not while Aileen had claimed it.

"What's that, the head of a robot minotaur?" Jason said, smiling, having entered Leslie's spare bedroom with a coffee in hand. He'd been looking through books on the coffee table; one on medical curiosities and one on supposedly true cases of ghosts, hauntings and poltergeists. The kind of books Aileen said Leslie left out in the open to shock people. Leslie had replied that she liked to shock herself, and – yes – others too. Shock them awake. Shock them to feel.

"A futuristic...shaman's icon," Aileen said, trying to mock Leslie's explanation but coming up short. "She calls it *Icon*."

"You have some imagination, Les. How long did it take you to do this?"

"I really don't know...I did it over a period of three weeks."

"You gonna hang it up in the house?"

"Maybe. In the kitchen."

"Naturally," said Aileen. "I'm glad I live downstairs." Three floors; two complete apartments plus a large attic and the basement. They rented from their maternal grandmother, who lived across the street. Aileen had claimed half of the bright attic, once a third apartment, as her studio; the rest was their mutual storage area. Leslie had the cellar. She was quite content with this arrangement.

"I think Leslie's apartment is fascinating. She has a unique touch."

"Jason, gluing dried-up dog turds on the walls would be a unique touch as well...but unique isn't always most important. Mood, feeling, intent...purpose. Much more meaningful. Les has the talent, but I'm trying to help guide her into more meaningful work instead of trying to assail people. H. R. Giger's stuff is unique too but it's just repetitious ugliness. He's wasting his talent, too."

"Many people like his stuff, and I like your sister's." Jason smiled at Leslie.

"Thank you." She smiled back, returned to her folding.

She loved Jason.

She loved her sister. She felt guilty whenever she thought how she'd love to trade with Aileen. She'd take Jason, and Aileen could have their father, who had molested Leslie, the quieter, meeker of the two girls...the vulnerable one...from the age of ten until she was fifteen, when her mother found out and divorced him. Leslie felt guilty that she was somewhat resentful that Aileen had never had to go through what she had – had never once been touched. It was almost as if Aileen and their father had betrayed her together, in a conspiracy to keep her down.

There was a going-away party for one of the paste-up girls at work. The crew was dwindling; the pay was bad. Burger King paid more to start. Second shift now had only one full-time pressman on the social line. Leslie felt like she'd been there for a decade. She felt left behind, and signed the going away card: "Good luck – Lucky! Leslie." Once she would have drawn in a quick little sketch, but she hardly drew anything at work anymore.

"Ah, okay, we're gonna have break in a little while so everybody should go back now, huh?" said the social stripping group leader, who was twenty. At twenty-four, Leslie was the oldest person in the prep department. She returned to commercial stripping. She sat in there alone.

A half hour later the commercial group leader, who was twenty-one, returned from wherever and settled down to go through an Avon catalog. Leslie developed a headache from staring into the light table. She excused herself, went to the small nonsmoking break room to down her aspirins with a cup of water.

The social group leader was still sitting in the break room with the girl who was leaving and the other paste-up girl, an hour since she'd told everyone to return to work. Another social stripper, a friend of the group leader, was using the pay phone.

She could sense the tension of the group leader, Sharon, at having been discovered. A few months ago Leslie had taken thirty extra minutes after a fifteen minute break on a slow night, and her group leader had burst into the caf and yelled at her in front of the others in there to go back to work. The next day, with the prep supervisor's blessings, both group leaders called her into the office to give her a verbal warning.

When she returned to work, there was a greater pile of negs on her desk, magically, and her group leader was gone; she'd been paged on the intercom to come down to a press where the operator, a burly handsome flirt who even flirted with Leslie, would fill the group
leader in nightly on the soaps he videotaped for when he came home. He spoke of the soap opera characters with the same authority with which he spoke of sports stars and hokey wrestlers.

The other commercial stripper, a twenty-year-old male friend of Sharon's who made three dollars an hour more than Leslie, had vanished into the camera room to chat with the camera operator...long ago.

Leslie complained of these things to her supervisor on first shift, though it was easier to do it in letters she left him. He had told Leslie during their last meeting, after she had started to tremble and raise her voice, that her bad attitude might affect her raise potential and her employment.

He'd probably thought she was close to tears that time. She wasn't. She was close to screaming at him. It was fury that had shaken her.

Leslie blew dust motes off the small crystal ball on the table in her grandmother's dark, cozy study with its built-in shelves of musty books. It was a house the Addams Family wouldn't live in, according to Aileen. Aileen often told their grandmother that one day she was going to rent a dumpster and just toss everything out for her. "Oh no you won't," said their grandmother, not amused by these teasing threats.

"Why don't you take that home with you, honey?" The grandmother, a mummy-like wizened gnome, lowered her body into a chair opposite Leslie.

"The ball? I bought it for you, Nana – as a present."

"Is that where I got that?"

"Yes, from me, last year, for Christmas."

"Oh...oh. Well, why don't you take it now? Your sister will just come in and steal it anyway."

"Nana, don't you let her scare you with that crap – she's just teasing you."

"She's come in here and stolen from me many times already – she took my best cactus book, she took my old clock and put some crummy cheap one in its place. She thinks I don't notice. Where did she get a key? Does she have one? I lock up *every* night." The grandmother looked bewildered. "I've heard her a couple times but by the time I get downstairs she's gone."

Leslie shivered with a nervous chill, her sympathy for her grandmother such that for a moment she almost believed someone was creeping through this house late in the night. She knew, however, that Aileen never sneaked in here or stole anything. Her grandmother was senile. And she'd always been a pack rat, a collector, very possessive of her heaps of junk treasure, the antiques, the boxes of old movie magazines, *Life* magazines with Monroe and JFK on the covers. "Anal retentive," according to Aileen, in Freud's lingo. "Won't part with her shit."

"She won't steal the ball, Nana. Just keep it."

"Did I tell you I spoke to Eddy in it one night?"

"Yes." Another shiver.

"He said he was happy and he was getting a big party

ready for me soon. I saw his face in it. If she ever tries to take that crystal and put a cheap fake in its place she'll hear from me...I haven't said anything yet but I'm about to blow my top at her, your sister. She stole my cactus book and my favorite old clock and put a cheap plastic one up there instead. I can tell the difference."

"Have you used the ball lately, Nana?"

"Oh no, I can't right now...I'm too tired and distracted all the time. I can't concentrate."

"I wish I could watch you contact Grand-dad."

"I have to be alone for that, honey. Remember when you were a little girl and your mother would leave you over here for the day, and we'd watch TV, and I'd show you the tarot cards?"

"And you taught me to read palms."

"And we used the ouija board, and the pendulum. Nothing much ever happened to me when someone else did it with me, but when I was alone I got through clear. I spoke to that Mr. Johnson all those times. It's been a long while since I talked to him, but Eddy said he'll be at the party. You have to be alone and concentrate but I can't anymore. You should take the ball and try it, honey. You'll do it some day. It doesn't matter how. Ouija board, séance, crystal, whatever. It's just a medium. Something you focus on to get your power concentrated. Better than having nothing to focus on. It could be a shoe, as long as you focused enough on it."

Leslie laughed. She adored this woman. She was so frightened leaving her alone as often as she did, but she tried to drop in at least for an hour every day. Her mother lived in Vermont with her new husband, and Aileen seldom crossed the street to this house directly opposite the one the two sisters shared.

"I'd like to try to develop my psychic abilities like that, communicate with the other side, foresee the future...but it's scary, too."

"Don't be scared; you can control it. You just have to concentrate. Take the ball and keep it, honey, I can't use it anymore. I'm going to die soon anyway...Eddy told me."

"Nana, don't say that. You're doing okay."

"Well take it. I want you to have it. I can't use it. I don't even know where I got it, but I want you to have it before your sister sneaks in here and steals it."

Leslie took the crystal sphere and its little ebony stand. She was surprised. Her grandmother was indeed possessive of her possessions and rarely parted with so much as a single magazine.

"Hey, no drawing in here," joked Rita, the commercial stripping group leader, leaving fresh folders of negs on Leslie's side table. She leaned over Leslie's shoulder. "What is it? A machine?"

"I guess so. An art project I thought of. An industrial sculpture."

"What does it do? Play movies?" There was a TV screen in the machine.

"I thought of putting a TV in there hooked up to a VCR and have it play tapes I'd make with a rented camera."

"Oh-kay," Rita chuckled, wagging her head. She went back to her own light table. "But you'd better not turn yourself into a giant fly with it." She laughed.

"I'll try not to." Leslie set her sketch aside. She hadn't drawn for weeks and Rita had gone from the room for a half hour, chatting in paste-up, but of course she had to walk in and catch her just then. Maybe she'd tell their supervisor tomorrow. Let her, Leslie thought.

Injustice ate at Leslie. Favoritism. Lack of integrity. Laziness and apathy. It all abounded here. Pressmen lounged talking, threw paper balls at each other, chased each other with spray water bottles. The supervisors lounged around talking about golf and skiing for hours. Leslie didn't want to see them all become mindless robots, hardworking ants. But she was hardworking while still remaining a strong individual.

Her individuality was all. They must never defeat that. Never break her spirit. To attempt that would be no different than an attempt to murder her.

But weren't they trying? Weren't they?

The rickety steps creaked, the entire bottom half of the staircase shifted as Leslie crept down to the basement with a dead black and white TV in her arms, a broken pre-ghetto blaster tape recorder on top of that, its circuits exposed and wires dangling out from an earlier project. She set these materials down amidst her growing collection. There were oddly shaped pieces of packing styrofoam from her new TV and VCR, and from Aileen's. More from her microwave. Smaller strips, a whole trash bag full, from the boxes of metal press plates at work. Two toasters, hubcaps, rain gutters, a toaster oven, a heavy old style blender, a rusty muffler and three old radios. She had a large box filled with sheets of cardboard, filed according to size, most of it from work.

Still, the base structure was not yet decided on and at this point she could only accumulate more potential components. The entire machine needn't be designed first — she'd rather improvise, let it unfold of its own will under her hands — but she needed that foundation. The meager materials she possessed failed her vision, for one thing. She saw the machine as filling the entire back wall of the basement where now there was sooty webbed stone, and the machine would be metal, probably a glossy obsidian black, with chrome-painted wheels and levers, dials and buttons, glass transformers and wood and leather like some old fashioned conception of a mad scientist's device. Something from Frankenstein's lab. A console from the spacecraft of a 50s B-movie. Something from the Industrial Age. All of these things, ominous and heavy, the foundation in welded metal plates. But she didn't know how to weld. And where would she get large plates of metal?

There was a bookcase-like utility shelf unit of metal in the shed adjacent to the house, upstairs. Maybe that. A removed refrigerator door leaned in there, too. She could solder, if not weld. She was good with tools. But she knew a lot of her creation was going to have to be wood. She would just have to cover it with extra coats of thick enamel paint to hide the grain, or cover the wood first in linoleum tiles. She had a stack of those.

Stove pipes, an air-conditioner, a box of car parts. She had enough to work with. She needed that basic design.

It would help, also, if she knew what the "purpose," as Aileen would say, of the sculpture was. The purpose of the machine.

Industrial Shrine, she thought, in keeping with the idea of her last project, the pink cow skull. Some updated primal or mythical concept.

If only her grandmother would let her go through her husband's great collection of tools, auto parts, pipes and building materials in her cellar. Leslie's grandfather had been as much of a pack rat in his way as his wife. Again Leslie distracted herself from the challenge of the design by thinking of the components and small detail. She hadn't had to create the foundation for the cow skull.

Thinking of her grandmother, Leslie suddenly realized the purpose of her machine.

It would be a modern-age focus for psychic energy. An Industrial Age crystal ball. She would even incorporate the crystal ball into it. A TV hooked up to a VCR, both hidden but for the screen, on which would be shown tarot cards, just one after another after another. She smiled, fresh inspiration lifting her from her inhibiting doubts.

Leslie's group leader Rita, the male commercial stripper Kenny, and Sharon came back to work an hour and fifteen minutes after the start of second shift's half hour lunch break. Kenny's eyes were red and glassy, and when Leslie asked Rita a question about work Rita hid her mouth behind her hand and actually hiccupped once. There was a Chinese restaurant just down the highway, though usually their half hour lunch breaks there didn't extend beyond forty to fifty minutes. Forty minutes was, however, their lowest limit. The thing was, they punched back in. The proof of their actions was stamped in ink.

A few months ago Leslie had been called into her supervisor Keith's office and given a verbal warning for being late several minutes about once a week. She was told a continuance of this behavior might "jeopardize" her employment. Now she came in at three every day though her shift began at three-thirty, just to be safe, and had a coffee.

Keith had to know *some* of it. He was simply afraid to speak to his group leaders for fear of scaring them off. There were few workers who had stayed with the company for more than several years, but these group leaders had been working here since high school. Though they each made around ten dollars an hour, it was the group leader status which most appealed to them, Leslie believed. Telling others what to do, the liberties they felt they warranted. Keith had to tolerate their behavior or he'd lose them...though Leslie saw them as lifers. If the company could stay in business that long, which was doubtful.

Injustice. And when she spoke up against it he told her she had a bad attitude, and threatened *her*. Yes, she did have a bad attitude. They had fostered it in her.

And it ate at her more every day. They were in their post-Thanksgiving slow period. Not enough work for all three commercial strippers...so Rita and Kenny disappeared into paste-up with Sharon to make paper chains for Christmas. The pay rate for this function was ten dollars an hour. Leslie made seven-fifty to strip negatives, after three and a half years here. People on second shift now started at six-fifty, with a pay raise in three months. Leslie spoke with a male Puerto Rican pressman who had admitted he made over eight-fifty an hour after one year of employment.

It wasn't the money. She could handle low pay – if the company were consistently stingy. It was what it represented. Exploitation. Lack of respect. She could work for too little pay or too little respect, but not both simultaneously. It made her feel weak, humiliated...victimized. She had been victimized as a child. It was an unpleasant feeling that lived in the gut like a nest of tapeworms.

She heard laughter from paste-up. Leslie lifted the flap titled "Don't Look" to expose her bloody series of cartoons, and pinned the flap open with a loose razor-sharp X-Acto blade. With her red marker she drew blood running down the inside of the flap from where the blade now punctured it.

It was Aileen who found their grandmother. She was lying on the floor of her study, the table on its side where she'd pulled it down with her. Aileen had called to find out if Nana wanted some dinner brought to her, and she and Jason had gone over when the phone went unanswered.

She was still alive for a few minutes, Aileen told Leslie. She asked who had stolen her crystal ball, accused Aileen of it, sobbed at her to go away. "Eddy is waiting for us...we can see him," she had finally said in a whispery child's voice, weirdly speaking of herself in the plural. And then she'd died just moments before the ambulance pulled up.

Leslie was both relieved that she hadn't been there for those final minutes, and agonized that she hadn't.

Several days later came the next, less foreseen, development.

The grandmother had left the house the girls lived in, Eddy's old station wagon, and ten thousand dollars to her daughter in Vermont. To Aileen she had left five thousand dollars. To Leslie she had left her remaining five thousand, and her house with everything in it.

The will was found to be legitimate. She had had it changed last year, and her daughter and granddaughters were never made aware. The previous arrangement had called for the daughter to receive the old house and its contents, the car, and the granddaughters would be awarded ten thousand each and split the newer house they rented. The change, as their grandmother's lawyer now confessed, had been implemented so that Leslie could live in the house and take good care of what she chose to retain of the vast collection of treasures therein. The grandmother knew Leslie would retain much of it...and reverently so.

"Of course you realize you have to restore the will to the way it was before," Aileen raved at the lawyer's glossy expansive table. "She was senile when she changed it – it's not valid. Crazy!"

Leslie avoided the eyes of her mother, gazed at her reflection in the table. "Nana wanted it this way...we have to honor her wishes."

"Oh right – yeah!" Aileen bolted up from the table, her face a clenched red fist. "Mom gets a house, you get a house full of antiques, and I get five thousand dollars. Of course you want to honor Nana's wishes – you're probably the one who got her to alter the will!"

"I didn't!" Now Leslie looked up at her sister, blue eyes moistening.

"Oh sure...you went over there every goddamn day."

"Maybe that's *why* she left me her house."

"You can't do this to me, Leslie, I wouldn't do it to you! Goddamn you, what did you do – huh?" Aileen slammed the table with the flat of her hand. "Huh?"

"Aileen," their mother said. "Sit down and calm down."

"Just shut up, ma... *Jesus!* How do you think I feel? Why is she leaving me out like this; I didn't do anything! I stayed with her while she died!" Aileen broke down into gasping, heaving sobs of frustration. Her moody all black garb was finally filling a more than chic function. "What kind of lawyer are you, anyway?"

The lawyer kept an even temper. "Her family physician was present and signed the will as a witness, if I might remind you."

"Then that old idiot is senile, too! All three of you were crazy! God, you can't fool me, I know how nutty she talked and forgetful she was! Even last year!" Aileen whirled on her sister. "Leslie, if you do this..."

"You can have my five thousand, too."

"I don't *want* your five thousand!" Aileen laughed hysterically. "I want my half of that *house!*"

"I'm sorry," Leslie said softly, looking down.

"You're just jealous of me, you ungrateful bitch!" Aileen stabbed a finger in Leslie's face. "This is your way of showing me up for your pathetic feelings of inferiority, isn't it? This is your revenge."

"*Aileen,*" said their mother.

"You can't even afford to live there alone!"

"The mortgage is paid for," the lawyer spoke up in Leslie's defense, seeing how Aileen was grouping them together. "The property taxes are under two hundred a month." You couldn't beat that for a rent.

"I'll give you all the money I make from the antiques I sell," Leslie said. "But I decide what to sell and what not to."

"I want my share! *All my share!*" Aileen thumped her chest.

"I'm giving you some of mine. It was Nana's stuff to

give away."

The finger in the face again. "You don't exist for me anymore, do you understand that? You are now a nonentity."

"Aileen, sit down for God's sake!" their mother yelled, tears streaming.

Leslie said no more in her or her grandmother's defense.

The machine had begun to take form, but not where Leslie had originally planned it. It would fill one narrow wall of the damp basement of her grandmother's old house. Leslie's new house.

Her grandfather had bequeathed to her a wealth of materials and tools. Even some of her grandmother's things from upstairs and the attic would be utilized. Leslie alternated between working on the machine and the intimidating challenge of organizing her grandmother's belongings. She really didn't want to give up any of it for sale, but knew she must.

She played tapes while she worked on the machine; the quiet of the old house and the unfamiliarity of this darker, damper cellar made her somewhat jumpy. Boards would creak softly overhead. She thought of her Nana's imagined phantom burglaries. A few times she even caught herself wondering if Aileen were skulking around up there. Did she have a key?

The obvious use for the psychic machine would be to contact her grandmother. This was her house, Leslie had the crystal ball – the energy was right. But still, the thought of it chilled her. She was so intrigued, yet so hesitant. But she kept building the machine. It would serve as an artwork now...an actual psychic medium later if she ever screwed up enough courage to try it.

There must be another way to test her psychic ability, she mused as she spray-painted some tarnished metal pieces a bright new silver, newspapers spread to protect the cement floor. Another kind of psychic energy could be concentrated through the machine. Maybe she would strive to contact some living person telepathically. Roll a pencil across the floor. Start a fire in a metal pail full of paper. The possibilities unfolded.

Sometimes instead of tapes she listened to the radio. A news report told her how a plant which would research and develop chemical warfare weapons was soon to open in Libya. The construction of the plant had been supervised, nominally, by America's current favorite villain, the much-hated and furious-faced General Jambiya. In several weeks Jambiya would attend the plant's opening ceremonies. Leslie despised Jambiya as much as any good American did. His face actually frightened her. Once while walking on the street she had chanced to look down at a discarded newspaper and had been startled by a photo of him. She had taken the face to be that of a monster, some demon, and actually had had to go back and retrieve the paper to discover the identity of what she'd seen. Leslie could easily imagine that this was the face of the Antichrist, of the one with the blue turban foretold by Nostradamus, who would bring about Armageddon. Like any good American, Leslie wanted to see General Jambiya dead.

Leslie was stripping a negative for an artist's representative out of New York. She copied the name down on a scrap of paper dutifully, without enthusiasm; she had few illusions as to how difficult it was to become recognized, to be accepted, especially since she had applied for a job in the art department here at work.

The position was posted, as required, over the punch clock. Two of the company's three artists, all young women, had left within about a month of each other. Leslie was encouraged – even excited. To work upstairs, to make good (presumably) money, to no longer be just some monkey in a corner down here. The company could get away with paying her less than someone straight out of art school, since she had no credentials, and also she was familiar with the company's tastes and needs. She believed her chances were very good. She phoned personnel and was accepted for an interview, a chance to show her portfolio to the head of personnel and the head of the art department.

But twenty people, she was told later, would be called

back for second interviews. She didn't know whether to believe this, since most of these people were said to be from outside, but she learned of four other people within the company besides herself who had applied.

The printing industry attracted many artists, despite its involving more craftwork and outright mechanical unskilled labor than artistry. But there were even other artistic people who didn't apply, and others Leslie had known who had quit by now.

Of the four, she had really only seen one other person's portfolio. A first shift commercial stripper named Craig. She had even been the one to tell Craig about the posted job, since he hadn't noticed, and had urged him to pursue it. He was a nice shy kid and she couldn't keep the opportunity hidden from him. But when she saw his portfolio she worried about her wisdom in her decision to prompt him. His pencil portraits of rock stars were fantastic, as good, probably, as her portraits of rock and movie stars in ball point pen, which were the pride of her portfolio. But other than that she had much more material to show, of a greater variety of styles and content and in a greater diversity of mediums. Other people told her, also, she was more talented than the other three. She still had a lot of optimism.

For several nights she had stayed up late drawing designs especially for the interview; birth announcement designs, stationery designs, a Bar Mitzvah invitation card design – as the company was Jewish-owned with a largely Jewish clientele – all on company stock. She had cartoons, portraits, high school newsletters she'd illustrated, and a few imaginative (but nonviolent) fantasy drawings.

The personnel manager was fairly generous with praise, the young head artist was coolly, professionally composed but did offer some compliments. *Inorganic Organism,* which showed a skeleton-like robot rabbit drawn in ball point, painstakingly detailed, one of Leslie's favorite drawings, was passed by without comment from either.

The work she'd done on company stock in the company style excited a bit of interest, but when Leslie left she couldn't tell what kind of impression she'd made. Her optimism had waned. They'd get back to her.

Several months later, after she had given up hope, she

was called for a second interview, this time with the head artist again and the owner of the company herself. Leslie was thrilled. Next week. It was her vacation next week but she wasn't going anywhere so she would be only too happy to come in.

As it turned out, the other four artistic employees were called back for a second interview also. "We've had a hard time choosing," the personnel head told Leslie by way of an apology for the long suspenseful wait.

This time the head artist seemed a little looser, but the company owner was pretty stony throughout except for an earnest smile one of the cuter birth announcement designs won from her.

"I was thinking," said the head artist, "it would be great to have Leslie illustrate the company newsletter."

"Mm," agreed the owner.

Two weeks later Leslie got a call. The job had been awarded to the first shift commercial stripping group leader, who'd graduated from the Rhode Island School of Design. She has a piece of paper to prove she's an artist, Leslie thought. But she began to think that they had probably made the proper choice; the woman had to be good to have graduated from a school like that.

But it couldn't have hurt that she was a group leader, or – as Leslie learned – that every day for some time the woman had taken her lunch with the head of the art department.

They were only placating me, Leslie told herself now as she moved on to the next neg. They have to post a job, even if they know already who they want. They have to act like they're giving everyone a fair shake. Two interviews for everyone...each ego stroked. But they never seriously considered me, she thought. I'm a whiner, a complainer, a prima donna and a trouble maker. I'm no robot clone zombie with her nose up someone's ass. I'm a sculptor, not clay. They don't want that.

She glanced up, around. She was alone in the room.

Leslie was tempted to take Rita's work and dab a touch of opaque paint over a letter or two here and there, to scratch a few negs with her X-Acto's blade, so Rita would get marked down for letting these errors get past her...but she couldn't bring herself to attack them so directly.

The new purpose for the machine and its new color came to her almost side-by-side as ideas at work.

Luckily she hadn't bought any black paint yet. The new color was red.

It clicked. That was it – she knew she had it locked now, and couldn't wait to get home and throw herself into it. She did, that night, and the next day bought the paint. A lot of it.

The title would be *Hate Machine*. She knew that the day-to-day stressful frustration of work was eating her up inside, fighting to rend its way out of her. This would serve as a release as much as an expression, a reflection of her emotions. As therapeutic as it was artistic. The psychic device could wait until a braver day, when her grandmother lying on the floor upstairs whispering about Eddy and her party wasn't so strong in her mind.

Hate was with her constantly, waiting to be vented. Hate was her frame of mind. Everything she felt now...frustration, sadness, loneliness...blended into one blood red ray. Her feelings would make it powerful as a work of art; authentic. And maybe it would suck much of the suffocating hatred out of her. Hate was the theme.

She began painting the skeletal structure, and her enthusiastic choice was confirmed and reinforced as she saw how it was coming out. It was a deep dark red she had wanted, a rich Chinese red, a glossy fire engine red, with silvery wheels and trim and knobs set out against it. She wasn't afraid to splatter the red paint on her white t-shirt and white coveralls and bare feet. Her hands were thickly caked in it. She imagined she was painting the machine in human blood.

She could barely restrain herself from adding the details – that would be the most fun, the most imaginative part – but she forced herself to wait. When she was ready for it, she called in sick to work. Let Rita do some work for a change.

This was the work that counted. Her life's work. Being a "stripper" was actually only the meaningless hobby. Here was her own little factory.

Across the entire top of the machine, jutting out, their

handles hidden inside the machine, were knife blades...thirteen gleaming kitchen knife blades in all, cheap ones bought for the purpose. There were clear glass telephone pole insulators. Sliding panels with red and blue wires inside like veins. There were three bottles with a large, dead black beetle in each, the bottles set into the hollows carved from a long piece of styrofoam painted in extra thick coats to mask the spongy texture. There was a red spray-painted typewriter keyboard (the rest of this machine disappearing into the greater machine), and fastened to either side of the machine were two horseshoe crabs, one above the other, painted glossy red.

The crystal ball was there as in her earlier design, just for more power. Wires seemed to come out from under it and vanished into other areas on a protruding shelf-like console. In the front center of the machine there were three silver wheels – the main controls. Switches to flip, a few knife handle levers to be thrown. Black rubber tubing snaked in and out in places. A small antique mirror of her Nana's was incorporated, the ornate frame painted red. Above the mirror was a cast-iron geisha mask decoration, maybe a mock Noh theater mask, once painted various colors, now all crimson but for the silver teeth.

A dead mouse she'd found was in another bottle with a silver-painted cap. In a styrofoam hollow, a trilobite fossil, and beside that a red-painted telephone with the receiver hooked into another part of the machine like a computer tie-in. There were four new meat thermometers plunged deep into styrofoam to form a row of gauges. Bills were behind, but this was more important. There was a red-painted old plastic radio set into the machine to be turned on for static, the dial glowing orange, and a string of large outdoors Christmas bulbs poked out of a long strip of styrofoam but all thirteen exposed bulbs glowed red. To make noise and vibrate the machine, behind a panel at its base she had hidden the air compressor for her airbrush set.

She'd decided against a TV and video recorder. Along the front of the machine under the wheels were four picture frames in a row painted red, and several smaller ones elsewhere. Under the mirror, in the very center of the machine, was a more ornate antique picture frame. That would be her main "screen."

The lesser ones she could fill now. Into one frame she

slipped a black and white photo of a Mafioso dead in his car, magazine ink streaming generously down his face. In another was a photo clipped from a book about death, written from pathological, psychological, philosophical, and theological viewpoints, showing the decapitated and partly mummified head of a fifteen-year-old Pakistani girl murdered by her own father. In a third frame she displayed another photo from this book: a man slumped against an ominous-looking factory machine which had apparently sucked his arm into it to the shoulder, killing him.

She used other pictures from this book and several others. She could order intact replacements later; for now the machine was all. She called in sick a second day – work was slow anyway, wasn't it? Clipping a picture, she bobbed her head to a song from her tape player, sitting cross-legged on a flattened box on the basement floor.

The evening of her second day off from work she crept down to a small cemetery a few streets over, where she remembered there was a tomb up against the bordering fence whose earthen roof was a little caved in near the stone of its front. She had worried that a child playing on top might fall through one day, but tonight she was grateful for it.

She wore white, though black would have been wiser. Let a spectator, if one came along, take her for a ghost. She lay on the cold frozen dome of the tomb and shone a flashlight down through the crevice. Her gratification was doubled, and now she began to employ the broomstick she had brought along, a coat hanger fitted at its end. She had to reach her entire arm to the shoulder into the hole and press her face to the dirt but she was too excited to be afraid that something would seize her from the other side.

The brittle brown skull lacked a bottom jaw, lacked upper teeth; what she took to be mummified brains rattled inside it. Smallish, perhaps that of a child or a small woman. Whether or not the pelvis and the femur belonged to the same individual she had no idea.

She painted the three components red and set them aside to dry, to be incorporated later. She would just have enough room to fit them in; she didn't want to crowd the machine with an overabundance of detail – it must have system and symmetry, be aesthetically balanced.

JEFFREY THOMAS | 189

As it was, she thought, regarding the nearly completed work, the machine looked like the main controls for hell's furnace. Or, she considered, it might be Satan's baroque and no doubt cacophonous upright piano, decorated with framed photos of the damned.

The final, missing component was the photograph to frame in the central place of honor. This subject would be the object of the machine's focus. It would be interchangeable. But what, or whom, to start off with?

She found the answer in a copy of *Newsweek* in the break room at work the next day. There, grinning, stood General Jambiya with several other men inside the chemical warfare research and development plant they had just ceremoniously opened this week.

Even grinning, Jambiya's face horrified her. The eyes were a gleaming black, more soulless than those of a shark. Maybe he was too obvious, too "popular" a target for her hate projector, but she couldn't resist. This would be the ceremonious opening of her machine. The reflection was too great, too humorous – too symmetrical – to resist.

When she had lit the red candles poking up from either end of the shelf console (the skull now in the center of this), had lit the string of red phallic-tipped Christmas bulbs, and switched on the radio's dim orange face – bringing to life a hissing crackling static – Leslie went and turned off the rest of the lights in the cellar. When she returned to the machine, the flickering candle light and the deep red glow played on the white canvas of her utterly naked body.

"General." She raised a glass of sparkling wine from the shelf, saluted the picture framed in the place of honor. Jambiya and friends in the factory. She sipped, set the glass down delicately, and took in a deep breath so as to begin.

She first knelt to reach in and activate the air compressor. It sputtered to life, droned muffledly behind its panel, making the great machine tremble with power. The beetles jiggled in their three bottles. With small circular patches cut from black electrical tape, Leslie fastened two red wires to her temples, the other two ends disappearing into an open panel in the machine. She fastened two others on her breasts above her nipples. Finally she pulled a black rubber hose from the machine and calmly plugged it into her body, between her legs, like an umbilical cord below her belly. She must siphon all her energy, all her power, into and through the machine.

She pushed a few levers, and smiled. She tapped out the keys that spelled *General Jambiya* on the keyboard, as if programming a computer. She flipped switches and turned some dials. Despite her smile, she did all this with the utmost intensity and concentration, slowly and methodically, as if acting out a precise Japanese tea ritual. Before she had come down here she had taken a hot bath in the completely dark bathroom to cleanse her mind of all else save her purpose. Of all else but hate.

Finally, all that remained were the three silver wheels.

She turned the first wheel once, twice, three times. The second wheel once, twice, three times. All the while she stared unblinking at the photograph of General Jambiya before her on her view screen. Leslie turned the third wheel once, twice, three times to the right.

She stared at the photo a bit longer, gripping her support handles, feet together on her black rubber mat, body rigid. And then it was over. She reversed the entire procedure. The wheels turned once, twice, three times to the left. She was just as gracefully methodical and unhurried now as before.

When the machine was fully off she slumped a little against it for support, and finally her nakedness made her cold.

There had been an explosion, the newspaper said. Ninety-two people had died. Among them, General Jambiya and the plant directors pictured in the photograph from *Newsweek*. Terrorist sabotage was suspected. The U.S. was being accused.

"My God," Leslie breathed, trembling as if still hooked up to the machine, "my *God*..."

Rita tapped her on the head with a rolled up piece of paper. "Back to work, Les." Rita left the break room. Leslie sat there for a few moments more.

Too bad those other men had had their picture taken with him, eh? And the plant itself, behind them.

Leslie shuddered and grinned.

She could hardly wait to go home.

Sympathetic magic, wasn't that what they called it? Leslie stood apart from the Hate Machine, clothed, regarding it, arms crossed against the chilly air. The Hate Machine was also a death machine, then. She hadn't intended to *actually* try to reach out and kill General Jambiya – had she?

Her desire had been real enough. And obviously the original notion of the machine as being a device to focus psychic energy like the sun through a magnifying glass had remained in the back of her mind throughout her creation of the machine, influencing the outcome.

What was the part that had most made this possible? The crystal ball? The skull? The photos? How could she understand her creation so little as to wonder that? It was obviously the entire composition, the sum of all the parts; wasn't that the whole point? The entire machine, and none of it. Just something to focus on...could have been a shoe.

But a chemical research and development plant had to be a volatile thing to begin with. She must experiment further.

Upstairs, she paged through the rest of today's newspaper she'd taken from work. She found it quickly. You didn't have to look far in a newspaper for horror. Len Huffman, on trial amid much media attention for the alleged rape and murder of his four-year-old adopted daughter. Alleged, but they had to say that, didn't they, even when it was pretty obvious, as it was here? Most people seemed to be pretty convinced of his guilt. Leslie read the article on him. Yes. She nodded. She felt sufficiently convinced.

The evening paper the next day reported that the alleged rapist/murderer of four-year-old Barbara Huffman, Len Huffman, had died in custody during the night between three and four in the morning, of cardiac arrest.

He had had no history of heart problems.

Leslie had plugged into her machine at exactly three o'clock AM.

The next day's paper related the death of reputed mafia don Dominic Chilorio, victim of a cerebral aneurysm. Two-thirty in the morning.

The following day's paper told of the death of the imprisoned, mesmeric George Ballard, whose strange cult had murdered a total of eight affluent Californians during the late sixties. Somehow he had managed to hang himself in his cell. Three-thirty in the morning, prison officials figured.

The next day it was eighteen-year-old Dave Capuccio, arraigned for vehicular homicide while driving under the influence, dead of a blow to the head while in his cell – apparently he'd tripped and struck his skull against something, though it hadn't yet been determined what. One in the morning. Leslie got out of work at twelve-thirty. She hadn't wasted any time, that night.

By now, of course, she was quite convinced.

She bought an alphabetical encyclopedia of contemporary murderers and criminals, but knew better than to kill too many of them all at once, and she certainly knew better than to go through it alphabetically. Also, she killed the first man at one o'clock in the afternoon, before work, so no one would detect a pattern forming. Not that she was much concerned about being traced. The ultimate murder weapon. She'd show these monsters how to commit the perfect murder.

She went through the papers, killed some more people she found in there.

She killed an Ayatollah, but his death wasn't reported by his people. There was always the possibility, too, that he had already been dead for a long time before she focused her sight on him.

The freedom, the reach, the *power*. She could change the world. Save the world. She must read more on politics. She must find out who it was most important to kill for the good of the common people, and the planet itself. Presidents, religious leaders, the heads of mammoth corporations, the members of the World Bank? Sooner or later people would know something very strange was happening, but how could they ever discover the machine? Just in case, she burned her clipped papers and magazines quickly, and the photos from her central view screen as soon as she was done with them. She padlocked the cellar door before she went to work.

She contemplated placing a photograph of, say, Hitler addressing a crowd in the machine. Would nothing happen? Would the past he affected? She wouldn't go down that route of experimentation now, but later...when she'd learned more.

The sleeves of her bulky white sweater were pushed back in rings, arms before her on the table, hands folded around a styrofoam cup of black coffee, the steaming heat growing painful to her hands but she didn't take them away, her eyes caught in the tangled steam tendrils.

The gray metal door clicked open. Rita pushed her upper body in.

"Did you go to lunch late?"

"No...my regular time," Leslie murmured, not looking up.

"Well, it's seven-fifty." Leslie was twenty minutes late.

"I'll be there when I'm ready."

Rita didn't respond or move for a moment or two. Leslie had never spoken to her in an arrogant way — except that time Rita had taken her into the boss's office.

"Ah, I think you should come back now...I just put some work on your desk."

"Why don't you do a little of it for a change? Or do we need some more paper chains for Christmas?"

Again Rita was at a loss for words. That time she had called Leslie in for a talk Leslie had snapped at her about how she extended her breaks, and Rita had snapped back it was none of her business. Leslie had started trembling badly and had barely been able to form words; luckily Sharon stepped in and soothed things out a little. But Leslie and Rita hadn't spoken for days. Now Rita could obviously sense the same situation building, but she was a *group leader,* and she'd be damned if she backed down.

She came fully into the room, holding the door wide open. "Come on, Leslie."

"I told you I'm not ready."

"Are you feeling sick or what?"

"No, I just don't feel like working. You know what that's like, don't you? When you and Sharon and Kenny go in the upstairs break room for an hour on your ten-minute break, and then into paste-up for an hour, and then down to the cafeteria for another hour, and if anybody asks, and nobody does, you just say you're on your ten minute break? Well, I'm just practicing to be a group leader. Maybe if I sit on my ass all night they'll promote me, too." Leslie hadn't once looked out of the steam.

"I get my work done," Rita hissed shakily.

"I get your work done."

"I won't leave until you go back to work, and I'm going to have to report this tomorrow, I'm sorry."

"Wow."

Rita slammed the metal door. The wall shook. Leslie casually lifted her drink, delicately sipped at it. Rita's voice over the intercom tremulously paging Marty, the night supervisor, who was actually primarily involved with the presses and not prep or upstairs. Several minutes later as Leslie was finishing her cooling coffee Rita reappeared triumphantly with Marty, a friendly and decent man Leslie had never had trouble with. Marty looked concerned.

"Are you all right, Leslie?"

Leslie got up, threw away the cup and approached them. "When they don't work, I don't work, from now on. I'm sorry, but I won't be taken for a fool. And tomorrow I think *I'll* have words with personnel...or maybe the president."

As Leslie began to pass Rita to go through the door Rita reached out and grabbed Leslie by the baggy sleeve of her sweater. "You'd better calm down, Leslie!" she hissed through her teeth, jaw thrust, her whole body shaking.

Leslie looked from Rita's fist clenching her sleeve slowly up into Rita's eyes, and smiled.

"Hey," said Marty to Rita, gently pushing her arm away.

Leslie continued on out of the room, her mind already made up to call in sick again tomorrow.

As much a pack rat as her grandmother (she just needed five or six more decades to catch up with her treasure), Leslie had saved every company newsletter since she'd started. She glanced at the clock while she snipped. She was upstairs; she stayed out of the cellar now when she wasn't using the machine, so she wouldn't grow jaded with its presence and dampen its fire. She sat cross-legged on the study floor, probably on the spot where Nana had died, but she wasn't afraid. Soon she would build a black machine, to communicate with her and others...great minds, so she might learn from them. She needed to know as much as she could about the world.

And a white machine. Yes, that would probably even come first. The opposite end of the cellar, so she wouldn't be distracted by one while at the other (she would have to hang curtains over them soon – yes, that would be dramatic, black velour or satin). The white machine would be the Love Machine. She didn't know what kind of love she might spread through it, but she would experiment. The spirits could lend her advice. Love that healed the body perhaps, or mind at least. One thing was certain...Jason would forget all about Aileen.

Leslie nodded her head to a darkly majestic song by Brian Setzer, *The Knife Feels Like Justice,* on her tape player. When it was over she rewound it and played it again. Tonight, again, her scissors felt like justice.

She went down to the cellar. It was twenty of seven...and seven was second shift's "lunch."

Her clothing neatly folded aside, she stepped onto the rubber mat. A nearby space heater would keep the chill air from distracting her.

Into the center frame, grinning Noh mask and mirror

above, Leslie slipped a piece of paper with tiny photographs of Rita, Sharon, and Kenny glued on it. All three decapitated black and white heads were smiling.

The machine came rumbling to life, hissed, glowed, quivered in anticipation. The dead beetles came to dancing life. Leslie hooked the four wires to her nude body, and inserted the hose. First the levers. Then three names punched in on the keyboard. Switches, knobs. At last, the wheels.

One turn...two turns...three turns. On to the second wheel.

It was one past seven. They would be in one of their cars together, on their way to the Chinese restaurant for drinks and an appetizer. All together like three yolks in one egg in her fist. She stared intently at their faces. Rita. She remembered her face from yesterday, the thrust jaw.

Sharon, next.

One turn...two turns...three turns...

And Kenny, smiling at her. She put her hands on the third, last, wheel.

She liked Kenny, even if he did follow Sharon like a puppy. But he had seniority over her. With both Rita and Kenny gone, Leslie would be made second shift commercial stripping group leader...wouldn't she?

One turn...

She stared at Kenny. She liked Kenny. He was even sweet...he had never been malicious to her...not even unpleasant.

Two turns...

She had liked *all* of them at one time.

Her knuckles were white, her fists felt bloodless.

Leslie jerked her hands away from the wheel as if electrified.

She would learn the next day that on the way to lunch, Kenny had nearly lost control of his car. Rita and Sharon had screamed as the car shot toward a telephone pole, but at the last second Kenny was able to wrestle back control. Something with the steering wheel.

The next day she would be standing with Kenny, Rita, Sharon, Marty, and many other employees watching firemen and police sift through the charred ruins of the printing company they worked for. Had worked for. It was flattened.

JEFFREY THOMAS 197

Marty said he had heard the explosion; it had rattled his house's windows. Thank God, he said, it had happened in the early morning hours when no one was inside it.

Leslie turned slightly when she heard Sharon sniffle. Rita was dabbing at an eye. Dethroned. Just monkeys now, like the rest of...

Us, Leslie almost completed. But she was no longer a monkey.

She believed her vengeance had been just and fair. It was about time justice was brought into the world.

The photograph of the printing company, snipped from a recent newsletter, burned in a metal bucket. Leslie stood over it. She was down here today, with no work to worry about, to begin work on the Love Machine.

I might not have to *use* a Love Machine, daddy, if it wasn't for you, Leslie thought as she dragged a box of car parts across the floor.

There had been the brief fantasy...only a brief fantasy...of putting her father's face into the Hate Machine.

She dismissed that memory, brushed it away as even now she brushed sooty cobwebs from the stone wall with a broom. The Love Machine would be tucked in the niche under the stairs. Smaller than the Hate Machine, but so nicely enclosed; putting up a curtain here to close her in would be easy. Squatting in this space, she swept old webs and spider husks with a small brush into a dust pan.

Footsteps above.

Leslie froze in her squatting position, nerves straining to pick up a vibration.

Had it been her imagination?

A muffled woman's voice.

Floorboards creaked. Closer...

Nana, Leslie thought, and shuddered.

The basement door squealed open. Leslie trembled, holding the dust pan sideways like a hatchet. Footsteps came clumping down over her head. She didn't breathe.

Men from the government.

It was a man. He turned to face her, his face registering shock.

"Jesus, Les, what are you doing under there?" Jason chuckled nervously, holding his chest. "You wanna give me a heart attack?"

"I was just sweeping up webs," Leslie said, smiling shyly. More clumping steps. Leslie came out and straightened as Aileen stepped before her.

"So this is where you hide. Like a little white cave worm."

"Aileen," said Jason, "come on, now."

"What do you mean walking in here like this?" Leslie said, blue eyes frigid.

"Why not?" Aileen smiled. "It's my house, too."

Leslie glanced at Jason, back to her sister. "No it isn't."

"It is, Les. Mom's been trying to call you but if you paid your bills you'd have a phone. She' s coming down tomorrow but I just couldn't wait to tell you. My lawyer has found that Nana's updated will was invalid."

"That's impossible! That's...*impossible!* It isn't invalid, how can it be?"

"Look, Mom wants us *both* to split this house like we're supposed to. And Nana did, too, before she got Alzheimer's disease, which she had...and she was on medication, also...she was always doped up."

"Her physician was a witness!"

"My lawyer talked to him."

Leslie's mouth hung open. She wagged her head, the ice eyes starting to melt into tears. "Don't do this, Aileen...please...don't do this."

"That's what I said to you, Les – don't you remember? Don't do this to me? Don't cut your own sister's *throat?* But you did...you did. Remember?" Aileen smiled tightly, began to stroll about the basement with hands in pockets. Jason stood by looking at the floor, helpless and embarrassed. "I'm not doing anything to you, Leslie...I'm just undoing what you did to me." She picked up an odd empty picture frame, its wire hanging. "Don't worry, I won't be living here with you. I'll just rent out my floor. I'll even let you decide which floor you want. But all of *this* – " she held up the antique frame " – gets split up evenly, too. All of it...*evenly.*"

"I won't let you do this," Leslie said, tears rolling

down her face in two symmetrical streams. She couldn't bring herself to look at Jason. Only his presence prevented her from crumpling into sobs of fear and anger.

"*Mom* wants it this way. What the hell is that?"

"*Don't go near that!*" Leslie hissed, feeling faint.

Jason looked up, startled, then over at Aileen.

They hadn't noticed it before. Looming in the shadows. Dark...still...

"Look at *this,* Jason." Aileen threw a lever. "Look at this. A skull. Where'd you get a *skull,* Les?"

"I told you not to touch it!" Leslie ran at her sister, pushed her away. "It's a fake skull like they use in schools. This is my artwork." She stood protectively in front of it, reached behind her to shut off the lever Aileen had thrown.

"It's sick, Leslie. *You're* sick. I mean it, you really are. It's sad." Aileen gave Jason a bitter smirk over her shoulder. "It's pretty pathetic, Les. I've tried to help you get out of this thing..."

"Go *away!* Leave me alone!" Now Leslie did crumple, Jason or no.

"Aileen, leave her alone," Jason snapped.

"What's...this?" Aileen said, a metal bucket at her feet. Black ash. A partially burned photograph...the fire had gone out before it had fully burned away. Aileen lifted it out. "Oh my God."

"Don't touch that! Don't do this, Aileen, don't *do* this!"

"Jason." Aileen held the picture up for him to see, no longer smiling. "They said it might be arson at the print shop she works at."

"It wasn't me!"

"Aileen, for God's sake."

Leslie snatched the picture from Aileen's hand and shredded it. "Leave me alone," she sobbed hysterically, "leave me *alone...*"

"Did you do it, Leslie? Are you that sick, or what?"

"She didn't do it, Aileen, now shut up and go upstairs." Jason got behind his girlfriend and pushed her along by the shoulders. "I mean it, give her a break."

"Did *she* give me a break?" Aileen said, but letting herself be pushed.

"Go on now, I told you to wait until your mother got here to do this."

Aileen hesitated on the stairs. "Just in case, Les, don't get any ideas about burning any other houses down, or you'll be very sorry."

"Come *on!*" Jason yelled at her. "Go!"

Aileen clumped up out of sight; Leslie watched her black legs through liquid vision. Jason came to her, touched her arm but she recoiled. Drew in on herself.

"Leave me alone, *please.*"

"Les, I'm sorry — she's hot over all this but she'll cool off...you're sisters. You'll both cool off. Don't let money come between you two."

"It isn't money," Leslie groaned. Couldn't look at him.

"Jason!" Aileen shouted upstairs.

"I'll cool her down," Jason promised.

"Please leave me alone."

"Are you going to be okay for now, Les?"

He seemed truly to care. How could Aileen have ever landed a guy like him?

Because she's confidant. Strong. I'm a crippled little weakling. A victim, she thought.

That was why she had landed Daddy.

No — I'm strong now. I'm very strong.

Leslie straightened up. "I'll be fine, Jason — thanks." She was able to compose her voice, even face him to smile. "Go to her or she'll have your head. We'll work this out."

"Good," he said. "Okay...I'll catch you later, then." Jason moved to the stairs. "I knew I was gonna have to referee today, but I know you two can reach some kind of compromise or something."

"Something will happen," Leslie assured him.

Jason hesitated a moment on the bottom step. Leslie's striking light blue eyes looked strange with the flesh around them, and the whites of the eyes themselves, so red.

The photograph showed both of them as teenagers, arms around each other's shoulders, bikini-clad at Hampton

Beach. Squinting into the camera. Both had long dark hair, and Aileen wore a white bikini top. The portion of Leslie's bikini top that showed was blue. Leslie stared at herself. This girl was a stranger. She had ceased to exist.

No tape music played. The scissors felt heavy and cold, like a gun.

She cut the picture down the middle. Then she cropped the bottom of the photo to remove her hand from Aileen's shoulder. Couldn't take any chances, could she?

The space heater glowed increasingly as it fired up. Radio static.

Leslie neatly folded her sweater onto an old chair.

Red row of Christmas bulbs. She lit the end candles. Shadows moved around the machine like hooded Druids.

She folded her blouse and bra on top of the sweater, smoothed back her ruffled choppy blond hair. Unzipped, stepped out of her white pants. Neatly folded them on the rest like a samurai ritualistically undoing his robes for seppuku.

This is my gun, she thought of the red machine. My Martian death ray. No...my rooftop sniper's rifle. And this – she slipped the photo into the center picture frame – is my scope.

Aileen grinned out at her, tiny. *Now* who was the victim? *Now* who was strong?

Why wait for the Love Machine when she could take Jason now?

"I tried to warn you," Leslie told her. "*Right?* I tried to warn you."

They had fun that time at Hampton Beach. Leslie had eventually felt left out, jealous of Aileen's flirtation with boys, but they'd still had fun.

A long time ago. Another life. Leslie stepped onto the rubber pad. The shadows quivered in the empty sockets of the glossy red skull.

What if Jason's with her? her mind whispered urgently out of nowhere. What if she doesn't die of a cerebral hemorrhage or cardiac arrest? What if it's a car crash? An explosion?

Leslie pictured Aileen collapsing, like Nana, dragging down a table, clutching at her chest or head. Blood from her nostrils, eyes ballooned. Feet thumping in spasms. The photograph grinned at her.

"I *hate* you," Leslie croaked at the picture. "I *hate* you!"

Tears started returning.

Stop it, Leslie, *stop it*, a cool voice inside her said. Gods don't cry.

"Jesus," Leslie sobbed at the picture, "why can't you *love* me? Why?" She bucked now with her sobs. "I love *you!* I love *you!*"

She threw the first levers. The machine shook. Firelight flashed on the row of knife blades above her head, the open jaws of a monster poised over her.

She's in my way, Leslie thought. She *knows* me, she suspects something...she can close in on the truth. I have to destroy her.

Kill her, the red machine told her. Let me have her.

There was another photo she could have used of the two of them together. Aileen was four, Leslie two. They were sitting on the couch in their pajamas. Daddy had taken the picture...

Leslie stuck the wires to her temples. Then to her breasts.

...and Aileen was hugging her little sister proudly.

"It isn't fair," Leslie droned, over and over. "It isn't fair." Hungry, the machine hissed in her mind. *Feed* her to me — like the others.

The black hose violated her. She had forgotten — or had wanted to forget — typing Aileen's name into the keyboard. She was mixing up the order of the procedure but it didn't matter; the machine was only too ready.

Could be a shoe, Nana had said.

Feed me, the machine said, and Leslie had to laugh out loud shakily at that. The knives suddenly reminded her of the teeth of the monster plant in the movie *Little Shop of Horrors*.

I'm not kidding, Leslie. You started this. You brought me to life. I'm your child and I'm hungry. *Now feed* her to me. She'll nourish me more than all the others put together. *You* know that.

"Go to hell!" Leslie said, stepping backward off the pad. The tube slipped out of her and the tape pulled away. "I made you and you'll do what I want," she shouted at it. "I made you...and I can destroy you!"

Naked, she danced with wild abandon to Jim Carroll singing about people that had died. Then, slower, to the Smiths, from *Meat is Murder,* singing the haunting *How Soon is Now?*. She rewound this song, played it again while she sipped a glass of sparkling wine. She toasted the machine.

She placed her feet together on the rubber pad. The hose, the electrodes. Hissing static, rumbling engine, the energy tubes glowing red and the candle flame fluttering inside the crystal ball like eager spirits. The captured souls of those gone before. The trilobite fossil rocked in its hollow, lending its ancient psychometric energy, stored up for six hundred million years. The gun was loaded and ready to be cocked.

She calmly tapped on the keyboard. She remembered the steps now.

Switches. Knobs. And last, the wheels.

Leslie felt a melancholy relief. A sad peace. She felt almost happy. Yes...yes, she did.

Into the center screen she had introduced the other half of the photo from Hampton Beach. She had been careful, however, to crop the bottom first to remove Aileen's hand from her shoulder. She couldn't take any chances.

But it was the mirror below the screen she stared into and concentrated on. The vivid blue crystal balls of her eyes.

Yes, relief. Peace.

This was what she'd wanted all along.

THE ENDLESS FALL

When he regained consciousness, he found himself facing a curved window. There was no way he couldn't be facing it; the window was situated a short distance in front of him, and he was fastened tightly in his seat.

Outside the concave window, autumn filled his view, so entirely that the space capsule could have been resting on the floor of an ocean of autumn, drowned in autumn. He was also viewing this sight through the concave face shield of the helmet he wore over his head. A succession of windows, like the multiple lenses of a microscope, or telescope.

He didn't remember his name, or how he had come to be here, yet somehow he had vague, dreamlike recollections of being a child who had loved the beauty of autumn and the month-long season of Halloween, but at the same time had dreaded the coming of fall for heralding in a new school year – forced once again to rejoin the laughing, shouting, taunting, bullying ranks of other children.

The scene he saw outside the capsule's one thick window looked identical to the impressions of many lost autumns that swam up from his fogged memory. Outside, there were no houses visible, no roads or paths or any other signs of humanity; only leaves above and leaves mirrored below, bridged by dark tree trunks. The carpet of leaves that had already fallen was more uniformly orange, with an undertone of brown, but the canopy of foliage supported by the receding columns of trunks was more varied in its hues. A conflagration of orange, yellow, red, with teasing contrasts of green woven throughout like the last of the summer leaves the inferno was consuming. Though not a speck of sky showed through the dense ceiling, the glow that seemed to emanate from the leaves themselves suggested the light of late afternoon burned behind and through them. In fact, the interior of the tiny capsule was awash in subtly shifting lattices of projected orange and yellow light, as if the air inside swarmed with ghostly koi fish. This mottled golden light played across the darkened instrument panels and blank, black monitor screens, and across his gloved hands, and his legs encased in the thickly padded, single-piece white suit he wore.

The instruments were not entirely dark. Here and there a tiny red ruby of light burned, or blinked in silent code. One small readout screen, though its message jiggled and jumped in place, displayed the glowing red letters: EMERGENCY POWER ENGAGED.

Some of the toggle switches, big clunky buttons, and knobs were labeled or numbered, but so many were not, and control panels thick with them encroached on him from all sides. Keyboards mostly just had their keys labeled with letters.

He might have panicked in his helplessness, in the face of all these incomprehensible controls, had no air been coming into his helmet, but this was not the case. He tested this by taking some deep breaths, and his lungs filled reassuringly. He looked down at his front, and saw three segmented tubes ran out from under the chair he was strapped into, plugged like umbilical cords into ports in his suit: one just below the edge of his helmet, another down near his abdomen, and a third at his groin. His guess was this third tube disposed of his urine. So, he had air, and apparently he needn't worry about relieving his bladder. But surely he couldn't sit here forever. The air might still run out, and though it might take a while, he would eventually die of thirst, even before he died of hunger.

It must be safe to go outside. Look at those trees: he most certainly had to be home. But was he? Something about the shapes of some of the leaves out there seemed subtly wrong. Nature loves symmetry, but one type of leaf in particular appeared oddly asymmetrical to him, with four small lobes on one side and one larger lobe on the opposite side, like the crude outline of a human hand. But how could he really tell from here? And even if this wasn't home, it was home-like in the extreme, wasn't it?

Still, home-like might not be good enough. Even a relatively minor difference in the atmosphere might prove fatal to him if he ventured outside and removed his helmet.

Ultimately, he might not have any choice. Still, he needn't be rash. For right now, escaping the security of the capsule should be a last resort. A retrieval party could be on the way even now, having tracked the capsule's descent.

Or...might an enemy of some type be on the way, if he was a stranger here, in the wrong country? On the wrong planet?

How long was it safe to wait?

What if a fire should start in the capsule, from some damage sustained in its fall?

Was it a capsule, or a lifeboat? Had he fled from a dangerous situation aboard some larger ship still in orbit? Or maybe a space station...a space prison? Was he a criminal? Had he been a prisoner of war, who had escaped and stolen a small craft?

Maybe...perhaps. All these *what ifs* sadistically goaded him to panic, to flee from this claustrophobic cockpit before it became a deathtrap.

But even if he were to give in to such panic, there was the question of *how* to get outside, when he couldn't readily decipher the staggering amount of controls crowded around his chair and the window.

Unfastening and throwing off the safety harness that had strapped him to his seat was easy enough to figure out, and relieved at least some of his feeling of helplessness. He then returned his attention to the instruments, trying to narrow his focus so as not to be so overwhelmed. He shifted his attention here, then there. If anything, the instruments seemed to be growing darker, blending together even more confusingly, until at last he realized why. He looked up sharply, out the window again.

The late afternoon light glowing through the ceiling of leaves had become dim, waning like a dying bonfire. Evening was coming in like a tide. Somewhere behind all the leaves, the sun (*his* sun?) was setting.

So, there would be no escaping the capsule tonight, even if he identified the means to do so. He was apparently in the middle of a dense forest, perhaps miles from civilization. Perhaps with no civilization to be found at all. He might walk right off a cliff edge in the darkness. There might be dangerous people out there. Dangerous animals.

He would wait, yes; there was now no question. Maybe he would sleep, to conserve his energy. But was that wise? What if his air ran out while he slept, or enemies surrounded the craft, or that imagined fire spread to the inside of the cockpit? He must stay vigilant through the night. He only hoped it was a terrestrial night...not some alien night of hours beyond counting.

The world outside purpled. The fire of the leaves went out and left only its negative afterimage. He watched, as if expecting a figure to emerge ghost-like from the gloomy trees. Watched, as the purple deepened, as if he expected to see the glowing eyes of a predatory animal lurking out there. He listened, but heard only his breathing inside the helmet, and now as the black of night arrived in its fullness he was confronted with pure nothingness. Even space, with its stars, could not be this black, though he couldn't recall being in space. There were no impressions like those he had of boyhood's autumns. Had he regained consciousness at this point, instead of several hours earlier, he might have believed himself to be in a bathysphere at the far, icy bottom of a sea.

Only the tiny ruby lights scattered across the control panels, brighter for the contrast of darkness – all he had in lieu of stars, red as dying stars – prevented him from feeling as though he were locked in a vault. Confined in a coffin. Already dead.

To force himself to stay awake, he tried thinking of how many words he could make from the stuttering red letters of EMERGENCY POWER ENGAGED. *MEN. EMERGE. COWER. ENRAGED.* But though he had vowed not to, at some point in this game he fell asleep.

He dreamed of plummeting through space, with star-bejeweled blackness looming at his back, and below him the vast cloud-swirled curve of a planet, its oceans blue, its land masses – aside from the ice caps – entirely orange-yellow, as if it was a world where autumn reigned completely and eternally. He wasn't plunging toward the planet in his capsule, however, but merely in his space suit and helmet, his three umbilical cords trailing out behind him. Soon he would be entering the glow of the planet's atmosphere, and as it filled his vision he spread his arms out wide, waiting for them to catch fire and burn up like the wings of a falling angel.

Silhouetted against the fiery continents below he noticed several drifting black shapes. They were triangular. Were they satellites, or space crafts in orbit? Was this what his capsule looked like from the outside? It was hard for him to guess at their scale, but he had the impression these remote shapes would be much larger than his capsule. As he continued to plummet, he thought he could make out a tangled mass of black cords hanging from the bottom of one of the triangular forms, passing directly below him, as if it were a balloon-type object and its mooring lines had torn free.

These black triangles gliding slowly above the autumnal land masses filled him with an inexplicable dread, where the expectation of burning up in the atmosphere like a meteor had not. He was suddenly desperate to arrest his fall, but of course he could not. All he could do to escape was...

...wake up, and he awoke with a jolt, to see that a bluish predawn glow had illuminated the forest spectrally, and that a person was just outside the curved capsule window peering in at him. He couldn't make out this person's features, however, because they wore a space helmet as he did, and from the outside its face shield was an opaque metallic gold.

His first impression was that the helmeted figure was his own reflection in the glass, but when the person saw that he had awakened they turned abruptly and darted away, running off toward the distant trees as quickly as they could in that cumbersome space suit. He sat there in his chair paralyzed with fear, until the white figure was swallowed up in the trees and the misty blue light, and gone like a hallucination.

He would not have felt fear if the individual had signaled to him reassuringly...had made an attempt to get the capsule open in a manner that did not seem threatening. But the person's startled flight was not at all reassuring. It mystified him, and that made him frightened.

Someone who was afraid of him might want to hurt him. They might come back with others to hurt him.

He couldn't allow himself to remain trapped and vulnerable any longer.

A mad crowd of *what ifs* prodded him toward the cliff edge of panic again, but his desperation lent a fresh keenness to his reexamination of the controls around him. He had noticed yesterday a lever switch with a red handle set into the underside of the panel directly in front of him, near his right knee. An identical lever was set in the base of his chair, within easy reach of his right hand. The two switches were not labeled, but their size and bright color made them stand out. They were extra important.

He considered that the switch in the chair might be the release for an ejector seat, to propel him and the chair (assuming he was still safely strapped into it) out of the capsule, with a parachute then opening to break his fall. Yes, that seemed very plausible to him, but then the switch near his knee? Could it be the release for the capsule's door or hatch? But where was that, anyway? He twisted around to look to his right, then to his left, then twisted more to look behind him. No outline of a hatch was apparent, but if this lever did in fact unseal one, it would soon make its presence known.

He reached to the handle in front of him and closed his fist around it. Hesitated. He put a little pressure on it. It wouldn't budge. He realized he had to simultaneously depress a button in one end of the handle to release it. Holding in this button with his thumb, he drew in a deep breath, then dragged the red switch down through its slot.

With a muffled, propulsive boom, the curved window in front of him was catapulted outward, spinning in the air several times until it crashed against the trunk of a tree and fell to the ground, where it lay rocking. The impact with the tree caused a cascade of yellow leaves to flutter down, joining those that already drifted earthward intermittently from above.

If that other person in the space suit, somewhere out there, hadn't already known he was here, they would have realized it now.

When his heartbeat slowed and his thoughts staggered forward again, with his gloved fingers he explored the coupling of the tube that ran into the socket at his abdomen. Though he had only seen the figure outside briefly, he had recognized it wore a suit just like his own, and he didn't recall seeing any tubes connected to the ports in it. If it was safe for them, it would be safe for him.

He pulled back on the rim of the tube's end, while also shifting aside a little switch with his thumb, and the hose came free of the port. The ear speakers inside his helmet permitted him to hear a brief hiss drain from the end of the tube, but the pressure change inside his suit was all but imperceptible. Next he undid the tube connected at his crotch, and when it came away he felt a subtle, odd sensation as if his penis had been released from a mild suction he hadn't been conscious of previously. Lastly, the tube at the base of his helmet. He hesitated, but reminded himself of the stranger who had been spying on him, their suit without tubes, and anyway what choice did he have any longer? He unplugged the last hose, and drew a breath into his helmet through the open port at his collar.

Crisp air flowed into his helmet, down his throat like cool water. It tasted of the autumn leaves above and the leaf litter below. The breath he drew into him was earthy, with a touch of dampness, and it almost brought those elusive boyhood memories into sharper focus but they resisted beguilingly. It was a good smell. It was good air.

Before climbing out of the cockpit he looked around for anything he might make use of, take with him. (Take with him *where?* Well, he'd address that question shortly. One thing at a time.) Set into a recess in the back of his chair he discovered a backpack in the form of a hard, white shell. A mobile air tank? He disconnected this backpack, rested it on the floor and opened its catches. Fitted inside were a variety of survival items. A first aid kit. A red flare gun. A small water purification unit. A container for water (filled). A tube of concentrated paste. (He unscrewed its cap and held the tube close to the port at his collar. A smell like peanut butter.) A fire-starting instrument. A flashlight. A multi-tool with an unfolding knife blade and various other unfolding heads. And a semiautomatic pistol with one spare magazine of cartridges.

He removed the gun, checked its magazine, chambered the first round and set the safety. Then he slipped his arms through the backpack's straps and buckled them across his chest.

He stepped up on the edge of the control panel that faced his vacated chair, and – careful not to depress any buttons or trip any switches with his feet – boosted himself up. He placed a foot on the edge of the blown-out window, then hopped out onto the ground.

He looked this way and that warily, turning his whole body because of his fitted helmet. If he had a gun in hand, the other space-suited figure might, too. No sign of that person, as yet. He switched his attention to the capsule.

Leaves that had drifted down during the night, or perhaps come loose when the craft had shattered through the treetops, plastered its white surface like scales, as if to camouflage the capsule, showing either their bright upper sides or their paler bottom sides. There was still a torn gap in the thick foliage directly above, exposing a tease of crystalline blue sky that he hadn't been able to see while within.

A name stenciled in large black letters on the craft's outer hull. UCSS FETCH.

U had to be United. SS must be Space Ship. But was the C for Countries? Colonies? Cosmos? Was this the name of the capsule itself, or a larger craft the capsule might have belonged to, or been a segment of?

Spread across the ground behind the capsule was a blue parachute, still attached by lines. He tucked his handgun under a strap of his backpack, and gathered the heavy parachute in his hands and dragged it back to the capsule, then set about shrouding the craft with the material to cover the opening left by the ejected window, if only to keep out rain and small animals (if any existed) in case he needed to make use of the capsule again. Certainly this makeshift tarp wouldn't keep out that stranger should they return. He weighed the edges of the chute down with rocks he dug with his fingers out of the black, moist soil beneath the thick layer of leaf litter.

As he worked, he paused frequently to look around him at the woods, as they came alive again gradually with the dawn-ignited colors of autumn.

He set off in the direction opposite to that in which the stranger had fled. If the stranger thought it best to avoid him, it was best he avoid them, too...at least for now. He needed to find out more about where he was. What was around.

To mark his trail, every so often he made a configuration of three stones at the base of a tree: a second rock atop the first, then a third rock against the left side of the first as a kind of arrow pointing the way back toward the capsule.

The ground dipped or rose a little sometimes, gently, but finally he came to a steeper slope and he climbed it, at times having to hold onto tree trunks so as not to lose his footing on the slippery leaves. He reached the crest of this hill and looked down ahead of him to see only more of the same autumnal forest, seemingly extending unto infinity. The only difference up ahead was that there were boulders scattered here and there, some split as if cleaved by the axes of gods, and coated unevenly with brilliant green moss.

He slid off his backpack and sat down atop the hill, his back propped against a trunk, and at last unfastened and removed his helmet. He got his gloves off and ran his hands back across his short hair, which bristled wetly with perspiration. He gulped in the refreshing air and the rich scent of the woods. He drank some water – fighting to keep it to just a few swallows – and squeezed a little bit of the concentrated food paste between his lips.

After this bit of rest he descended the other side of the hill and walked on, pistol in one hand and helmet in the other. He didn't like how it bumped against his leg but he liked having his head free, being able to look around by turning his neck, the cool breeze against his face.

The mild breeze rustled through the treetops. Leaves fell, rocking, as if in slow motion, adding to the carpet on the forest floor.

The noon sun arced overhead, splintered through the foliage into glinting coppery shards. He paused again, set down his helmet with the gun inside it, to build another marker of stones. Paused again, to drink some more water, eat some more protein paste.

Still, he had come across no roads, no habitations, no sign at all of humanity or anything approximating humanity.

He walked on, and the sun started on its descent toward late afternoon and evening beyond.

Was it safe to rest somewhere for the night? But he *must* rest somewhere for the night.

He came to a boulder that had been cleft into two halves, and a tree had grown between them, perhaps having wedged them further apart over the years. The gap was enough for him to squeeze into and lie down in. So he did this, crawling in all the way to the tree trunk, pushing his backpack in ahead of him. He lay his helmet on top of it. He propped his head on his bent arm and, gun in hand, watched through the crack in the stone as twilight again fell upon the forest. Purple...more purple...blackness.

He dozed off, and dreamed that he was back at his capsule with the stenciled name UCSS FETCH. He was again staring up through the irregular hole made when the craft had torn through the treetops to half embed itself in the forest floor. This time, though, across the crisp blue sky there coasted a massive black shape, triangular in outline – a pyramid, actually – from the flat bottom of which dangled a nest of sluggishly coiling cords or tubes.

The space traveler's eyes flicked open. Absolute darkness, but he oriented himself by the close smell of decaying leaves blanketing soft soil. He remained very still, careful not to make any noise by shifting his body, because something was out there in the blackness, crunching drying leaves under its feet.

Light approached, yellow like a patch of sunset that had been left behind and was trying to catch up. It grew brighter, as the footsteps crunched more loudly. He propped the butt of the pistol on his thigh, pointing it toward the opening of his shelter. The light became a flame. Someone was carrying a torch. He heard it snap even over the crackle of the torch bearer's footfalls. Was the light enough to expose him in his lair? Was the torch bearer hunting for him?

The glare as the fire came even with the cleft hurt his eyes and he curled his finger around the trigger.

Whether they were hunting him or not, the flame passed by. The footfalls receded. Eventually, both were gone. He had gone unnoticed.

It was a long time before he was able to doze off again. Close to dawn, he slept another hour at best.

He reopened his eyes to the bluish haze of pre-dawn, with a subtle hum shivering inside his body as if he were feeling the vibration of a powerful machine through the ground. Was it this vibration that had awakened him?

He saw something strange in front of him through the crevice. At first he thought he'd only imagined it. When he saw it happen again, he thought he might still be dreaming...but he wasn't dreaming.

He'd seen a leaf – one of those with a mitten-like shape – rise from the forest floor and continue climbing upward, rocking, as if in slow motion. Borne by the breeze? But why had only this one leaf been stirred? Then another leaf rose up, climbed in lazy spirals. It floated toward a tree he could see straight ahead of him through the crack. When it reached the underside of the tree's foliage, the leaf appeared to rejoin it. As if it had reattached itself to the twig from which it had dropped away at some earlier time.

Was it possible? Was this how the trees here, though always shedding leaves, never depleted themselves? By being continually replenished? But how was it possible? Even on an alien world, it defied any kind of natural law. At least, the natural laws he knew.

As he lay there throughout the unfolding of this mystery, he was so disoriented and disturbed it was as if he were unable to move, even if he'd willed it with every muscle working in concert; even his breathing seemed suspended. Eventually, though – after he witnessed no more leaves returning to their branches – the strange spell was broken.

He noticed that odd vibration had passed away.

He inched out of the crack in the boulder like a newborn soul, born feet first. He ate a dab more paste, swallowed a few more gulps of water. He'd need more water very soon. He feared running out of water, now, more than he did the stranger or strangers he shared these woods with.

And on again, still thirsty and ill-rested.

Incongruous color showed through the clouds of leaves ahead of him, like snatches of blue sky, but this was too near to the ground to be that. A body of water, then, reflecting sky?

He stealthily crept up on the color, seeing more and more blue between the trees, until finally he peered cautiously around the black pillar of a trunk at the color's source. In an open spot too small to be called a clearing, a tent had been erected. Someone had made it from the blue material of his capsule's parachute.

Yet it couldn't be; it had to be a tarp of a similar hue. This material looked too old and faded. Ragged at the edges, almost worn through in spots, and plastered with leaves as if it had been here a long time. The tent dipped in the middle, and fallen leaves had collected thickly there. But then again, it was a parachute like his own and not a tarp, after all: he could see where its suspension lines had once been attached, and it was segments of these cords that had been used to support the tent, their ends attached to sticks hammered into the ground.

He noted there was a fire pit just outside the tent's opening, ringed in stones and full of gray ashes and fallen leaves. It hadn't been lit in a while.

After watching the tent for long minutes, and seeing no one emerge from it, and hearing no sounds from within, he stepped out from behind the tree and stole up on it, pistol in hand.

He crouched, set his helmet down, shifted aside the opening's flap with his free hand and pointed the handgun inside. The tent was unoccupied.

After glancing over his shoulder, he crawled in on hands and knees.

The ground inside had been cleared of leaves and stones. In the far corner was a small pile of rotting mushrooms, deep red in color like liver but breaking down into a white gelatinous mass. The mushrooms when fresh must be edible, or else why would they have been collected? Yet they had been abandoned along with the camp. These specimens were beyond eating, but if one could find them so could another.

The only other item in the tent was a hard white backpack just like his own. He opened it to find it empty except for the first aid kit, which still contained some of its supplies.

Why had the tent been forsaken? Camped out in the open like this, had the tent's occupant been surprised, dragged out and killed? Had these meager leavings been considered too inconsequential to take? Or, venturing out to search for water or more food, had this person met with misfortune, and never returned? Maybe he or she had discovered better shelter?

He was sorely tempted to make use of the tent himself, but it was so conspicuous, so vulnerable. Then again, eventually he would have to risk camping somewhere, in order to get more sleep.

He decided to decide on whether to use the camp later. For now, he would search in the immediate area for more mushrooms, and for water.

After what he would have gauged to be only an hour he found a number of large mushrooms, beautifully dark red, nestled between the roots of several trees. He took a nibble from the edge of one and found its taste not bad, though he wondered if he might try roasting them over a fire. He refrained from eating another bite, in case the mushroom ended up disagreeing with him or set off an allergic reaction, but in the meantime he picked the rest that he had found and placed them in the bowl of his helmet.

As he was plucking the last of them, he noticed an odd, soft pattering sound...on the leaves overhead, and the ground all around him. Then a drop of cold water struck the back of his neck and he flinched. He tilted back his head and another drop struck the center of his forehead like a liquid bullet. It had begun to rain.

His decision had been made for him; he started back hastily in the direction of the tent.

He managed to get there before the rain had strengthened too much, though it had wetted his hair. He scooped up the rotting mushrooms, carried them outside and tossed them, then dumped the new mushrooms inside on a little bed he made of fallen leaves. He put his helmet outside, propped by stones with the open end up, to catch water. He carried the forsaken backpack outside, removed the first aid kit and left the backpack open on the ground to collect more water. He also cleared away the leaves that had gathered atop the tent in its slumped hollow, hoping to catch some water there, too.

The rain finally mounted to a downpour that came crashing unhindered through the leaves above, and he was grateful to be inside. He weighed the trailing flap of the opening shut with his own backpack. Then, he stretched out on his side in the murk and listened to the rain tapping all across the blue membrane, his pistol on the ground by his hand.

The sound of the rain made him feel insulated inside this fragile womb, soon coaxing him to sleep.

JEFFREY THOMAS 217

He awoke in the night, finding the rain hadn't ceased but had at least become subdued again. He drank some water from his container. He peeked out through the tent's flap but was greeted only by unmitigated blackness.

As he lay back again he mused that he did not feel lonely. His anxiousness was not for company, but only for survival. He still could recall nothing concrete of his life back home, wherever home had been, but he felt no hint of an aching void such as would be filled by returning to a wife or children, or even close friends. He might have all of these things, for all he knew, or he might have had them once and lost them over time, but whatever the case his current aloneness was not in itself vexing. He could keep himself alive, but other people might try to prevent him from that. Other people might wish him harm, wish him dead. People were like that; he didn't need to remember any names or faces to know it. The way he felt right now, at least, was that he wouldn't mind being alone for the rest of his life.

Under his bulky space suit he wore a closefitting long-sleeved top and long johns, white in color, and warm enough that he stripped down to just these. Thin sneaker-like shoes inside his boots enabled him to put the heavy boots into a corner. He folded his space suit and left it in the tent to use as a pillow. He drank as much water as he wanted now (emptying the helmet), ate a bit of his paste and chanced a few larger bites of mushroom for his breakfast. He left his spare backpack, still holding water, in the tent but brought his own backpack with him as he set off to do some more exploring. His intention, though – after having comfortably bonded with the tent last night – was to maintain the camp as his base of operations until something more secure presented itself. He had his gun, and maybe he could set some booby-traps around the camp.

Now that he was not trapped in a space capsule, and had found that both water and food were to be had, his early state of fear had dulled to a more feral kind of wariness. He just had to stay on his toes and avoid these other...survivors?

As he walked along, stopping occasionally to leave

more markers, he asked himself what it was he hoped to discover or achieve, beyond finding better shelter and more nourishment. Of course he wanted to determine where he was, to learn whether he was on his home world. But if not, did he hope there was a way to be rescued, or to acquire a craft to take into space again? Well, he supposed he did want to return home. Maybe home was actually a worse place for him than this, but wasn't going home what one would be expected to want? Mainly, though, truth be told, right now he just wanted to understand more in general, to fill the frustratingly shrunken chamber of his mind. He felt like a newborn with no parents to instruct or guide him. Well, he would have to be his own parent. Born again.

He found a mushroom growing against the base of a tree, and as he stooped to collect it and place it in his helmet he noticed one of his stone markers arranged beside it. One small stone atop a larger stone, and a stone to the left of these pointing back in the direction he had come from. And yet, he didn't think he had left a marker here previously. No, he was sure he hadn't been this way yet. If so, he would have already plucked the mushrooms, unless they grew that quickly. Was someone copying his markers, intending to confuse him, to get him to lost in circles? It would be odd if another person had devised the same exact method of marking their trail.

He straightened up, scanning about him as if he thought he might see someone in the distance half hidden behind a tree, giggling at him, but he was still alone. Well, as it happened this marker pointed him back toward his camp and saved him the trouble of having to lay down a new one himself. It left him uneasy, though, as he resumed his exploration.

Just a short while later, he came upon the space capsule.

Another space capsule. He knew it wasn't his own for several reasons. For one, it was badly burned from a too precipitous descent, its smooth white shell scorched back. (Maybe its retrorockets hadn't fired?) Instead of lying across the ground like his capsule's chute, the parachute – still attached, though it might not have deployed correctly – was snagged in the branches directly above, intact but also blackened. For another thing, the cockpit window was still in place, not ejected.

He wiped at the window with his sleeve, clearing the greasy black grime away just enough for him to see something of the shadowy interior. It looked blackened by fire in there, too, without even the tiny red jewels that would indicate emergency power. But he flinched back from the window when he saw that the pilot's chair was not unoccupied.

After composing himself, he stepped up to the window again and cupped his hands around the spot he had cleaned.

The pilot in his blackened space suit was slumped a little to one side, his seat thrown harness off. His helmet's visor was up; maybe he had lost air to his suit and in desperation had lifted it. The face framed within the helmet was that of a charred skull. Had the flames trapped within the capsule eaten his flesh, or had time done that?

He backed away from the window, examined the outside of the craft again. Moving around to one side, this time he spotted letters showing a little more black under the charring. Again he used his sleeve to wipe at the capsule, to give himself a better look. Then he backed off and read the letters he had uncovered. They spelled: UCSS FETCH.

This craft couldn't have the same name as his own. That is, multiple craft wouldn't bear a single name. This could only mean, he reckoned, that FETCH was the name of a mother ship and these capsules were just lifepods, as he had speculated earlier. What other explanation could there be?

In any case, this poor bastard had not been as lucky as he.

There was nothing to be salvaged here. He could do no more than move on, but he felt a little goodwill toward the dead man because he didn't pose a threat to him, so he gave the burnt pilot a little salute before he slipped past the capsule into the forested depths ahead.

He was following a hum. He had noticed it a little while ago. Not so much an audible hum, as a deep bass resonance in his chest. It only deepened the further he went on, growing to an almost uncomfortable inner vibration. It reminded him of the vibration he had felt while sheltering in the halved boulder, but more intense.

The hum led him to a great clearing, larger than anything he had thus far encountered and floored with long, blondish grass. He hung back at its edge, though, hiding himself behind a tree, as he gazed in fear and wonder at the source of the heavy vibration quivering through him. A structure had been built within the field, or maybe this spot of land has originally been cleared of trees to accommodate it.

It was a pyramid, towering imposingly against the vivid blue sky. It called forth images of a series of famous pyramids in a desert of his home world, but he didn't know if this one was quite as tall as those, and the angles of its sides seemed more steep. Also, rather than being composed of millions of blocks of limestone, this structure appeared to be carved from one titanic mass of coal-black matter, its surfaces oddly textured, giving the impression of black clay covered in the thumbprints of some giant that had molded it.

As he stared at the black pyramid, he realized another of those odd paralyzing spells had come over him. He couldn't will himself to move the hand he had placed on the tree trunk. He wasn't even sure if he was drawing breath into his lungs. He could not blink, and he was peripherally aware that mitten-shaped fallen leaves were floating up from the ground around him, spiraling upward and reattaching themselves to branches overhead.

The vibration inside him suddenly spiked to an internalized earthquake, as the pyramid began floating upward off the grass it had crushed flat.

Beneath it, a slowly writhing tangle of sinuous black appendages – like colossal tentacles – were revealed, rooted to the hovering pyramid's base. They coiled ponderously as the looming structure rose higher, blotting out much of the beautiful sky like some triangular-shaped heavenly body.

Higher it rose, higher, until it seemed as far above the world as an airplane. Then, the pyramid moved laterally...until finally it passed beyond his range of sight and was gone, leaving that open circle of blue sky marred only by an innocuous fleet of white clouds.

As the thing had ascended, the vibration had gradually weakened again, tapering off and then disappearing altogether as the pyramid was lost from sight. When that happened, he was released from his paralysis. He dropped to his knees and vomited.

The leaves had stopped floating in reverse.

When he was able to stand again, he turned back toward his camp, and rested in his tent until his organs no longer felt shaken and poisoned by the vibration that had filled him.

He stayed on at the camp he'd discovered, but he never let down his guard. He found a less plentiful, smaller and white variety of mushroom, and after risking a tentative bite established that it was edible, too. Though he never encountered any higher animals such as squirrels, birds, or even insects, he learned that if he dug down into the black soil he could easily uncover good-sized earthworms. And it rained often enough that water was no longer a concern. He could even spare it to wash himself occasionally.

He thought to shave by scraping his face with the blade of his multi-tool, but why should he shave? For whom? He became bearded.

Then one afternoon, after returning from foraging with his helmet full of mushrooms and squirming worms, he discovered two men at his camp. He dropped the helmet and drew his gun from his waistband.

One man, with long graying hair and a thick beard like a wild man, his closefitting long-sleeved shirt and long johns dark with grime, lay on his back with a bullet hole in the center of his forehead, blood streaming thickly down the sides of his face. He lay just outside the tent, having partially fallen across the fire pit, which was currently only full of ashes.

The other man's clothing was similar but whiter, his hair short and face clean-shaven. He sat with his legs splayed out and his back propped against a tree trunk. In his hand was the gun with which he had killed the older man. A makeshift spear, formed from a long straight branch with a sharpened tip, had been thrust into the front of his neck, a good foot of it having emerged out the back. Blood had saturated the front of his shirt and pooled in his lap. The young man's face was almost gray, almost lifeless, and yet he recognized that face. Though he had no mirror in which to see himself, and had never returned to his own capsule where he might find reflective surfaces, he knew that this man possessed the same face he did.

Though his eyes were going glassy, the young man became aware of him and started to raise his pistol from the ground. He pointed his own gun, which he had not fired up until now, and pulled the trigger once. There was a loud cracking report that rolled off between the trees in all directions. With a bullet through its forehead and the back of its skull gaping, the young man's head slumped heavily.

He went over to the older man and stood over him. Despite the long graying hair and wild beard, and the wrinkles and ingrained grime, he saw that this man possessed his face, as well.

He figured the two men had independently thought to raid or acquire his camp. The old man had actually already stolen all his stored mushrooms and placed them into a crude sack made from parachute material. The only other thing of value belonging to the old man was the spear, and this he tugged out of the young man's body. The young man had more to offer, though. He wore a backpack full of supplies, the tube of food paste only half empty. And now he had two pistols.

He made the decision to only eat the young man.

He had no way of preserving meat, and the young man was, well, younger and cleaner, his flesh more full. So he dragged the old man far enough away into the woods that the decomposition shouldn't bother him, and awkwardly dug a shallow grave with the spear and his hands. In the process he exposed a bounty of worms.

He kept the young man's clothes as a spare set, then hung the nude body upside-down from a tree branch somewhat distant from his camp, using a section of parachute line to bind the ankles. Then he cut the man's already damaged throat with his multi-tool's blade to drain out as much blood as he could. He decided not to save and drink the blood.

When he felt he had emptied a sufficient amount of blood, he cut the body down and sliced thick steaks from the thighs and buttocks. Having taken all he felt he could eat before the meat started to go bad, he dragged the body off into the woods to bury it beside the body of the older version of themselves.

Now, he knew why the other men who haunted these endless autumnal woods feared and avoided each other.

Eating the cooked and delicious meat that evening in front of his snapping campfire, he didn't feel bad for the dead man at all. Had it been someone else he believed he would have, but he had only harmed himself.

He had never seen one of the titan pyramid creatures set down in the field again, but he sometimes ventured there to have a view of the sky, and he would see one or more of them gliding past, piercing slowly through the clouds. At such a distance their vibrations were bearable. It was his feeling that, either intentionally or accidentally, these creatures were responsible for disrupting time, but of course he knew too little to prove that.

Then one day, when his hair and beard had grown long, during a visit to the great clearing he saw more than just a pair of distant black pyramids drifting high above.

As he was gazing up and shielding his eyes against a sun that he now knew to be an alien star, watching the pyramids and feeling their tuning fork murmur inside his heart, the sky flickered as if he had blinked several times, but he hadn't. For just a moment, he was looking up into a night sky, infinitely black and strewn with countless stars glittering like pulverized glass. Then it was day again, but the blue sky was now full of new objects that seemed to have taken the place of the many stars.

They were brightly white space capsules, hanging from the wide bells of blue parachutes and descending gracefully, none of them having burned in the atmosphere. He had no idea how many. From where he stood he would guess scores of them. Maybe a hundred. Maybe more, out of his range of seeing.

All of them, he had no doubt, stenciled with the letters that spelled UCSS FETCH.

The sight made him afraid. If two men had discovered his camp at the same time, others would no doubt be coming soon enough. He would need a more secure shelter, after all, but where could he be truly safe from himself?

He supposed he shouldn't be afraid...afraid of himself. If he was killed, he would still live on.

There would come even more capsules after these – he knew it.

More and more. Always falling.

– With thanks to Nick Gucker for his artistic inspiration

About the Author

Jeffrey Thomas is an American author of weird fiction, the creator of the milieu Punktown. Books in the Punktown universe include the short story collections *Punktown* and *Ghosts of Punktown*, and the novels *Deadstock* and *Blue War*. Thomas's other books include the short story collections *Worship The Night*, *Thirteen Specimens*, and *Unholy Dimensions*, and the novels *Letters From Hades*, *Boneland*, and *Subject 11*. His stories have been selected for inclusion in *The Year's Best Horror Stories* (Editor, Karl Edward Wagner), *The Year's Best Fantasy and Horror* (Editors, Ellen Datlow and Terri Windling), and *Year's Best Weird Fiction* (Editor, Laird Barron). Though his work is often inspired by his travels in Viet Nam, Thomas makes his home in Massachusetts.

Painting by Nicolas Huck.

ALSO FROM
LOVECRAFT EZINE PRESS

Whispers, by Kristin Dearborn

Nightmare's Disciple, by Joseph S. Pulver, Sr.

Autumn Cthulhu, edited by Mike Davis

The Lurking Chronology, by Pete Rawlik

The Sea of Ash, by Scott Thomas

The King in Yellow Tales volume I, by Joseph S. Pulver, Sr.

Made in the USA
San Bernardino, CA
22 May 2018